The Sand Dollar

Maggie Christensen

In memory of Maxine,
who introduced me to the Oregon Coast.

Prologue

Florence Oregon, July 1950

The red Chevy convertible roars into life, breaking the silence of the early morning and throwing the young couple back in their seats. The girl turns to her companion and laughs, her long dark hair rippling on her shoulders.

"We've done it!"

"Not yet, but we'll be in Mexico tomorrow if we drive all night. We'll be safe then."

"Dad'll never think of looking for us there." She hugs herself in glee. "We couldn't have managed without help."

The boy pushes a hand through his jet black mane and looks over with a tolerant smile. "We'd have found a way. You and me, we belong together." He reaches over and grabs her hand.

"Together forever!" The girl stretches out, head back against the seat. "Faster, honey. I can't wait to get there."

The car speeds on. It's early morning and the roads are clear. All is well, till they come to a sharp corner with a rock face on one side and a steep drop on the other. The car accelerates into the bend throwing the girl hard against her companion.

"Not that fast," she laughs, then her laugh turns to a scream as the car hits the rock face and ricochets out of control. "What's the matter?" she finally manages to yell, as they sway from side to side down what is now a steep incline.

"The brakes…they won't…"

The girl screams again and her hands reach down to protect her unborn child before she is engulfed in darkness, oblivious to the crash and the continuous blare of the horn which follows.

One

"I didn't get it!" Jenny's shoulders drooped as she sank into the chair beside her friend's desk, her eyes beginning to mist. She wiped them angrily with the back of her hand. She'd held the tears back this far, she could last out a bit longer.

"Hang on a tick." Rosa finished the email she was writing and pressed *Send*. "Now, let's grab a coffee and you can tell all. You can't go back to the office looking like that."

Trust Rosa to be honest with her. She must look like death warmed up if the chill in her bones was anything to go by. Jenny's friend picked up her purse and mobile and shooed her out the door. "Coffee's on me today."

"I'll just pop to the loo first."

Somehow Jenny stumbled to the nearest toilet. *What is it about women that we take our sorrows to the loo?* she thought, using a tissue to mop up the tears, which were now streaming down her face.

"What a mess," she said aloud, as she looked at her face in the mirror. *Did they consider her too old?* Jenny examined herself carefully. She might be close to sixty, but she wasn't quite over the hill yet. An open face with wide violet eyes looked back at her. A few lines around the eyes, a few more round the mouth. Too much laughing – though not today. Her hair looked tidy, the dark bob framing her face suited her sharp features; the high cheekbones and pointed chin. She stepped

3

away from the mirror as the door opened.

*

Jenny gazed out of the window while Rosa bought the coffees. The palm trees trembled in the breeze and the bright red, orange and purples of the bougainvillea assaulted her eyes. The heat haze shimmered on the hard surface of the car park, reminding her summer was not yet over. She loved the ambiance here. This hospital campus had been part of her working life for as long as she could remember, but she might not be seeing it for much longer. Suddenly the familiar view blurred. It was as if she was viewing it through a haze. Jenny brushed a hand across her eyes, as tears threatened to erupt again.

"Now tell me." Rosa placed two coffees on the table and looked up expectantly.

"Well, I didn't get it. That's all. They didn't appoint anyone. They're going to re-advertise and I've been offered a redundancy and/or an executive coaching session. Just like that. I don't know why they advertised the position in the new structure if they didn't intend to appoint any of the local candidates." Jenny dropped her eyes and played with her spoon as she spoke.

"Wow. Well, I did say you were too good for them. You'd have shown them up in no time at all. Talk about the blind leading the blind..."

"It hasn't sunk in yet. How will I tell my team? How can I face them looking like this?"

"Send them an email and go home," advised Rosa. "It'll all look better after the weekend. And think of the opportunities."

Opportunities! Jenny sniffed. That wasn't the word she'd use. She thought of her ten staff members. She'd been their leader and mentor for the past ten years. They'd never considered anything like this could happen. An email would certainly be an easy way out; give her time to consider her options. *What would she do? How was she going to handle the humiliation of being tossed aside with everyone knowing?*

"Tell you what," Rosa offered. "Do it from my office then you won't have to avoid anyone on the way."

"What would I do without you? What *will* I do without you?"

Jenny sighed, as the reality of the situation began to sink in. "I guess they would find me another position, but I won't become a victim. I've seen that happen too often. I'm not ready for the scrapheap yet." She sat up, stiffening her back and straightening her long, elegant neck as she considered her options.

"First things first. Get through the weekend. Use it to relax, then come back refreshed on Monday."

Refreshed? Who did Rosa think she was talking to? This was the Jenny who was the perfectionist in everything she did, the high achiever from way back. How could she relax with all of this happening and her future uncertain? She should be making plans. Plans had always been her lifesaver when times got tough, and this was a tough time – no doubt about that.

*

Thank goodness for the weekend, Jenny thought when she awoke next morning to the raucous cackle of a kookaburra, and the sunlight streaming in her bedroom window. She didn't need to face anything or anyone for two whole days. Nevertheless, the meeting with Carmel, her boss, was still going around and around in her head as she started on the routine Saturday chores. She realized that it was the apparent devaluing of all she'd achieved over the past ten years that saddened her the most. Jenny knew she needed to rise above it and move on, but it wouldn't be easy. She'd been aware of her bravado when speaking with Rosa, but today she was alone and she couldn't fool herself. It was okay to talk about moving on, but moving on to where?

Jenny's eyes began to fill. Now she was on her own, she could give way to her emotions. The tears trickled down her cheeks as she indulged in a bout of self-pity. She let them flow unchecked, washing away all the anger and unfulfilled ambitions. *Everything had been going so well. It just wasn't fair!*

Around lunchtime Jenny received the weekly phone call from her daughter. At first it was the usual catch-up call, but after Jenny had recounted what she thought was a humorous account of her work situation, something in her daughter's voice caught her by surprise.

"Is everything alright, Helen? You sound a bit stressed."

"Oh, Mum," Helen's usually self-contained voice broke, "it's the baby. He's not sleeping, and Bradley's going through a difficult stage. And Alan is working late most nights. I don't know how I can cope." There was a pause. "You couldn't... no, I guess you're going to fight this decision in your usual stubborn way. Your career has always come first, and now, when it looks like folding, you'll still be putting yourself first."

Jenny sat down with a thump, swallowing the angry words which threatened to erupt. This, on top of everything else. Helen had been fiercely independent since she left home at eighteen. Now, ten years later, she lived on the leafy North Shore of Sydney with her architect husband and two children. This was the first inkling Jenny had that everything wasn't right in Helen's world. She took a deep breath before replying.

"Now hold on, Helen. You know I'm always here for you." They talked for another half hour by which time Helen had calmed down and was sounding more like herself.

"Thanks, Mum. You've really helped. It was good to talk to you like this. Tom is beginning to drop off so I'll put him down. Just caught me at a bad time."

As she hung up, Jenny started thinking. If she gave up work, took the redundancy, she could be there for Helen, move closer, take some of the load, offer to babysit and maybe Helen could even go back to work. She knew some of her friends had taken on this role in retirement and seemed to be enjoying it. They loved to talk about their trips to the zoo, the aquarium, the beach. It was food for thought, but was it really what she wanted to do with the rest of her life?

The call made Jenny think back too. She'd sacrificed a lot for her kids over the years and thought they'd been proud of her. She remembered Helen asking her advice regarding careers in her late teens. Jenny had been glad at that time she had something to offer, that she'd not been one of these stay-at-home mums. Not like the mothers of many of Helen's friends. Had her daughter forgotten all of that? So it seemed.

She went back to her weekend routine, more unsettled than before. Maybe Helen did resent the time she'd spent away from her and her brother. Maybe now was the time to make up for that by being there for Helen and her children and allowing her to enjoy the sort of career path Jenny herself had followed. By the time she was ready for bed she still hadn't reached a decision.

*

Jenny was awakened on Sunday by a call from her son, Hugh. It was as if she'd been sending out smoke signals. She should have known her news would get around. Helen and Hugh had been very close all of their lives, and the story of her impending redundancy was sure to be no secret.

"Never mind, Mum. You couldn't have stayed there forever anyway." *When had her son become so patronizing?* After voicing a few platitudes, Hugh asked, "Why don't you move to Brisbane? You could see more of your grandchildren and Karen is dying to go back to work again. It would fill in your time too."

Jenny really had to bite her tongue this time. *Were these the children she'd raised?* She came off the phone more thoughtful than ever. While it was nice of her children to be concerned about her future, she was a bit surprised they saw their mother as no more than a glorified babysitter, someone who was past it and needed something to keep her busy. She should have been amused, but was so shocked she lost her sense of humor. However, the idea of a change of some sort did have its merits. She'd allowed herself to get into a rut. She needed time to ponder her future.

After dinner, Jenny set to emptying out the bottom drawer of her bedside table, a task she'd been putting off for ages. A round object fell to the floor. She picked it up and rubbed her thumb over the surface. She looked down at the white object dotted with five holes and her fingers traced the star-like shape on its surface. It took her back to her childhood. She had been about six or seven and wandering on an Oregon beach when she'd picked it up.

"Look what I've found, Maddy!"

Her godmother had bent down to the height of the little girl and explained. "It's a sand dollar, Jenny Wren. It was once a sea creature and this bleached skeleton is all that's left." Maddy had gone on to spell out its significance, which Jenny had long forgotten. What she *did* remember was her belief as a child that this white disc held magical qualities.

Jenny sighed as she absentmindedly dropped it into her pocket. She could do with some magic right now.

*

San Francisco California

"Are you sure about this?"

Mike Halliday looked up from the box he was filling with books. "There's nothing to keep me here now. Oregon calls," was his terse reply.

His colleague sat down on the desk, fixing him with a level gaze. "Mike, Mary died only two weeks ago. Don't you want to wait a bit longer? It's a drastic step you're taking."

Mike stood still, book in hand, and sighed. "Thanks, Bob. Appreciate your concern. But you know Mary has been gone from me for more than three years. Alzheimer's took the Mary I knew. It's just her shell I've been visiting in the nursing home. Now even that's gone, best I go too... to Oregon I mean," he quickly added, seeing Bob's shocked expression. "We have a great place up there. Always meant to retire there together." He looked into the distance. After a long pause he went on, "There's only me now, and I'm going."

"Why not finish the semester? It's not like you to leave anything half finished."

"You're right there, but I don't have a teaching load this semester. I'm really on sabbatical. I only stayed around the university to be close to Mary. I can do my research just as well in Seal Rock, better in fact."

"So you're still on about the Native American tribes in that region?"

"Yeah, the Confederated Tribes of Coos, Lower Umpqua and Siuslaw Indians. It's an interesting story..."

"Not now," Bob laughed. "I don't want to get you started on your pet hobby horse. Remember you're having dinner with Cathy and me tonight. Remind you of what you'll be missing up there in the sticks."

"The smog, the traffic, the hectic lifestyle, I know. It'll actually be good to get away from all that. I feel as if I'm starting a new life. I told you I'd put the house on the market, didn't I? It's far too big for one person."

As Bob left with a cheery wave, Mike reflected how he'd be glad to get rid of the old place. Since Mary had gone into the nursing home, it had been so depressing going back to the empty house every night. The place had been like an albatross hanging around his neck. He really spent very little time there. This office had been more of a home to him. He looked around the now denuded bookshelves and the piles of discarded papers and folders lying beside the overfull wastepaper bin. Well, it would belong to someone else soon; some bright young academic, no doubt, full of how he was going to change the world. It had been a long time since Mike had thought that way. Now he was content with the research for his book.

He hadn't been completely honest with Bob. There were some things he *would* miss. Mike ran his fingers through his thick hair and tugged on his beard, a habit he'd developed over the years. He'd miss the camaraderie of the staffroom, having like-minded individuals with whom to discuss his ideas; the delightful moment when one of his graduate students made a breakthrough in a research project. But who was he kidding? He certainly wouldn't miss the backbiting, the jockeying for promotion, the lack of respect for his own area of research. The Dean had suggested he continue with some postgrad students, but he'd decided to make a clean break. He was looking forward to leading a solitary life in a spot which held such fond memories for him.

Back home, Mike was greeted by Ben, the black labrador he and Mary had raised from a pup, and who was now his faithful companion. Once inside the house, Mike's gaze took in the boxes he'd packed for his trip north. They contained mainly books and a few clothes. The realtor had told him the house would sell better furnished, so everything else was still in place, just as it had been for years. He ran his hand over the arm of the sofa, the feel of its soft surface bringing back memories of happier times. He sat down in what had been his favorite armchair, the springs sagging under his weight with the wear of over twenty years. He rubbed his eyes, tired already at the thought of the long drive ahead and wishing he could avoid the farewell Bob had planned for him. He'd never been a social animal. Mary had understood that. His eyes fell on the letter he'd been handed by his lawyer after the funeral. It was lying on the coffee table where he'd thrown it, unable to handle what it contained. He picked it up, the words blurring as he tried to read it a second time. His darling Mary had been thinking of him, even as the darkness of her illness engulfed her. She spoke of their love and the wonderful years they'd shared, but it was the final words that had thrown him, and still did as he re-read them.

"I know you are a solitary soul, my darling, but you do occasionally need a companion to share your days and your thoughts. I know that, alongside everything else we shared, I was there for you. I hope you won't draw so deeply into your shell that you forget our closeness and the comfort it gave both of us. I want you to find that closeness with another. Should the right person appear, please think of my wish for you, and let her into your life."

Mike folded the letter carefully and slowly replaced it on the table. His fingers reached down to touch Ben's head. The dog nudged his master gently.

Two

The alarm buzzed. Jenny opened her eyes. Monday morning. From her bed she could see the sun creeping in through the drapes, lighting up the well-worn furniture. Family photos crowded each other on the top of the chest of drawers: her own wedding photo, those of her children and a few of the grandchildren. This was her home and she had no intention of leaving it. But other parts of her life were due for a shake-up. Maybe this was just the kick in the butt she'd been needing. Jenny had a few matters to take care of, then had arranged to meet with Rosa after work for a drink.

The most difficult part of the day was telling the news to her staff, but the Friday email had dulled their shock. To their credit, they were more concerned for her than themselves, and there were a few tears.

"What will you do?" her personal assistant voiced the question for all of them.

"I'll find something." She needed today to work everything out. She might even accept this executive coaching thing. At least it would give her breathing space. It could even help, though she doubted that. She'd always been one to make her own decisions, and she didn't intend to stop now.

The meeting with Carmel wasn't as stressful as the previous one had been. For a start, Jenny had already made some decisions. Walking across to her manager's office, she felt more in control than before, and control was important to her. She'd decided to take one step at a time and took three deep breaths along the way to help reinforce her decision and calm the butterflies doing summersaults in her stomach.

"Thanks for the offer of an executive coach, Carmel. I'd like to take that up. What timeframe did you have in mind?"

As Carmel put on her glasses and consulted a sheaf of papers, Jenny became aware of the slightly glacial atmosphere in the office. Surely she wasn't imagining it? Where was the warm supportive manager of the past five years? Perhaps Carmel's position was under threat too, and Jenny's own situation was just the tip of the iceberg.

"Doctor Carter will be conducting interviews next Tuesday." The words broke into Jenny's ruminations so much she had to ask the other woman to repeat them.

"Pat, in HR, is coordinating the times. She'll be in touch." Carmel shuffled the papers together and looked up expectantly. The interview was at an end. It seemed to Jenny that Carmel had now wiped her hands of her, and had passed her on to this executive coach no one knew anything about.

Jenny spent the afternoon going through her shelves of folders and updating her resumé. The drink with Rosa at a local wine bar would complete her day.

*

"Well, you're looking heaps better. The weekend worked its magic as I predicted," Rosa said as she placed the two glasses of Merlot on the table. "What have you decided?"

"It was a couple of calls from the kids that helped me make up my mind. I'm sure they see this as a god-sent opportunity to turn me into a babysitting grandma."

Rosa looked shocked. "Don't make up your mind too soon. You know you'd be bored stupid in a week," she warned.

"Don't worry. I don't intend to do anything rash, but I don't really think I can stick around." Jenny bit her lip, twirling the stem of the wineglass between her fingers. "I'd feel like an old worn-out shoe and I don't want to be here to see what they do. I get the feeling the whole department's in line for the chop. Took ten years to build up and it can disappear with a stroke of a pen. It's called outsourcing. Think I'll take some leave and use this coaching program to help plan my future, which won't be here. Probably not quite what Carmel had in mind, but I'm afraid she's lost my loyalty now."

*

Jenny looked around at what was soon to be her former office. She had done quite a bit of tidying up in the past two weeks, and binned a lot of old documents she'd been hoarding for some unknown reason. It certainly looked as if someone was on the move, she thought, as she prepared herself for this first session with the executive coach. Her fingers drummed nervously on the desk while she wondered what it would be like. Jenny wasn't the sort of person to bare her soul to a stranger. She'd always been very private, private and in control. But with all that had been happening recently, events seemed to be spiraling out of her control. On the surface nothing had changed. Jenny was still there. The department continued to operate much as before. The difference was subtle. The staff were on edge, not knowing what was going to happen or if their own jobs were safe. Jenny, herself, didn't feel the same commitment to the organization. How could she? She didn't know what the future held. Her eyes fell on the email. The appointment was with someone called Alex Carter from ABC Coaching and was in the small meeting room at eleven o'clock. It was five minutes to. She'd best be off. A nervous tremor fluttered in her stomach, which was crazy. She wasn't on trial here. It wasn't a job interview. That was over. This was the guy who was going to help her plan her future. It was a positive step!

*

"You'll never guess." Jenny bounced into Rosa's office smiling.

"You look as if you've won the lottery. What's happened?"

"I've had this crazy idea. I know what to do, at least, what I'm going to do next." Jenny suddenly felt exhausted and sank into a chair.

"What?" Rosa swung her chair round to face Jenny. "What's cheered you up like this?"

Jenny took the sand dollar out of her pocket turned it over and over in her fingers. "I found this last night. I've had it for most of my life, but it's been hidden away."

"Is it something special to you?" Rosa reached over to take the object. but Jenny closed her fist over it and gripped it tightly.

"It's a sand dollar. It comes from Oregon. And... and when I was a child I believed it was magic." Jenny smiled in reminiscence. "Amazing what we choose to believe as children. My godmother told me that it was mermaid's money and would always bring me good luck. I found it on the weekend when I was doing some clearing out."

Rosa cleared her throat, but remained silent. She appeared to be waiting while Jenny gathered her thoughts. Jenny continued.

"I know this sounds crazy, but it occurred to me it's a sign. A sign I should visit her." The words sounded strange, even to Jenny. Was the normally clear-headed Jenny actually suggesting she should visit Oregon on the basis of having found a sand dollar she'd picked up over fifty years ago? Looking up, she saw Rosa gazing at her intently.

"What would take you to Oregon?"

"I know. I sound crazy, but Maddy's there."

"Maddy?"

"Maddy." Jenny closed her eyes as she imagined herself being welcomed into her godmother's arms. She could almost smell the wood smoke from the stove. It had always been lit. The tang of smoke had mingled with the smell of the timber in the walls of her godmother's home. Scenes flashed through her mind: Maddy's warm embrace, the comfort of the old house, the wild ocean beach; running against the wind, collecting shells and driftwood; the never-ending supply of food. She shook herself. These were childhood memories. She hadn't been there for years. She opened her eyes again. "Maddy's my godmother."

"Have you kept in touch with her at all?" Rosa queried. "Or is she a stranger to you?"

"Oh yes, we've kept in touch. It was only Christmas and birthdays, the usual things, till Mum died. Gosh, that was about ten years ago now. Then we began to communicate more often. Maddy's even on email. Quite tech savvy for someone of her advanced years." Jenny laughed.

"Well, sounds like you have a plan."

"It may be a crazy idea, but I'm going to visit Maddy in Oregon. It'll give me time to decide what to do with my life, but whatever it is it won't be with this organization, that's for sure. It'll be something completely different."

"Good on you. You know, I read about women like you the other day."

"Women like me?"

"Women who change direction at sixty. They're calling you downagers."

"Downagers," she savored the word, "I think I like that, though it may be a bit too much like dowagers." She laughed again. "That's what I'll be, a downager. You mean you think it's a good idea? It would get me out of this place and if I stay here I'll either vegetate or die."

"That's a bit strong." Rosa was pretending to look shocked, but both of them knew of several staff who had developed serious illnesses during the past year. "Though I know what you mean. I may not stay long myself."

"You're safe. They won't get rid of the finance staff. Still, it wouldn't do you any harm to look around. It's a bit like deserting the sinking ship, though it may not be actually sinking, just going round in circles."

Rosa smiled. "Great to see that sense of humor coming out again. It's been a serious few weeks."

*

Jenny felt more settled as she drove home that night. She wasn't there yet, but now there was something to focus on. Her self-confidence had taken more of a beating than she'd realized and it was good to have something to look forward to again.

Driving past the Noosa River, Jenny slowed down and thought again what a beautiful spot this was. The sun was setting and the water glistened in its fading rays. She saw a flock of red and green lorikeets rise into the treetops and knew that if she opened the window, she would hear their loud screeching as they headed for their evening roosts.

She and John had bought here when they first married, before it had become such a popular holiday and retirement spot, the warm climate and the beaches attracting people from the southern states. Jenny still lived in the home they'd chosen back then, probably a bit big for her these days, but it was great when the family came for holidays. That didn't happen so much these days, she mused. They seemed to prefer camping, or overseas trips, to visiting her up here. Still, this wasn't the time to think of changing her living arrangements. There was to be enough change in her life with whatever her future plans might hold. Jenny liked the sound of change and smiled as she drove into the garage and walked into the house. As always, she was lulled by the view over the lake from her living room and decided not to pull the drapes. Instead of turning on the television, she loaded a CD of restful music and began to prepare her meal. Her mind was full of what she needed to do. She needed to make a list. She'd do that after dinner, and first thing tomorrow would check with the pay office on what sort of payout to expect. Better to know that before making any decisions she might regret. But she already knew there would be no regrets. This felt right.

*

It was going to be a long trip. Mike switched the radio to his favorite country and western station and settled himself into the driving seat of his Chevrolet pickup, with Ben lying beside him in the passenger seat. He felt free, free at last; no longer tied to the tedium of departmental meetings, the frustration of marking assignments, counseling students. He even relished the freedom from the agonizing visits to the nursing home to the wife he loved. He was looking forward to reaching his destination. The peace of Seal Rock beckoned, and in two days he'd be there. With no distractions he could write the book he'd been researching for the past two years.

As darkness began to fall, Mike started looking out for a roadside motel where he could stretch out for the night. It didn't have to be fancy; there was only himself and Ben to consider. It wasn't long before some flashing lights ahead caught his eye and he pulled into the parking lot of a Holiday Inn. Guessing that his gear, such as it was, would be safe in the back of the vehicle, he and Ben went into the allocated room. He had eaten sparingly on the drive up, but found he really wasn't hungry, just tired. This trip was taking more out of him than he'd anticipated. Must be getting old, he thought, standing in the shower, the hot water flowing over him as the stiffness gradually disappeared from his limbs.

Ben had already found his spot and was asleep on the mat when Mike emerged dripping, a towel around his waist. Not bad for an old fellow, he thought, catching sight of himself in the mirror. He was about to turn in when he remembered he'd promised to let Maddy know his ETA.

"Mike, is that you?" Her clear, educated voice immediately called up a picture of his elegant neighbor. In her eighties, Madeline de Ruiz was the epitome of the grande dame. Never married, she had lived in the house next to theirs for as long he and Mary had owned it and longer. She enjoyed the solitary life, and Mike couldn't have wished for a better neighbor. "Are you on your way already?" she continued, interrupting his thoughts.

"Just stopped for the night. Should be there tomorrow. Guess it's cold up there, huh?"

"A bit colder than you'd be having in San Francisco, but the air is clear and the wind hasn't been too bad today. Will you let me cook you some dinner tomorrow night? That'll give you time to stock up."

"That'd be great, thanks. I'll see you then." Mike hung up. Maddy had been a good friend to Mary and him, and she'd understood when he'd not been able to get up so often over the past three years. One of the things he liked most about her was her ability to maintain silence. Apart from his Mary, Maddy was the only woman he'd met who didn't feel the need to fill every available moment with chatter. Maddy would understand his need for peace and quiet; his need to get away from the life he had known and to forge a new life for himself.

Mike's mind went back to the dinner with Bob and Cathy. They really had no inkling of how he felt; his need to be alone. He could still hear Cathy's high-pitched voice, "Won't you be lonely up there, Mike? Now that Mary's gone." She had coughed and continued, undeterred by her husband's hand on her arm. "If you stay in San Francisco there's

a better social life. You could meet someone. In fact I know several..."
At that point she must have become aware of the tension emanating
from the two men, because she hadn't finished her sentence. Mike had
taken the opportunity to leave soon after.

He knew quite well that if he stayed there, he'd become the prey
for every unmarried woman from thirty-five to sixty, and a few of the
married ones too. He'd been considered off limits while Mary was
alive, but now he was a widower... Mike had seen what happened to
another colleague. His wife had barely been cold in her grave when the
harpies appeared. He had succumbed and married again within the
year. At least it had kept the others at bay. Mike grinned. He'd be safe
where he was going. Only one woman around and that was Maddy.
She certainly wouldn't be chasing him.

As he settled down to sleep, Mike felt secure in the knowledge
he'd made the right decision. It had been a bit of a wrench to leave
the home he and Mary had made for themselves, but it was time. The
family they anticipated had never eventuated and, after a few years of
unfulfilled hopes, they'd both devoted themselves to their careers and
each other. It had been a happy life until she became sick. The cabin
at Seal Rock had been a weekend haven for them: a place to get away
from the rat race of university life. Now it would provide him with the
bolt hole he sought – a place where he could find peace and write to
his heart's content.

Three

Jenny wakened early the following morning. Looking out at the sunshine dappling the garden, she almost regretted her decision of the previous day, almost but not quite. And now she'd made the decision, she couldn't wait to get away. However, there were a few matters to take care of first. Most importantly she had to contact Maddy. Her godmother wasn't a young woman, and it would certainly disturb her routine to have Jenny land in on her. She mightn't even want her there.

As she prepared breakfast, Jenny checked out the time difference and debated whether to call or email her godmother. An email would be best, she decided. That would give Maddy time to consider the proposition, and she'd be able to prepare herself before they spoke on the phone. Logging into her computer, a quick check of her incoming mail made Jenny gasp with astonishment. There was one from Maddy to her. A shiver ran down her spine. It was as if fate had decided to take a hand. Opening it quickly, she couldn't believe her eyes. Her godmother was inviting her to visit, no, she was almost pleading with her to visit. The coincidence was staggering.

*

"And can you believe it; she says she needs to talk to me face to face and wonders if I could possibly take time off to visit her." As Jenny

19

recounted this to Rosa over their morning coffee, she was still having trouble believing it.

"So you're definitely going." Her friend smiled.

"Well, yes. Maddy was my mother's best friend. She doesn't mention what she wants to talk about."

"Does she have children of her own?"

"No. She never married. I think there was someone, but the war seemed to put paid to that, and she never met anyone else. Sad really. She's lived alone for eons, in this big house. At least it's always seemed big to me, but I guess I was only about five or six when I first saw it, so it might not be as big as I remember."

"And you haven't seen her since?"

"She visited us when I was about twelve, and we met briefly when I travelled to the US in my gap year, but I had other things on my mind then."

"I'll bet. Aren't you curious about what she wants?"

"I guess, but I'm just glad she's invited me. I was feeling a bit strange suggesting I visit after all this time on the basis of finding that sand dollar."

"So you replied and told her, did you?"

"Yes, and I'll call tomorrow. That'll give her time to digest my email. I can't believe I'm really going. There's so much to do. Tell the kids for one thing." She stopped, imagining the outcry when Helen and Hugh learned of her plans.

"That'll put their noses out of joint. Do them good, realizing you're not going to be at their beck and call." Rosa went silent as if wondering if she'd said too much.

Jenny smiled. She knew that, close as she was to her children and grandchildren, her friend believed they often took advantage of her.

"Are you going to accept the redundancy right away then?"

Jenny thought for a moment. "Well, maybe not right away. I don't want to make any rash decisions, though it *is* what I want to do," she added quickly. "But I might just take some leave first. I have about three months long service leave owing to me plus some annual leave."

"Yes, you always were too conscientious to take leave when you should have, unlike everyone else."

"Well, it'll come in handy now, won't it? That's if they'll let me go off at such short notice." Jenny suddenly sounded deflated as she realized the organization might not take kindly to her request for immediate leave.

"I bet they jump at it. You'll be one less person to worry about when they put all the new plans into place. Your only worry will be what you come back to."

"Oh, I'm not concerned about that." Jenny finished her coffee and stood up. "I'll fill in the forms now. Get in while the going's good."

Once Jenny's leave was granted, she began to prepare for her trip. She delayed telling her children until everything was settled as she had no doubt they'd try to change her mind. Just a quick visit to each, she decided, then she'd be off. As she began to make lists for everything that needed to be done prior to such an extensive trip, she picked up the sand dollar again. Such a little object, she contemplated, and yet, here she was making plans to travel across the world to visit the place it had come from.

Four

Seal Rock, Oregon

Mike typed the final word for the day, and pushing his chair back from the desk, linked his hands behind his head and stretched. He looked out at the wild Pacific Ocean in the distance and contemplated, not for the first time, how peaceful he felt here.

This won't do, he thought, rising and signaling to Ben, lying at his feet. The dog jumped up at his master's bidding and led the way to the door, pausing by the hook where his lead hung.

"Come on, boy." Mike shrugged into the checked bomber jacket, which showed the wear and tear of many of his own sixty-three years, and let himself and his dog out into the brisk air.

As they made their way down the rough roadway which led to the beach, Mike glanced up at the neighboring house. Seeing a movement at the door, he stopped.

"Have you time for a coffee?" The voice, though old, was strong, and came from the erect grey-haired matron who was the only other human to inhabit this quiet roadway.

"Always time for you, Maddy. Come, Ben." Mike changed direction to head towards the high-roofed dwelling standing back from the road. "You're braving the cold this afternoon?"

Maddy looked up at the sky. "Might be some rain later. It's true Oregon spring weather," she laughed. "Come on in. I must have known you'd be out and about. I've some coffee already brewing. I want you to hear my news."

"News?" Mike followed the elegant figure into the house and, looking around, admired again the warmth of the décor. Maddy had lived in the same spot for over fifty years, and the whole place reflected her exquisite taste.

His companion waited till they were settled by the wood stove with Ben at their feet, before continuing. "It's Jenny. Remember my telling you about her?" Without waiting for his response, she added, "Looks as if she's going to lose her job."

"Isn't she the super-efficient multitasking robot who lives in Australia?" Mike said, wrapping both hands around his mug of coffee. "Surely she'll find it easy to get another position. Or maybe take time to relax?" he joked, sipping his coffee with enjoyment.

"That's just it. She seems to be taking it badly, and as you know, I need to think of my future here. Jenny's the closest thing I have to family."

"You'll go on forever." Mike's eyes focused on the woman sitting opposite. "You haven't changed in the ten years I've been coming up here." He looked around at the immaculate home. "And you don't do too badly on the home front either."

"Thanks, you're a tonic to an old lady. But we can't get away from the fact that I'm not getting any younger. I need to think of the future, both for me and this house." Maddy looked reflectively into the fire. "I wouldn't like to think of strangers living here."

"Maddy, be realistic. She lives in Australia. It's the other side of the world, and doesn't she have children too?"

"And grandchildren. Something I haven't been blessed with." She looked over at the photo on the wall of the soldier who hadn't returned from the Second World War.

"That's something we have in common." Mike moved restlessly in the chair. "Mary and I would have liked children, but it wasn't to be. Anyway is that your news; that this Jenny's job is going belly up on her?"

"That's only part of it. She's coming here. Should arrive in two to three weeks. It'll be a bit of a break for her, give her time to work out what she wants to do, and time for us to get reacquainted." She smiled. "She found the sand dollar. She was only about six when she visited, and she picked up a sand dollar on the beach. She believed me when I told her it was magic. She's kept it all these years... and now it's bringing her back."

Mike scratched his head. "A sand dollar, but they're ten a penny. They sell them in all the souvenir shops around here. There's nothing magic in them. Isn't there some story?"

"Well, I remember telling her it was mermaid's money washed up on the beach and was very special. I believe there's a story about some religious symbolism, but I prefer the magical explanation myself."

"Sounds as if your peace'll be shattered. How long does she intend to stay?" Mike was wondering if Jenny's visit was going to disturb *his* peace too. He enjoyed the quiet and privacy of this neck of the woods. He didn't want it spoiled by a visitor from overseas.

"Open-ended." Maddy appeared smug. "But I expect she'll soon sort herself out and be off again. She's about your age," she added with a glint in her eye.

"You're not going to try matchmaking, I hope." Mike smiled grimly. "I'm past all that."

"I wouldn't dare." Maddy looked down into her coffee as if working out what to say next. "I just meant that you two may have things in common, being from the same era."

"Oh, yes. You mean we'd like the same music? Doubt it. I've never been in sync with guys of my generation. That's probably why you and I get on so well." He stood up. "Thanks for the coffee, Maddy. Might be best if I keep out of the way when your visitor is here. Ben and I'll catch up with you before she arrives. Let me know if there's anything I can do to help you prepare for her visit."

Walking along the windswept beach, Mike pondered as he threw pieces of driftwood for Ben to fetch. He'd quickly become accustomed to this solitary existence. Maddy scarcely counted since she was as solitary as he was. They rubbed together well as neighbors; there when needed, but keeping to themselves most of the time. Of course, he could understand Maddy's concern about the future. She didn't seem to have any relatives, at least none that came to visit. But this visitor from Australia. What would that do to their peaceful existence? He zipped up his jacket as the wind buffeted him. It was so strong he could feel the grains of sand hitting his face as if he was being sandblasted.

The wind would keep away the rain Maddy had predicted though, he had to admit, a day without rain was unusual at this time of year.

It wasn't surprising, Mike reflected, that he and Ben had the beach to themselves. This was the way they liked it. Mike had come to regard it as *his* beach, this long stretch of white sand, just the spot to find the sand dollars Maddy had talked about. As Ben began his favorite game of chasing the waves, Mike sat down on one of the large logs washed up by a recent storm and gazed out at the ocean.

*

Back home again Mike took off his jacket and turned up the heat. The house, built as a hunting cabin some twenty years ago, had been modernized by the previous owners, and it provided a cozy home, well suited to his present needs. Sitting down at his desk once more, he took one glance at the growing clouds outside and settled to outline his next chapter. The Siuslaw Indians were proving a great distraction from everything around him as he researched their history. Once living in kinship villages prior to the advent of the white man, and now part of the Confederated Tribes of Coos, Lower Umpqua and Siuslaw Indians, the descendants owned the Three Rivers Casino in neighboring Florence. As he trawled through on-line documents, Mike became lost in another world, one in which the Indian reigned supreme in his territory. It was dark when he finally raised his head to hear Ben's protests that it was well past mealtime.

Five

Mike slammed the door of his pickup and brushed his hand through his hair, reflecting that his good genes had ensured its continuing thickness. Even though he was in his early sixties, his thatch still retained much of its original reddish color albeit somewhat faded, though his beard was letting him down by turning white.

He'd driven down to Florence from Seal Rock to keep an appointment which could prove vital to his research. Pushing open the door to the coffee house, Mike was met by a welcome blast of hot air. Oregon in April was cold. A long lanky figure unfolded itself from a table in the back corner.

"You'd be Mike." The voice was slow, but more cultured than he'd expected, and he silently castigated himself for his unwitting prejudice.

"Paul, good to meet you at last."

"Yeah. Emails are okay, but I'm glad to see the man behind them. Let's get you tanked up, then we'll see how I can help you."

A few minutes later both men were nursing extra-large mugs of strong black coffee, while contemplating the river outside the window. Mike broke into the comfortable silence. "You mentioned you're a member of one of the Native American tribes around here. As I said, I'm writing a history of the tribes and would be most grateful for any information you could help me with."

"We...ell." There was a long pause during which Mike wondered if he'd hit a raw nerve by jumping straight in. "I'm a card-carrying Native American, you might say," Paul replied at last. "That means I have some Native American ancestry. In fact, I'm what you call one eighth Native American. I can locate Native American blood on both sides; Mother and Father. But I'm not really part of the community here in Oregon, though I do have some connections with it. What sort of book are you writing? As I said, I don't know if I can be of much help."

"As I explained in my emails, I've been researching the tribes around here for a few years now. It's a bit of a historical treatise and I'd like to get some hands-on info; speak to a few of the guys. Need to make sure I'm not treading on any toes. Seemed like you could help. So now I've moved to Seal Rock..."

"Nice spot," said Paul, taking a sip of his coffee. "You living there permanent now?"

"Yeah. I was hoping you might be able to introduce me to some of the Native American community up here. I know you said you're only on the periphery of the group. Do you know anyone who'd be willing to talk with me?"

There was as long pause, while Paul seemed to be working out what to say. Then he began slowly. "We...ll, let me see. There's Ron... yeah, I guess he'd be your best bet. Ron Williams. He's pretty involved up at the casino, and he goes to all the gatherings. Don't do that myself. He'd be good for a yarn about what happened in the old days."

"Great." At last Mike felt he was getting somewhere. He downed the remainder of his coffee in one gulp. "Can you introduce me to him? How does that work?"

Another long pause. Mike was just about to give up when Paul replied, "He lives a way up, at Yachats. Can try to reach him. Will it be okay if I call you?"

"Sure. That would be best. Will you want to be there when we meet?" he queried.

"See what Ron wants," was the laconic reply, and with that Mike had to be satisfied. The two men rose and left the coffee shop together, shaking hands before they hopped into their respective vehicles. As Mike drove off, he noticed Paul had taken time to make a call on his mobile before starting the engine and wondered what that was about. Probably nothing to do with him, Mike decided.

*

Looking at her caller's number, Ellen was tempted to let the phone ring. She'd agreed to go to dinner with Paul the previous night only because he'd caught her in a weak moment. He was a friend of her brother, and not her type at all, if she did have a type, that is. She'd been on her own for so long she'd forgotten what her type was. Anyway he'd been asking her for some time. She'd finally agreed to meet him the night before and it hadn't gone well. Nothing against him, but a meal at the Casino just wasn't her thing. She'd hated the noise and the smoke, though she had to admit the food had been good, and Paul had made an amusing companion.

She picked up the phone. "Hi Paul, thanks for last night." She tried to be polite, but knew her voice lacked enthusiasm. However, he didn't seem to notice the absence of her usual friendly tone. Peering out of the window she could see his pickup parked across the street. What was the man thinking of, ringing her from right across the road?

He got straight to the point, but there was no mention of their date, nor, to her surprise and relief, of any future one. "Glad you're there, Ellen. I've just met this fellow. Been sending emails back and forth for a time. He's writing a book about our people, and I thought maybe you and Ron could help." Ellen held the phone away from her ear and laughed to herself. Here was she thinking he was calling for another date, and he was on a different planet altogether. And what was this with *our people*? Paul only identified as Native American when it suited him. Clearly it suited him right now.

"What do you expect me to do?" She thought quickly, a talent she'd developed over the years. Maybe she could shunt him off on her brother. That way she could avoid a repeat of the previous evening. "I think you'd better talk with Ron. He's most likely to have more time than I do right now." She looked around her bookshop and lamented, not for the first time, her lack of staff.

"Yeah that's what I'm calling about. Where's the best place to reach him? Will he be back up at Yachats yet?"

Ellen checked her watch. It was almost noon. "Right now, you'll probably find him down at the boat ramp. He's there most days at this time." Hanging up, Ellen reflected that her brother managed to while away most of his days. Since being invalided out of the forces after Vietnam, he'd shunned any idea of finding gainful employment.

She and Ron were both disappointments to their parents. Ellen sighed. Rita and Dick Williams had expected to be grandparents by now, such store did they set on the continuance of the family. Brother Ron had been a sporting hero at school and popular with the girls, but Vietnam had put paid to any dreams of a sporting career or family life. He had returned a broken man, in body and spirit and, to the despair of his family, was content to spend his time with old comrades rehashing what he saw as the highlight of his life.

Ellen's parents had held out more hope for her. But she had disappointed them too, the expected marriage failing to materialize. Always the bridesmaid, never the bride was how she categorized herself and, though godmother to the children of several friends, she'd failed to provide her parents with the longed-for grandchildren. Not that her single state bothered her unduly. Even as a child she'd been content with her own company; content with the invisible friends she talked to and played with. As she'd grown older, these "friends" had developed into visions and premonitions, which didn't always make sense to her at the time. She had come to accept that this was her destiny, her means of contributing to her community and to society in general.

Re-shelving her wide collection of romance novels, Ellen took time to reflect on her own series of on/off relationships. The most recent had ended only two years earlier, when Will had decided to move to Canada to be with his daughter and grandchildren. So much for his commitment to their relationship. But her bookshop meant more to her than had any of the men in her life, and even if Will had asked her to go with him, she'd have found it hard to agree.

Patting the last book in place, she looked around, filled with gratitude at what she had created here. Every day she gave thanks she'd been guided to this spot. It had been a rundown old tobacconists when she first saw it, but she knew it had potential, and here it was – The Reading Nook, aptly named. It was her private place and she'd fashioned it so that her customers could treat it as their private place too. The shelves were placed at odd angles to provide lots of corners. These corners held chairs sporting brightly colored squashy cushions, perfect for relaxed reading. That's what brought people back again and again.

Ellen sniffed up the familiar aroma, a blend of books, print and the scented candle she always kept lit behind the counter. As she made her way back there, she wondered exactly what this friend of Paul's wanted of Ron, but immediately dismissed it. It wouldn't have anything to do with her.

Six

Jenny was full of vitality when she picked up her hire car at Portland airport. It had been a long trip, but she'd managed to get some sleep, and the walk between terminals at Los Angeles had helped by taking her out into the fresh air, though fresh was probably the wrong word for it. The exhaust fumes from traffic, and the large number of smokers she'd had to walk past, did nothing to endear her to the United States. She'd been bombarded by loud announcements in Spanish, and had her passport requested by heavily built security guards who called her ma'am.

Now, however, she'd packed her luggage into the red PT Cruiser that was to be her vehicle for the next few months or so, and set out to become familiar with driving on the right hand side of the road. Once she'd left the city behind, Jenny was feeling more comfortable with the driving, and dared to turn on the radio. Finding a country and western station, she began to sing along, enjoying the scenery so different from home, and fascinated by the enormously large road signs and plethora of roadside diners.

Darkness was beginning to fall as she drove down Highway 101 and, passing through Newport, spied the sign for Seal Rock. She stopped to check the directions Maddy had sent her. She had to look for a dirt road opposite the beach on the left, and two mailboxes, one of which was topped by a metal cockerel. Driving slowly, and peering into the gloaming, Jenny could see there wasn't much to the township. All too soon, it seemed she'd passed right through and there, sure enough, on the left, were the two mailboxes. She turned the headlights on full, and made a left turn up a rough dirt road. In the distance, she could see the lights of a house.

As she drove into the yard, the door was flung open, and a tall figure was silhouetted in the light spilling out from the house.

"Welcome, my dear Jenny Wren," the familiar voice with its American lilt greeted her as she opened the car door.

Jenny ran to embrace her godmother. "Oh, Maddy, it's so good to see you after all this time."

Maddy returned the embrace warmly, then held her goddaughter at arm's length as if to inspect her. "You've worn well, honey. But you must be tired. You've had a long journey. How does a nice bowl of pumpkin soup with some of my home-made bread sound?"

"To die for," was Jenny's fervent reply, as she was ushered into the main room.

"It's just as I remember it," she cried joyfully, looking around to see the warm rag rugs lying as if thrown down haphazardly on the wooden floor; the wood stove on one wall providing firelight to the corners; the dried flowers and décor hanging from high rafters, and the walls filled with artifacts collected by Maddy on her travels.

"Come in here." Maddy drew Jenny into the kitchen area, where a steaming pot of soup was bubbling away on the stove. The scent of newly baked bread met Jenny's nostrils, and she sniffed it up greedily, closing her eyes to recapture the memories of her childhood.

It wasn't long before Jenny had finished her soup, and was soaking up the remnants with the last piece of bread.

"You don't seem to have aged at all," she said. It was difficult to accept that the erect elegant woman sitting opposite was in her eighties. Apart from the white hair, now in a neat bun on top of her head, and the faint lines on her otherwise smooth skin, she looked no different from how Jenny remembered her looking almost forty years earlier.

"Now, tell me what's been happening to you," Maddy began. "You've given your life to that organization, and you say they're going to toss you out with no thanks."

"It's not quite like that," Jenny said. "There have been major changes, and I guess I'm not part of them. But I'm okay with it," she grimaced. "I am now, anyway. I'm looking at this as a chance to move on, do something else. I'm not sure what at this stage, but something will come to me. I plan to use this trip as time out; time to consider what I want to do with the rest of my life."

"But your children, what do they think about all this?"

Jenny sat back. "They think it's their time; that I should be prepared to spend the rest of my life child minding." When Maddy didn't respond, she added, "I love my kids, and the grandkids too. Don't get me wrong. But I can't see myself spending all day every day with them. We'd drive each other mad. They need to stand on their own feet." As she spoke, Jenny had a picture of Helen and Alan as she'd left them. They'd been coping well. Alan had a good job, and Helen seemed to have accepted she couldn't rely on her mother to step in. Hugh had been quite a different matter, encouraging her to take the trip, while predicting she'd miss them all more than she expected. He might be right. Time would tell.

"Well, you're very welcome here. Take as long as you like. It's a good place to think. But I don't imagine you want to start thinking tonight. A good night's sleep is called for. We can have a chat in the morning."

Jenny yawned. The long trip was finally catching up with her. "I'll just fetch my things from the car."

In no time at all, Jenny was ensconced in the bedroom she remembered. The last thing she saw before she closed her eyes was the sand dollar, which she'd brought with her and placed on the bedside table. She'd brought it back to where it belonged.

*

Jenny awakened to unfamiliar sounds and a watery sunlight creeping through the curtains. It took her a few seconds to work out where she was. Looking at her watch, which she had left lying on the bedside table, she saw it was eight o'clock. Swinging her legs over the side of the bed, Jenny picked up the sand dollar lying beside her watch. She turned it over in her hands. It was a very ordinary round white disc, yet it had seemed important enough to bring her all this way.

Jenny quickly shrugged on her robe and stepped into the large room which was the hub of this house. Maddy was in the kitchen, and there were some delicious aromas wafting towards Jenny.

"Pancakes, my favorite! Sorry I overslept."

Maddy turned around from the stove. "Not at all, dear, but I thought you'd make it up soon, so I was just getting these started. Would you like to shower or eat first?"

"Shower if I've time." Jenny realized she was going to be spoiled here if she wasn't careful. The table held a large platter of pancakes along with butter, maple syrup and a bowl of chopped fruit. Freshly brewed coffee bubbled away on the stove, and her godmother was already dressed for the day in tailored black pants topped with a red sweater.

"If you're quick. They won't stay hot for long. And wear something warm. It's going to be a bit fresh today," Maddy said, pouring some coffee for herself and sitting down to read the paper.

Jenny was soon ready, and the pancakes were still warm when she appeared again and took her seat opposite Maddy. She had taken the older woman's advice and was wearing pants and a white roll neck sweater teamed with a navy fleece waistcoat.

"You look good," Maddy approved. "Now tuck in. I don't want to hear any silly nonsense about diets while you're here. Food is meant to be enjoyed, and it's not often I have someone to cook for."

Maddy filled her in on the local area, suggesting she might like to check out the beach later in the day.

"What was the important thing you wanted to talk with me about?" Jenny asked finally, when the last pancake had been eaten, and the coffee mugs emptied for the second time.

"It'll keep," Maddy smiled cagily. "Now, how about you come shopping with me? I wasn't sure of your tastes, so didn't do a full shop before you arrived. It'll give you a chance to check out our local shops too. You'll probably find them a tad different from what you're used to in Australia," she chuckled.

As they drove out of Maddy's garage, a white pickup went past in a flurry of dust, and Jenny heard a horn toot and saw a hand wave. "Who...," she began.

"That's Mike. He's my nearest neighbor, the owner of the other mailbox. But you won't see much of him." Maddy's voice became solemn. "He's recently lost his wife, and come up here to retire in a cabin a ways up the road. I think he's scared of women his own age. He reckons he's safe with me," she chortled, as if amused by the idea.

"Oh." Jenny expressed no interest in this piece of information. If she thought anything at all, it was that she certainly had no desire to meet a grumpy old man. Although she didn't consider *herself* to be old, she knew many of her age, men in particular, had given up on life.

Driving along, Jenny took the opportunity to ask her godmother a question she'd often wondered about. "Maddy, why do you call me Jenny Wren? I love your pet name for me, but I've often wondered where it came from. A wren isn't an American bird is it?"

"Bless you. We do have wrens in Oregon, but it's not after the bird. Jenny Wren's a favorite character in Dickens' *Our Mutual Friend*. She's a doll's dressmaker, and when you were little, you loved dressing up your dolls in all sorts of bits and pieces."

"Umm." Jenny was silent as she digested this information.

Once in the local supermarket, Jenny saw what her godmother had meant. While much of the layout was similar to what she was accustomed to back home, everything was on a much larger scale, from the size of the building and the layout of merchandise to the actual packaging of the food itself. Who on earth would want to buy ten pounds of smoked salmon, she wondered. She was used to packs more in the order of five hundred grams. Then there was the inclusion of a liquor section, with some Australian wines, she was glad to see, and guns. No wonder there were so many shooting incidents reported in this country, she figured, if they were readily available in the supermarket. It certainly was a one stop shop, and the service was amazing. Her jaw dropped when they were greeted in the aisles by assistants asking if they'd found everything they wanted, as well as wishing them a good day, and sounding as if they really meant it.

"Well?" When they were back in the car again, Maddy turned to her house guest. "What did you think?"

Looking at the figures hurrying around the parking lot, many on the large side, Jenny smiled. "I'm surprised everyone here isn't overweight," she joked. "All that hefty packaging makes it look as if everyone is feeding an army. How do you manage with just yourself to cook for?"

"There are some smaller packs if you know where to look, and I shop carefully. I don't buy prepackaged. I have them weigh out what I need."

*

Jenny surprised herself by having an afternoon nap and wakened feeling refreshed. "I could get used to this," she said, emerging from her bedroom to find Maddy sipping a cup of herbal tea.

"Why not? It's what I do most afternoons. Sets me up for the rest of the day. It's my version of happy hour." Maddy certainly looked full of energy as she offered Jenny a cup of tea.

"No thanks." Jenny was pulling on a thick parka she'd found hanging by the door. "I think I'll take up that idea of yours to walk along the beach before it gets dark. Okay if I wear this? Sure you don't want to come with me?" She looked at Maddy expectantly.

"No, you go on. I'd just hold you back. I'll have some dinner ready for you. Don't be too long. It'll be dark soon, and it comes down quickly here."

"Dinner! I feel as if I've just had lunch. All I seem to do here is eat," Jenny muttered, making her way out of the door.

She enjoyed the brisk walk down the dirt track and soon found herself crossing the road to the beach. Once there, she stood amazed. It was exactly as she remembered it; maybe even wilder than she remembered. High waves crashed up onto the rocky shore, which was strewn with white driftwood. A couple of utes, or what would be called trucks or pickups here – she had still to work out the difference – were parked at the roadside, and she could see a few people down by the water. They seemed to be gathering the driftwood into piles, and one was carrying an armful toward one of the vehicles. Jenny wondered what they were going to do with the wood. It looked too nice to use as firewood, but that would make sense in this cold climate.

Seeing the sun begin to dip on the horizon, she turned back towards her erstwhile home and hurried up the track. She'd almost reached the turn off to Maddy's house when she was nearly blinded by the lights of a vehicle coming towards her. Jumping quickly out of the way, she cursed. That had been a near thing. It must have been the neighbor, the grumpy misogynist. Well, she'd certainly keep out of his way.

Seven

Stepping out of the house to greet the morning, Jenny stretched luxuriantly. She'd been in Oregon two weeks already and was still none the wiser as to why Maddy had been so keen for her to visit. But she was glad she'd come. Already the peace of this place was having an effect on her. Jenny could feel all of her cares falling away. She was insulated from the stresses of job and family. Time enough to think of them later, much later.

With a sigh, she turned and went back into the warmth, rubbing her hands up her arms.

"Cold out there this morning?" Maddy was already standing by the stove, brewing the inevitable coffee.

"Coffee, yum. What's the plan for today?" Jenny yawned, as she sat down at the well-worn table, feeling quite at home.

"I think we'll go into town, to Waldport. There's someone I want you to meet."

Jenny's head bobbed up. This was something new. "What? Who?"

Maddy brought two mugs of coffee and sat down on the opposite side of the table. "I'm not getting any younger." As Jenny moved to say something, she held up her hand. "Just listen. I know I may seem hale and hearty, and that's the way I feel right now, but there's no getting away from the fact. I'm eighty-three and I'm not going to live forever."

Jenny felt the tears come to her eyes as she looked across the table. She started to speak, but Maddy beat her to it.

"No, dear, I'm just being realistic. But I've needed to make

preparations. To work out what to do with this place when I'm gone."
She looked around the house with affection. "I'd like to think it went
to someone who could care about it like I do." She leant her elbows on
the table and, leaning her chin on her hands, looked across at Jenny.
"That's why it'll go to you when I pass away."

"Me?" Jenny's voice squeaked in surprise. "But surely…"

"You're closest to me, and in the last couple of weeks, I've seen how
you've come to love it here."

Finding her voice again, Jenny began to remonstrate. "It's very kind
of you, Maddy dear, but think of it. My life is in Australia. I'm sure it
would be better…" But she didn't go on, because she couldn't think of
what would be better. The thought of having this haven of tranquility
to escape to was bringing all her emotions to the fore. She brushed the
back of her hand across her eyes to stem the threatening tears and said,
"How lovely of you to think of me in that way."

"I knew it was the right decision." Smiling, Maddy stretched over
to cover Jenny's hand with her own. The older hand felt frail to Jenny.
She could sense the fine bones through the stretched skin. Affection
for the older woman welled up, and her voice choked with emotion.
"Thank you."

Seeming unmoved by the emotion, Maddy continued briskly. "I
want to take you in to meet my lawyer today. Young George needs
your signature on a couple of documents."

"My signature?" Jenny was surprised. "Why does he need that?"

"There are a few other things I need to get in place. You'll be my
executor, of course, along with Mike up the road here, but I'm also
putting in place a revocable trust to avoid probate. I also have a living
will. I want everyone to be clear I never want to be on one of those
life support things. I've lived long enough. I don't want the quacks
keeping me alive just because they can." Maddy's voice was as strong
as ever, and Jenny smiled through damp eyes at the thought of anyone
trying to do anything to Maddy against her will. She was a force to be
reckoned with. I hope I can be as strong as that when I'm her age, was
the thought uppermost in Jenny's mind.

"Now, let's have breakfast. What about some bacon and eggs to
prepare us for our trip?"

"I'll make it," responded Jenny, still bemused by the conversation, and needing something to keep her occupied. As she broke the eggs and dropped the bacon into the pan, she turned over the conversation. She couldn't quite come to grips with someone cold-bloodedly making plans for her own demise, as Maddy was doing. But then, she'd never been close to anyone of Maddy's age before now, or anyone so strong-minded.

Now that she'd got her message across, Maddy seemed more relaxed and turned the conversation to Jenny herself. "Have you thought any more about what you're going to do when you go back home?" she asked, quickly adding, "I hope it's not for a while yet. You did say that you had three months leave, didn't you?"

"Yes." Jenny turned from her cooking. "I feel as if I've been here an age already, but I've lots of time. So long as everything is okay at home." As she spoke, Jenny realized she hadn't given any thought to matters at home in the last few days. For a moment she felt a few qualms, wondering what was happening, then she gave herself a shake. No, she was taking this time off, completely off. She'd forget about work, and even family, for a bit longer.

Breakfast over, Maddy seemed eager to be off and was hurrying Jenny along as she shrugged into a warm jacket. Jenny was beginning to realize the weather here was quite a bit cooler than she'd anticipated. Spring in Oregon was much colder than a Queensland winter, and the clothes she'd packed didn't quite suit.

"Can we check out some clothes shops when we're in town?" she said, as the two women piled into the car. "I'm going to need some warmer wear. I can't keep borrowing your outer garments."

"Sure thing, honey. I know just the place. We'll have a spot of lunch too. There's a great Mexican I favor."

Food again, thought Jenny. I can't believe how it seems to dominate our day. She settled to enjoy the view out the window as they sped along. She loved the outlook of the wild ocean on one side, paired with the tall forests on the other. It was quite primitive country, reminiscent of a trip she'd made to the northern part of Scotland several years earlier.

The meeting with the solicitor took up most of the morning. He was very chatty and interested in hearing Jenny talk about Australia. He said it was somewhere he and his wife were keen to visit, and he wanted to take this opportunity to find out as much as he could about the best places to see on their trip. However, in the midst of all this friendly chatter, they managed to complete the business of the day, and the pair left with Maddy satisfied with the result.

"Now, clothes." Maddy was in fine form, seemingly much relieved her legal business had been concluded. "We'll drive down to Florence. It's only about an hour away. There's a little place down there." The two women were silent as they drove along the coastal highway. Jenny was a bit stunned by it all. What would she do with a house in Seal Rock, Oregon? Well, she figured, shooting a glance at Maddy whose total focus was on the road ahead of them, it didn't look as if she'd have to worry about that for some time to come.

"This part is called Old Town," Maddy explained as they stepped out into a narrow street, bounded on both sides with shops and restaurants. "It's built along the river, and is a great haunt for tourists." Looking around, Jenny could see what she meant. She found herself anxious to explore, but decided that, for this trip, she'd better confine herself to the task in hand.

"Here we are," Maddy said. As she spoke, she led the way across the street, stopping by a double fronted window which displayed a range of casual women's fashions. "I think you'll find something to suit here. It's run by a group of women, and they cater to most tastes, mature tastes that is, not for the twenty year olds."

Pushing open the door, Jenny was surprised to hear singing coming from the back of the shop. "They're all in a choir, too," Maddy said. "It adds to the atmosphere, don't you think?" As she searched through the racks, Jenny discovered she was thoroughly enjoying herself. It had been ages since she'd taken time to shop for herself, and it was nice to be able to choose garments which didn't need to be suitable for the office.

Jenny left with an armful of bags containing pants, sweaters, and a weatherproof, fleece-lined jacket with a hood, perfect for the changeable weather here. She'd also snuck in a pale blue cotton ribbed jacket with stud fastening, designed for the summer Oregon weather, but perfect for a winter back home. "Thanks so much, Maddy. I'd never have found a place like that on my own. Do you go there often?" she asked, in recognition that the ladies behind the counter seemed to be on friendly terms with her godmother.

"My favorite place to shop," returned the older woman. "You may have noticed my indoor clothes are all-season ones." She looked down at her heavy cotton pants and top. "I buy nearly all of them here. I love the Oregon cotton clothes. Just change the weight of the top layer with the seasons."

That's certainly a simple way to do things, thought Jenny, beginning to wonder if a change in lifestyle would mean she'd change her style of dressing. Maybe her business suits were a thing of the past. It was certainly food for thought. Piling into the car again, she said, "You mentioned lunch. There seem to be lots of places here."

"Yes, but I want to take you to the Mexican on Highway 101. I don't get there very often and it's authentic food. You'll love it." Five minutes later the two were poring over the menu at a wide wooden table which sported a large basket of corn chips and two dips.

"What do you recommend?" Jenny couldn't remember the last time she'd eaten Mexican. She rather thought it was the time she'd felt her head almost blown off when she'd gulped down an icy cold margarita. She had no memory of what she'd eaten that night.

"Depends how hungry you are. I always go for a combination dish. That way you get to taste a variety. It doesn't matter if you don't eat it all," Maddy advised. "The servings are pretty large."

"Okay. I'm willing to try anything, but maybe a beer to wash it down?"

"Sure. I'll just have a Coke. I like to keep my alcohol consumption to the evenings when I can fall into bed afterwards."

"I've eaten far too much." Jenny viewed the empty plate in front of her in surprise. "But it was delicious. I couldn't do that too often," she said. "This is my treat," she added, taking the bill and placing her credit card alongside it. "Thank you so much. What a day. Home now?"

"I think so. Would you mind driving?" Maddy was beginning to look a bit tired. "I think I've worn myself out. But it's been fun. It's nice to have someone to do these things with for a change."

Jenny enjoyed the drive back. She needed practice to get used to driving on the right, and Maddy's car was a tad heavier than the PT Cruiser she'd hired. Still, they arrived home unscathed, and both retired for an afternoon nap. It would be easy to become used to this relaxed lifestyle, Jenny reflected, but it wasn't the answer for her. She was going to need something to get her teeth into and, so far, she'd no idea what.

It was already becoming dark when Jenny opened her eyes again, so she decided to give her beach walk a miss, planning to rise early the next morning instead. Given their heavy lunch, she set about preparing an omelet as a light supper. It was almost ready when Maddy appeared.

"Oh dear, I'm afraid I left you to your own devices. What kind of a hostess does that make me?" she said.

"I enjoyed it. I'm sorry if I tired you out today."

"You're right. We tried to do too much. Should have kept Florence for another day. I'll have an early night and may take things a bit easier tomorrow. This smells delicious and exactly what we need after that big lunch."

As Jenny prepared for bed that night she caught sight of a set of headlights travelling up the track. The neighbor, she guessed, wondering if he'd manage to keep out of her way for her entire visit. It would suit her just fine if he did. She didn't need her visit to be spoiled by someone whom she had already decided to dislike.

Eight

Mike felt he was making progress with his research. Paul had introduced him to his mate Ron, and the three had met for a bit of a chinwag. This Ron fellow had proved to be a mine of information, and what he didn't know, others would and he'd offered to find them. The plan was for Mike and Ron to get together again, and for Ron to introduce Mike to one of the elders of the Community. With a bit of luck he could wangle an invite to one of the tribal gatherings.

He had been up before the sun, working on a chapter that had been giving him problems, and was brewing some coffee when Ben dropped a ball at his feet. "Sorry, old fellow. Have I been neglecting you?" Mike picked the ball up and threw it gently across the room. Ben skidded after it and rucked up the rag rug which had been lovingly made by Mary several years earlier. "I guess this isn't the place. What say we hit the beach before it gets crowded?" Ben was a great companion, always agreed and never answered back. The dog wagged his tail frantically, as Mike found his jacket on the hall stand and let them both out.

It was a quick jog down to the beach which, as he'd expected, was deserted at this time in the morning. Lifting his face to the sky, Mike drank in the fresh air. This was what he'd come to Oregon to find: peace and tranquility. He took a deep breath. *Yes, it had been the right decision. This was a place he could be happy, could start again.*

Conscious of the dog bounding around his feet, he picked up one of the many pieces of driftwood lying around and began to play Ben's favorite game of fetch which, he knew, would go on till one of them tired of it, usually Mike. Ben's energy seemed boundless for an old dog. After about an hour of this, Mike was aware of an empty ache in his stomach and, seeing they'd strayed some way from where they'd started, called out, "Here Ben. Home," and started to jog back the way they'd come.

As they reached the roadway, Mike looked curiously at a red-coated figure walking towards the sea. It didn't appear to be anyone he knew. Must be a tourist, he decided, though it was a bit early in the season for them. He admired the long-legged figure in the distance. There weren't too many people who'd brave the beach this early in the morning. As he and Ben crossed the road toward the track home, Mike realized he hadn't seen a car. Where could the figure on the beach have come from? It was only as he made his way up the track past Maddy's home that the penny dropped. Of course, it must be the goddaughter from Australia. She was still here. Well, now he knew to keep away for a bit longer. Mike hoped his neighbor's peace wasn't being disturbed too much. He knew how much she valued it.

*

Jenny had noticed the man and dog on the beach as soon as she arrived. She was a bit disappointed, as she'd hoped to have it all to herself at this time of the morning. However, they seemed intent on their game and were moving away from her so she walked right down to the edge of the water and gazed out. It was so wonderful, this vast expanse of ocean. She stood breathing in the sea air as if her lungs couldn't get enough of it. Raising her arms to the sky she turned around full circle, then, realizing she might look strange to anyone watching, slowly let her arms drop and stuffed her hands into her pockets. Taking a quick peek, she saw the man and his dog were still moving away from her, but as she watched, they turned, so she quickly looked out to sea again and started to walk in the other direction.

Jenny wondered if the man was the neighbor Maddy had mentioned. She really couldn't tell from this distance, but his movements weren't those of the old codger she'd expected, and his hair looked blonde in the early sunlight. Even though Maddy had told her he was around her age, somehow Jenny had imagined someone old and staid, not someone like this man who was bounding along the beach with a black dog at his heels.

Despite her warm clothes, the cold was beginning to bite, so Jenny made her way back to the house. "I'm really loving it here," she burst out to Maddy who was sitting at the table with the local paper. "But I need to make plans."

"For what?" Maddy lowered the paper and peered over her glasses. "I thought you came here to relax. This is time out, right?"

"Right." Jenny bit her lip. "But I'll have to go back sometime, and I'll need a plan. It's wonderful here, but you know I can't stay. My life is in Australia. My children are there."

"Of course, I know that, and I'd never try to encourage you to stay here. But this place has a healing effect, and I can see it's beginning to work its magic on you. When I invited you here, it was for selfish reasons, I'm afraid." Maddy removed her glasses, placing them carefully on the table next to her half-empty coffee mug. "I needed to set my affairs in order, and I wanted you here to help get that done. But when you arrived you were as taut as the wire in that fence. You're beginning to loosen up, but you've still a way to go."

Jenny listened open-mouthed. This was news to her. She thought back to the day she'd arrived. *Yes, she'd been her usual super organized self. Had she really changed in the short weeks she'd been here?* She looked down at her mode of dress. *Well, that had changed for sure. And, yes, she was conscious of feeling more relaxed about things. What things? Well, her future. Was this desire for a plan only a way of trying to get back to the woman she'd been when she arrived?* "That's interesting," she said at last. "I wasn't aware, but now you mention it, yes, I do feel somewhat different. It must be the air here," she added flippantly.

"It is." Maddy's voice was serious. "It seems to me that you've spent your life in service of either your children or your job. You haven't taken time to work out what *you* want. Oh, I know," she continued, as Jenny opened her mouth to reply, "you think it's been your choice, and I guess it has been to some extent, but you've been a victim of circumstances, and have done exceptionally well with what you've been handed."

Shocked, Jenny sat down with a thump. She slid her jacket off her shoulders, and leaning her elbows on the table, her eyes went out of focus. A picture of Jenny Sullivan, executive manager and mother flashed across her vision. This was a person who spent her time on the priorities of others, whose own needs and desires had taken a back seat. Giving herself a shake, she found her voice. "You may be right, but what choice did I have? I did what I had to do."

"Of course you did and more power to you. You were left with two young children, and you certainly rose to the occasion. No one could fault you for that. But now life is giving you another chance. Can you see that? I know you're not one to sit back and believe it's all over. But try to get beyond that. Try to believe that for you this can be a new beginning." Maddy rose to leave the table. "Now, eat your breakfast. We have a lot to do today."

Watching Maddy fold up the paper and place it carefully in her magazine rack, Jenny, almost absentmindedly, reached for a cinnamon bun from the plate in the center of the table. As she bit into it the thought crossed her mind that she'd be like a house end when she returned to Australia if she kept on like this. She ignored the fact she hadn't gained a pound since her arrival, despite her apparent increased intake of food. When Maddy returned Jenny was peeling a banana.

Maddy appeared to read her mind. "It's the fresh sea air giving you an appetite," she said, "and the unaccustomed exercise is burning it off as fast as you take it in. Let me know when you're finished there."

"I'm done." Jenny took her last bite and rose. "What do you have in mind for today?" She still wasn't used to the energy of her companion.

"I thought you could help me do some clearing out. The local church is having a yard sale and I thought, since you're here to help, it would be a good opportunity to get rid of some of the things I've been hanging on to for years. Save you doing it when I pass," she chuckled, as if aware how morbid that sounded.

"Sounds fun. Let me clean my teeth, then I'll be with you."

Two hours later, Jenny was realizing that 'fun' may not have been the most accurate word, as they rifled through piles of accumulated junk which had collected in the attic over the past forty or so years. They were back downstairs in Maddy's bedroom, sorting it into bundles of items to keep, those for the sale, and those which were just rubbish, when Jenny came across an old photo album.

"Hey, look at this!" She began leafing through it. "Is this you and Mum when you were at school?" Peering over her shoulder, Maddy adjusted her glasses to get a better look.

"Yes, I remember that day. We thought we were the bee's knees in those outfits." Both women laughed at the old-fashioned styles.

Jenny continued to turn the pages. "Here you are again. Oh, who's this?" She was pointing to a photo of three girls, two of them were clearly her mother and Maddy, but in this photo they were accompanied by an exceedingly pretty leggy younger girl who was smiling gaily at the other two and pointing at the camera. "Maddy?" Jenny raised her voice as she realized her companion had left the room, and heard her footsteps moving across the other room combined with the insistent ringing of the telephone.

Suddenly she heard the steps falter and there was a loud thump, followed by a sharp cry. The telephone continued to ring, then there was silence. "Maddy?" Jenny repeated, dropping the album and rising quickly. She ran into the room to see her godmother lying on the floor, her right leg twisted beneath her. A tennis ball was rolling around close by. "What's happened?" Jenny rushed to the inert figure and bent over her. "What have you done? Can you move? We need to get you up."

"Just give me a minute. It was that dratted ball." The older woman was having trouble gaining her breath. Jenny turned round and picked up the tennis ball. Where on earth had that come from? Though, given the abundance of objects they'd uncovered in the rummage in the attic, it wouldn't be surprising if this had been one of them. She turned her attention back to her godmother, wondering how she was going to move her, but knowing she couldn't leave her lying there on the wooden floor.

Jenny bent over to brush Maddy's hair back, stroking the older woman's forehead with her fingers. "We need to move you. You can't stay here." She was beginning to experience some panic. They were alone, and Maddy was pretty heavy for Jenny to move by herself. She was wondering how she could do it, trying to remember courses on 'moving not lifting' she had sat through in a past life, when Maddy spoke again. "Fetch Mike. Number by the phone."

The dreaded Mike. Well, Jenny supposed any port in a storm, and this was a storm of emergency. "I'll be right back." She moved to pick up the phone, and sure enough, there was a list of emergency numbers lying beside it. She was amused to see her own number there as she dialed the local one.

The phone rang a couple of times before she heard a deep voice answer, "Mike Halliday."

"Hi, it's Jenny Sullivan here." She paused, unsure how to begin. "I'm Maddy's…"

"Oh, yes, the goddaughter from Australia." The voice was curious and a little distant. "How can I help you?"

"It's Maddy. She's had a fall. I need help. She said to call," the words burst out, tumbling over each other. Jenny's voice had a catch in it as she continued, "Can you come over?"

"Right away." The strength in Mike's voice was evident even over the phone. "Keep her warm till I get there."

Cursing herself for not thinking of this, Jenny hung up, and dragging a throw rug from the sofa, placed it over Maddy, then sat down by her side and offered what comfort she could. It wasn't long before she heard a car door slam, and there was a loud rap at the front door. Before she could move towards the door, it was flung open, and in strode the man she had seen on the beach. She recognized the wide shoulders and sturdy body topping a set of long legs and found herself gazing into a pair of grey eyes set above a white beard, which seemed incongruous with the reddish blonde thatch on his head.

"You must be…"

"Mike, and you're Jenny." The voice was deep and authoritative, someone used to getting his own way. Then it took on a more tender tone. "And what have we here?" He bent down beside Jenny and Maddy. He was so close Jenny could see the wrinkles at the corners of his eyes, and the etched smile lines crisscrossing the vertical creases on his cheeks. He looked as if he hadn't had much to smile about recently.

Maddy tried without success to sit up. "I don't think my leg's broken," she muttered, "but my ankle hurts, and something's not right further up. I can't seem to move."

"Are you in pain?" Mike was gently feeling over her body with his large hands. "Where does it hurt most?"

"Everywhere, it seems. I must have jarred everything as I went down. I don't know what happened."

"I do." Holding up the ball, Jenny said, "This is the culprit. It must have rolled out from somewhere, and you tripped as you were going to answer the phone."

"Oh, mea culpa," said Mike, clearly chagrined. "Looks like one of Ben's. We must have left it here when we were over one time."

"You play ball with your dog inside the house?" Jenny's tone was tinged with disapproval.

"We...ell..." Mike had the grace to look penitent. "Ben's used to being inside and..."

"It's only a ball, for goodness sake. It could have been worse. I could have fallen down the steps from the attic." Maddy's voice interrupted them, sounding stronger than before.

Mike turned to her and shook his head, "Methinks it's an ambulance for you today. You're going to need more care than we can give you here."

"Oh dear, I was afraid of that. Can you raise me up a bit for now?" Maddy was struggling to get up as she spoke.

"Better not. We don't know what damage you've done to your insides. Let the professionals handle it. As long as you're not too uncomfortable lying there for a little bit longer. You're warm enough?" Mike pulled the throw closer around her.

Jenny sat back watching in amazement. He'd just walked in and taken over. Even more surprising was the fact she'd let him do it. The old Jenny would have insisted on doing things for Maddy herself. Rising to her feet now, she found her voice. "I can call for the ambulance," she offered. "I think I saw the number by the phone, when I called you, Mike," she said, speaking directly to him for the first time.

"Great, then maybe a cup of tea, sweet tea. Your godmother's probably suffering from delayed shock."

"Sure thing." Shit, why didn't I think of that instead of sitting here like a stunned mullet, she thought, as she hurried to comply? He must think I'm a complete dill.

*

In fact Mike was thinking anything but that. He was pleasantly surprised to find the master of super organization he'd been anticipating, didn't know what to what to do.

He looked across the room as she made the call, then started fiddling with tea makings in the kitchen. "You'd better make a cup for yourself," he suggested. "You've had a shock too." His glance took in the swing of dark hair, which was obscuring the high-boned face and large violet eyes he'd noted earlier. She was wearing the same sort of casual clothes as Maddy; pants and a thick cotton top and, like her godmother, managed to look like elegance itself. However, whereas Maddy always seemed at home in this gear, the younger woman seemed a bit awkward, as if she was accustomed to a more tailored look. That figured, he thought, remembering what he'd heard about her; a high-powered executive who'd been made redundant. Must be difficult to cope with, he reflected. He'd made his own decision to move on, but to have it thrust upon you, well, that'd take some getting used to.

He turned his attention back to his neighbor. "What were you thinking of, Maddy, dear? You're usually so careful moving around. We're going to have to take more care of you," he joked.

"I was… it was… the phone rang." Maddy sounded weak and confused, and her energy levels seemed low.

"Don't you worry about anything now. The paramedics will be here soon and whisk you off. They'll take good care of you."

"But Jenny…" Maddy's voice was becoming weaker.

"She'll be fine. I'll look in on her," Mike found himself promising.

"I'll be okay. I'm not a kid." Jenny was back with the tea and had overheard his last words. "Here you are, Maddy." She passed a mug over and helped raise her head to allow her to take a sip. "Bet that tastes good."

The older woman sipped greedily then pushed the mug away. "That's enough for now, thanks." Her voice was coming out stronger as she added. "Now, I want you two to behave yourselves when I'm not here. It's a quiet spot, and it's important to be neighborly."

The two looked at each other. Mike felt he was being chastised like a kid for keeping away. Maddy was the only person he'd ever met as an adult, who could make him feel that way. He shot a glance at Jenny. She appeared to be stunned. Mike was the first to speak. "You do like telling us what to do, it seems. Can't be too much wrong with you.

You'll be back here with us in no time at all." The serious look on his face belied the flippancy in his voice. He saw Jenny give him a warning look so continued, addressing her, "Do you think we can cope without her, Jenny? Are we grown up enough?"

"That's enough from you, smartass." But Maddy's voice was fading again.

"How long do you think it'll be...?" Jenny was just starting to say, when they heard the siren of the ambulance driving up, followed by a door slamming and a loud knock at the front door.

In the confusion that followed, Maddy was placed on a stretcher and loaded into the ambulance. After a moment's hesitation Jenny followed her in.

"I'll follow in the pickup so I can give you a ride home," Mike said, an offer which Jenny seemed set to refuse.

"Oh, that's okay," she began as she rugged up for the cool outdoors. "I can make my own way."

"You may not want my company," Mike said, thinking he really didn't want to be cooped up in the cab of the pickup with her either, "but we have to consider Maddy. It's what she'd expect. And we don't know how long it'll be before you can leave again."

"That's what I mean. You don't want to be sitting around there all day waiting with me," Jenny said.

"Probably not." Mike was honest. "But you're a stranger here. There's not much public transport, and the taxi service is never there when you want it. I'm pleased to do this for you and for Maddy. It's a small thing." Not really, he reflected, thinking longingly of his computer sitting idle on the desk at home. Well, it wouldn't kill him. Maddy had been good to him, and they *were* neighbors, even if they did tend to keep out of each other's lives.

Once at the hospital the nursing staff took over, and Jenny and Mike were left to sit in the waiting room, while Maddy was wheeled off to be examined. Alone together for the first time, Mike glanced surreptitiously at Jenny who was pacing up and down the room, arms folded as if to ward off bad news. "You're close? You and Maddy, I mean," he added, thinking how much Jenny resembled her godmother, standing there erect with her head tilted to one side as if wondering how to reply.

"Yes and no." She seemed prepared to unbend a little and sat down two seats away from him, arms still folded. "She was a good friend of my mother's, and we've kept in touch."

"Your mother's American?"

"She was. She died around ten years ago. It was then Maddy and I started to communicate more. She and my mother were old schoolmates, and it seemed like a link to Mum. I guess it was for her too," she added thoughtfully.

"And you live in Australia. Which part?" Mike had decided that if they were going to be stuck here together, they might as well talk to each other. Whereas a couple of men could sit in companionable silence, he'd discovered over the years that the female of the species did like to talk.

As if reading his mind, Jenny replied rather sharply. "Don't feel you need to talk to me. It won't keep my mind off what's happening to Maddy, if that's what you think. But yes, as you probably already know, I do live in Australia, north of Brisbane, in Queensland, if you know where that is."

Yow, what did I do to deserve that! Mike stifled a smile. *She's a feisty one, for sure.* Deciding to give Jenny the benefit of the doubt – after all she was surely worried about her godmother – Mike ignored her sharp repartee and replied, "I do, as a matter of fact. Attended a conference in Brisbane a few years back, University of Queensland. Beautiful campus, as I recall."

"Oh." Jenny gave him a surprised look. "What sort of conference was that?"

"It was on indigenous people. I've been making a study of the Native American tribes in North America for some years and…" But he was interrupted by another "Oh" from Jenny who was looking over his shoulder. Turning around Mike saw a woman in a white coat heading towards them. They both stood up.

"You're both with Madeline de Ruiz?" she asked briskly, looking from one to the other.

"I am," Jenny replied quickly turning her back on Mike. "How is she?"

"I'm afraid the x-rays show she has broken her pelvis. We'll be keeping her here for a couple of weeks, then she'll need care if she's to go home. Do you live with her?" Again the doctor looked from one to the other.

"I'm visiting... from Australia."

"I'm her neighbor."

The two spoke at once.

"Well," Looking at Jenny, the doctor sought an answer, "Will you be there when she goes home? She'll need care for another four to six weeks at least."

"Yes, I can be here."

Mike looked at Jenny in surprise.

"I have some leave," she countered. "Can I see her now?" she asked eagerly.

"For a few moments, then it's best if you leave her to rest. We may be looking at surgery tomorrow. The specialist will decide when he's examined the x-rays. You can come back in to see her then."

"You wait here," Jenny instructed, following the doctor into the ward.

Left to himself, Mike stood up and fetched a coffee from a vending machine in the corner, grimacing at the bitter taste as he gulped it down. It was better than nothing, but not much. He realized this had all been a shock to him too. He'd operated on autopilot, and the effect was beginning to kick in. He'd have a Jack Daniels when he got home, he promised himself, then a night at his computer to make up for lost time.

It was about ten minutes later, when Jenny finally emerged looking white and shaken. "How is she?" Mike tried to take Jenny's arm as they walked out, but she brushed his hand away.

"She looks so frail lying there in that hospital bed. Not like herself at all. They've given her some painkillers, so she's not making much sense. We'd better get back. I've taken up too much of your time already." Jenny strode out to the vehicle ahead of Mike and waited impatiently for him to unlock it. They drove back in almost complete silence. Mike decided that he'd made an effort to be friendly, it was up to Jenny if she wanted to talk more. Clearly she didn't.

When they reached Seal Rock and Maddy's house, Mike got out, only to find Jenny had hurried into the house ahead of him. Tempted to go back behind the wheel and carry on home, his friendship for

Maddy prevented him, and taking a deep breath, he followed the hurrying figure up the path. His hand reached the door just as she was about to close it.

"What do you want?"

A thank you might be nice he thought, but his words were, "I'll bring in some wood for you, from the woodpile." He gestured to the pile of logs leaning against the far side of the house.

"No need." Jenny was clearly eager to be rid of him as, by now, he was of her, but he persisted.

"I'd do it for Maddy. It's not the easiest job for a woman on her own." He realized he might be tempting fate with these words, but some inbuilt sense of honor forced him to continue. "It's going to be a cold night. You'll want to bank up the fire."

As if realizing she'd been ungracious after his help with her godmother, Jenny lightened, "That'd be good," she said. "Thanks."

As he stepped back into his pickup for the short trip up the track, Mike welcomed the thought of returning to normal. Ben and him, alone. This was why he was here, not to get involved in his neighbor's affairs. He'd have to remember that. He'd keep away, just as he'd planned, until Jenny had gone home. Especially as his involvement was proving to be unwelcome.

Nine

Next morning Jenny awoke to a warm house. The place seemed quieter than usual. Suddenly she remembered. Maddy! She showered and dressed quickly, wondering how Maddy was feeling this morning. She debated whether to go for a walk, but decided against it. She'd had enough of being neighborly to that Mike guy the day before. Even though he hadn't turned out to be quite the cretin she'd expected, she preferred her own company, and if she bumped into him on the beach, she'd be forced to be polite.

Jenny relived the events of the previous day as she prepared her usual breakfast of cereal and coffee. It had all happened so fast. One minute they were laughing over the old photos, the next Maddy was lying there. Jenny's eyes began to mist as she remembered her fear at the sight of her godmother's twisted body. For a brief moment she'd thought...

She shook her head and picked up the phone.

"I'm calling to inquire about Madeline de Ruiz," she said, in response to the clinical voice which answered her, only to be amazed at the reply.

"Oh, Maddy," said the voice. "Would you like to speak to her? The doctor's been to see her, and I believe she's up to taking calls."

"Yes please." Jenny hadn't expected this. Almost before she had time to gather her thoughts, her godmother's voice was on the line, sounding weak but firm.

"You're not to worry about me. They're so good here. It's like being

56

on vacation, if it wasn't for this blasted pelvis. I can't have anything to eat or drink till they do some more of their damned tests, so it's probably best you don't come in this morning. How's Mike?"

"He brought some wood in for me."

"Good man. He's a kind fellow, bit of a loner, but then so am I," she gave a weak chuckle. "This has messed up our plans a bit, hasn't it?"

"You concentrate on getting well. I can stay till you're up and about again. I'll see you this afternoon." As she hung up, it crossed Jenny's mind that Maddy might not recover her health sufficiently to live on her own again, or might lose confidence in her ability to get around unaided. Well, they'd face that if and when it happened. For the moment Jenny was left to her own devices, and had the morning all to herself.

Looking around the house, Jenny decided to do as best she could to continue the clean-out process she and Maddy had started. The box of photos was still lying open in Maddy's bedroom with the albums and several loose photos scattered around. Figuring her godmother would want to hold on to these for sentimental value, Jenny started to put them aside, but became engrossed in looking at the early photos of her mother, many of which she hadn't seen before. In fact, she didn't remember ever seeing any photos of her mother's early years. It was as if her mother's life hadn't started until Jenny was born.

She was smiling at a couple of teenage shots of her mother and Maddy when the phone rang. Hoping it wasn't bad news, Jenny tentatively lifted the phone, "Hello? Maddy's phone. This is Jenny."

"Hello, stranger, what's up?"

Smiling with relief at the familiar voice, Jenny took the phone to the large armchair and curled her feet under her. "Rosa! What a surprise. You don't know how good it is to hear your voice."

"Wow. Didn't think I'd get a reception like that. What's been happening? Are you managing to chill out over there?"

"Chill is the operative word. It's pretty cold here. A lot cooler than back home. I've had to invest in some warmer clothes. And Maddy had a fall yesterday. It was such a shock as she's pretty lively for her age." Jenny's eyes began to fill as she spoke and she brushed them with the back of her hand. "She had to go to hospital, so I'm all alone here right now." Her voice broke.

"Oh my God! What a thing to happen. How is she? How are you holding up?" Rosa's voice radiated concern. It was so good to hear her old friend's voice, even though it was from the other side of the world. Goodness knows what time it was there. Pretty early, Jenny was sure.

"I think she's going to be all right, but she's not so young any more. I spoke to her earlier, and they're going to do some procedure this morning, so I'll go in to see her this afternoon. We managed to get the paramedics to her pretty quickly yesterday, though she was in a lot of pain."

"We?" Rosa was quick on the uptake. "Who's we? I thought it was just you and your godmother."

"It is. But I couldn't move her so I called the neighbor. He took charge." As she said it, Jenny realized how completely Mike *had* taken charge and that, to her surprise, she hadn't really minded.

"He?" Rosa's voice rose in surprise. "Sounds as if you've got a nice thing going there."

"Don't be daft. Have you ever seen me with a man?" The image of Mike's concerned face rose up as if to taunt her. Jenny shook her head and changed the subject. "Now tell me all the goss. What's been happening since I left?"

It was a full hour later when Jenny put down the phone, buoyed by the talk with her friend, but somewhat concerned with the way the restructure seemed to have escalated in her absence.

Oh, well, she knew she was going to leave anyway. This just affirmed it. She would email them today and confirm her request for redundancy. This called for a coffee, a strong one.

As she brewed her drink and fixed some lunch, Jenny realized how, in the short space of time she'd been here, her tastes were changing. Back home, coffee meant dropping into the local café for a cappuccino, here, having discovered no one knew how to make one to her taste, she'd come to enjoy the brewed coffee favored by the locals, strong as it was.

Later that afternoon, driving into town to visit her godmother, Jenny came to the conclusion that she now felt quite confident driving on the wrong side of the road. As she swung into the hospital car park, she reflected it was a good thing, as Maddy wasn't going to be able to drive anywhere anytime soon.

Turning up her collar against the wind that was beginning to blow up, Jenny hurried into the building.

"On your own today?" greeted the nurse who'd attended Maddy the day before.

"Just me," she responded brightly. "How's the patient this afternoon?"

"Still a bit drowsy, but you can go on in and see for yourself."

"Hello, Maddy," Jenny spoke softly, drawing back the screen and sitting down by the bedside. "How're you feeling? A bit tired?" She took the older woman's hand and stroked it gently.

Maddy opened her eyes slowly. "Is that you, Jenny Wren? Oh, you are a dear. I…" She seemed to drift off to sleep again. Jenny held her hand for a bit longer, then carefully released it. Wondering what to do, she stood up and gazed out of the window. Hearing a sound behind her, she turned.

"What are you doing here?" The words burst out of her as she saw Mike standing there.

"The same as you, I expect. I've come to visit Maddy. I assume that's permitted. I was concerned about her," he added in a softer tone. "Looks as if she's asleep."

"Yes… She just drifted off. I don't think there's much point in either of us being here right now."

"How about a coffee? There's a coffee shop downstairs where we can get a decent brew." Mike gave Jenny a quizzical glance as if to enquire whether she would be willing to suffer his presence for the time it would take to drink a cup of coffee.

"Why not?" Jenny decided it would be churlish to refuse, since they were both here now. "I'd like to have a word with the doctor first, if I can. Meet you down there?"

"Sure thing. I'll grab a spot and order."

Jenny wondered what she had let herself in for, and was debating the wisdom of her decision when she caught sight of the doctor she'd seen the previous evening. "Excuse me," she stepped quickly towards her. "I wanted to ask you about my godmother, Madeline de Ruiz."

"Right. You're Maddy's goddaughter. I can see the resemblance. Maddy'll be all right. She's a strong one. We'd like to keep her in for at least a week, then if you can guarantee she'll have good care, we can let her go home."

"Oh, yes. I'll be there for her." Jenny had a fleeting thought of her family back home, which she quickly suppressed. They'd be fine. She'd been emailing both Helen and Hugh regularly since she arrived in Oregon, and all was well there.

As she headed for the café, Jenny geared herself up for her next encounter with Mike. There was really nothing wrong with him, she told herself, and he hadn't made any unwelcome advances. If she were to be honest with herself, he seemed as unwilling as she was to take their association any further. Okay, she thought, let's get this over with. I should be grateful Maddy has such a considerate neighbor.

"Hi there," Jenny greeted him. "Thanks for getting the coffee in. You didn't need to do that."

It was nice for someone else to take charge. Something she hadn't experienced for so many years she'd forgotten what it felt like. She sat down and took a sip from the extra-large mug. Everything in this country seemed extra-large, including the man sitting opposite.

"So you're becoming accustomed to our brand of coffee?" Mike asked, with a faint twinkle in his eye. "I remember from my trip to Australia there were a lot of fancy styles."

"It's the Italian influence. I guess it was a later influence there," she said, knowing full well there'd been a lot of Italian immigration to the US too. The conversation stalled, then they both spoke at once,

"Maddy..."

"What did...?"

They laughed awkwardly, and Jenny tried again. "Maddy seems to be on the mend. The doctor gives her another week or so, then home."

"Great. And what will you do with yourself?"

Stifling the impulse to tell him not to worry about her, Jenny waved her hand in the air. "Oh, you know. There's always lots to do. Maddy and I were doing some clearing out. I'll get on with that. And I'd like to poke around the place. There's lots I've still to see. For instance, when we went to Florence last week, I promised myself I'd go back." Jenny could see from the relieved look on his face he'd been worried she might turn into a problem for him, so she quickly added, "I actually came over here to sort myself out. This time alone will be good for me; help me work out what I want to do next." That should satisfy him, she thought.

But it seemed to have the opposite effect. Mike swirled his mug to drain the last drop of coffee and, almost as if against his will, asked, "What needed sorting?" before tipping up the last drop and drawing the back of his hand over his mouth.

Not sure whether he really wanted a reply or was just being polite, Jenny decided to offer something without being too specific. "I'm thinking of changing jobs; finding a new career path." She stopped there. No need for him to know the sordid details, that she'd been dumped on the scrapheap like a piece of unwanted garbage, garbage that didn't fit with the new order.

"Yeah, happens," was his brief comment before he lapsed into silence again.

Drat the man. He could have sounded more interested. Jenny drummed her fingers on the table, realizing how unreasonable she was being. She didn't want his interest, then she was pissed off when he didn't express any.

"It's time I was off." She pushed her chair back from the table and rose. "I should get on the road. Thanks for the coffee," she added, trying not to sound ungracious, and walked out with as much dignity as she could muster.

*

Mike watched Jenny's erect back leave the café. Now what had he done to annoy the woman? Here he'd been, trying his manly best to entertain her, to sound interested in what she was doing, even if he wasn't, and she walked out like he'd insulted her. He'd never understand women, not if he lived to be a hundred. Mary was the only one he'd had any time for, and now she was gone. Maddy was different. He didn't consider her in the same bag. She was older, for one thing. Maddy was a mate. She'd have understood that he was trying to put Jenny at ease. She'd also have understood why it didn't work. He wasn't sure why, but this tall Australian woman was managing to get under his skin and penetrate the barrier he'd erected against women of all sorts, predatory or otherwise.

Ten

The next few days passed uneventfully for Jenny. She visited her godmother, walked on the beach only when she was sure that Mike had driven off somewhere, and continued sifting through the contents of the attic. She also made time to drive around the locality as she had promised herself she'd do. It was on one of these trips she made another visit to Old Town in Florence. When she'd been there with Maddy, they'd limited their visit to the clothes shop, and Jenny was keen to explore the other little stores she'd seen.

Poking around in the souvenir stores she made an amazing discovery. The sand dollar, which had been so special to her, was now a common object for the tourist trade. In fact they were on sale for two dollars. So much for the magical sand dollar. But, for Jenny, her own sand dollar still held its special magic. She fingered it in her pocket.

After a warming cup of clam chowder by the river, Jenny was set to return home when she spied a bookstore hidden away on a corner of the main street.

Still in exploring mode, Jenny pushed on the old wooden door and ventured inside to find herself in another world. She looked around in delight at the rows of shelves, the collection of books, old and new and the comfy seats, almost hidden by the stacks, where the avid reader could slake her thirst for books to her heart's content.

Jenny had been browsing for a time and had already collected an armful of books, having discovered some American authors with whom she wasn't familiar, when she was surprised by a melodious voice.

"I was going to ask if there was anything I could help you with, but you seem to be doing quite well on your own." The voice held a warm laugh, and Jenny saw a woman of close to her own age, whose graying hair, tied back from a round merry face, hung to her waist in a long plait. She was a large woman, as tall as Jenny herself, and wearing what appeared to be the uniform dress around here – pants with a checked flannelette shirt over a plain white T-shirt. On this woman, with her almost regal bearing, it looked like a fashion statement.

"Yes, I am." Jenny laughed back. "Is this your shop? It's wonderful. Like a..." She was lost for words. "Like a magic cave," she said eventually.

"Yes, it is, and thank you. I haven't seen you in here before. Are you visiting?"

"I'm visiting my godmother. She lives up in Seal Rock, but she's in hospital at the moment, so I'm poking around the area."

"Well, I'm glad you came in this direction." The woman's eyes seemed to see right through Jenny as she added, seemingly inconsequentially, "It was right for you to come here today."

What does that mean? thought Jenny, but in a swift movement, the woman stepped away. Jenny shook herself. It felt as if someone had walked over her grave, or more accurately as if this woman knew things about Jenny she didn't know herself. How foolish. Jenny had always been pragmatic and had rubbished such intimations of special powers or insights. Taking her purchases to the counter, she paid without any further conversation,

"Thank you for your custom. I look forward to seeing you again soon."

Jenny left the shop wondering if she would return. She was intrigued by both the shop and its owner. It would be nice to have somewhere like that herself. She'd always loved books and the atmosphere in bookshops and libraries. Books, yes, and libraries, but there the books all went back on the shelves. She once wanted to be a librarian, loved the peace and the books. She pictured her shelves of books at home – she'd read them all. She'd love to be surrounded by them all day and help others find the enjoyment that she found in them. Maybe that's what she should do when she got back home – buy a bookshop. She'd like to have one like that, a warm welcoming place.

Back at Maddy's home, it was as if the ambiance of the bookshop had attached itself to the books Jenny had purchased. They sat where she'd placed them in a pile on the table, but seemed to be calling to her as if trying to tell her something. She shook her head to rid herself of such fanciful notions.

*

It was a couple of days before Jenny ventured up into the attic again. This time she found a small suitcase hidden away in a dark corner. Pulling it down after her, she placed it on the coffee table, and opening the case, was amazed to find it contained not only more photos, but a bundle of letters tied together with blue ribbon.

Love letters, was Jenny's immediate thought, and anxious not to violate her godmother's privacy, her hand was moving to put them aside when she recognized the writing on the top envelope. It was her mother's. Jenny hadn't seen that writing since her mother had died over ten years ago, but she would know it anywhere. She flipped through the bundle. They were all in the same handwriting. All of the letters were from her mother, and they appeared to be in chronological order. Curiously she took the top letter out of the ribbon and turned it over and over in her hands. Would it be wrong to open it? Although she was eager to see what the two women had said to each other, she felt reluctant. Some force she didn't recognize seemed to be trying to prevent her from doing so. Still working out what to do, she went into the kitchen to brew up some coffee, taking the letter with her. It sat on the kitchen surface while the coffee was brewing.

Finally, taking her coffee and a macadamia nut cookie back into the main room, Jenny sat down and looked at the letter. What was she making such a fuss about? The letter was from her mother. What could possibly be in there that she shouldn't see? She began to drink her coffee and took a bite out of the cookie as she checked the date. It was dated in the year she had been born, sixty years ago. Whatever was in it was ancient history. Nevertheless, her hand shook when she tentatively opened the envelope

As her fingers slid inside to remove the flimsy airmail pages a photo fell out. It was a baby photo, of Jenny. That settled her qualms. This was probably the letter asking Maddy to be godmother. It would be fun to read – a bit of her own early history. She settled down in the chair and curled her legs under her, preparing to enjoy it.

My dear Maddy,

We've arrived home safely with our little bundle. She is a dear and was so good on the journey. We've decided to call her Jennifer Thea. Jenny for short. She has the largest violet eyes I've ever seen, and a cap of jet black hair.

Jenny smiled. It was just as she'd thought. How comforting it was to read this. It was almost like hearing her mother's voice again. She read on through the news about the sea voyage and arrival back in Australia then:

I appreciate your agreeing to be Jenny's godmother. I felt it was the least we could do. But I think you'll agree that it will have to be godmother at a distance. We've decided it would be best if Jenny never knows that she's not our child. Steve and I plan to keep her adoption secret. After all, I was pregnant when we left. No one here knows I miscarried on the ship over. But it might bring everything up again if we visit Oregon too often. She's ours now, the little girl we wanted and that's how it will be.

Jenny's hand shook and the letter fluttered to the floor. How could this be true? Adopted?

Coffee forgotten, she buried her face in her hands. Tears welled up and began to trickle down her cheeks. She let them flow. Jenny didn't know how long she sat there, but it was turning dark when she finally recovered her composure. She shivered. Her thoughts were in turmoil. She had to get out of the house for some fresh air. Regardless of the growing darkness, Jenny drew on a warm jacket and headed down to the beach.

Once there, she walked briskly along the edge of the water, careless of the incoming tide. The fierceness of the waves was in tune with her mood. As she strode along, she relished the abrading feeling of the sand on her face. When the water started lapping around her feet, however, common sense prevailed, and she made her way back towards the road, but stopped to rest on one of the large pieces of driftwood. She hugged herself, bending over to stare at the sand. She felt bereft. Her job had gone, now it seemed as if her whole history had gone too.

Jenny needed to talk to someone about this. Maddy was the obvious choice, but how could she bring it up with her now? She was making a good recovery, and Jenny didn't want to prejudice that. Who could she talk to about this? She turned over all possibilities. The children were out of the equation. This was going to affect them too. Rosa was another possibility, but the time wasn't right for a call to Australia. Rosa would be at work. Maybe she could wait till morning and call then, but what good would that do?

"What are you doing sitting here in the gloom?" The voice seemed to come from nowhere. Suddenly there was a black hairy shape rubbing against her and a hot tongue trying to lick her face.

"Oh," Jenny looked up to see the bearded face of the neighbor she had been successfully avoiding for the past few days. "It's you."

"You should be glad it's me and not some drunk. There are some unsavory characters who sometimes float around here after dark. Let's get you home." Mike reached down to help Jenny up, and although she brushed away his hand, she walked back with him across the road and up the track. "I don't know how long you've been sitting there," he said, "but you look frozen. Why don't I come in and pour you a glass of something to warm you up?"

Despite the obvious reluctance in his voice, Mike seemed pretty determined, so Jenny found herself allowing him to accompany her into the house. Turning on the lights, Mike looked at her in surprise. "You've let the stove go out. How did that happen?" He quickly added wood to the still-glowing embers and soon there was a bright blaze again. "Come and sit here. What were you thinking of?"

"I had a shock." Jenny was loath to say any more, but realized some explanation was going to be required. Then it occurred to her that Mike might be the ideal person to talk with. From what she knew of him, he was a private person, just like her. "I was reading this." She picked up the letter and handed it to him.

"I don't think..." he began, clearly unwilling to read what was obviously a piece of private correspondence. He made a movement as if to hand it back to her.

"No. Please do read it. I need someone else to know." She hesitated, while Mike stood awkwardly in the middle of the room. He looked as if he'd rather be anywhere but here, and was probably wishing he'd left her sitting on the beach. But he hadn't, so now he was stuck with her. "Please just read it," she insisted, and watched as he stood reading the letter.

Holding the sheet of paper in both hands, Mike looked up at her tenderly. "And you had no idea?" he asked gently.

Jenny shook her head, blinking madly to stop the tears which threatened. Mike stretched out his hand towards her shoulder as if to offer comfort, then let it drop away. Jenny hugged her arms to her body to ward off any physical contact.

"We definitely need that drink now." He put the letter down on the coffee table and went to the drinks trolley where he poured two large measures. "Get that down you," he said, handing one to Jenny.

"What is it?" she asked, sniffing the glass.

"Jack Daniels. The answer to the shock you've sustained. It'll burn going down, but it'll help."

Jenny took a sip.

"Don't sip it. Take a gulp. Put some fire in your belly."

Giving him a glare, Jenny emptied the glass, almost choking. "There, are you happy now?"

"When did you last have something to eat? You should have something now or that'll go straight to your head."

"I don't need being told what to do." Jenny's tone was abrupt. "Look," she said more gently, pushing her hands through her hair. "I'm grateful to you and all that. I needed someone to talk to, to share this with, but…"

"But now it's me, you're thinking better of it?"

"No, not at all. Actually I'm glad it's you. You won't…"

"Won't what?" Mike raised his eyebrows.

"Won't make a big thing of it, I guess is what I mean. But I'd rather be alone now, if you don't mind. I will have something to eat," she added, seeing he was about to say something else.

"That wasn't what I was going to say. I wondered…" he paused. "I wondered what you were going to do about this. I mean, it's a bit of a bummer being thrown this one. How do you intend to deal with it?"

"I really don't know. The whole thing's come from left field. It's… it's not anything I expected. Mum and Dad…" Jenny dragged her fingers through her hair again and started to walk with Mike to the door. "You've been great. I know I have to handle it. I guess I should bring it up with Maddy, but I can't do that right now. When she's better. I'll need some answers."

"I sure would if I were you. Okay. I'll be off. Umm, if… or… I'm just a bit up the track if you want an ear." Mike sounded awkward.

Jenny's eyes opened wide in surprise. An offer like this was the last thing she'd expected from this reticent man. "Thanks, I'll remember that." Her voice shook a little as she said goodbye and closed the door behind him.

Alone again, she busied herself heating up a can of soup and cut a thick slice of sour dough bread to go with it. Taking her solitary seat at the table she went over the events of the day, in particular her reaction to the contents of the letter. She tried to work out why she'd been so upset, finally figuring out it was because it was something completely beyond her control. The Jenny who had been the perfectly organized executive who made momentous decisions without losing sleep, had been shaken by the threat of redundancy. But she'd been recovering from that in these peaceful surroundings, and this past week, had even been considering a new life back home, maybe as a bookshop owner. This latest blow had taken her by surprise and had blasted through all of her defenses. Why, it even had her turning to the neighbor for solace. Well, she wouldn't be doing that again. At least she didn't think so. She felt herself hesitating as she remembered for a moment how comforting it had felt to have someone else take charge. He really was a bit like her, she mused, prickly on the outside with a soft center, the one he'd revealed to her today. But, no, she wouldn't let that happen again.

Eleven

Mike was excited. It had been a couple of weeks since his first meeting with Ron Williams, and now they were to meet again. He hoped that, this time, there would be news of the community and he'd be able to meet some more active members. He was rubbing his hands to warm them as, entering the coffee house, he looked around, seeing Ron in the corner.

"Hi there, good to see you again. Come and meet Ellen, my little sister."

"Hey, less of the little."

"Younger, then. But I can still beat you at baskets." Mike listened, amused at the clearly familiar sibling banter. Ron became serious again. "Ellen, this is the guy I've been telling you about. Reckons he's going to write a history of our people. Mike's his handle."

"I think there's been a few who've done that already." Her voice had a singsong quality and Mike could see she was a few years younger than her brother.

"You're right, of course," Mike answered comfortably. "I guess we all think we're going to provide the seminal work. It's a history and culture that has fascinated me for years."

"Ron tells me you're from Seal Rock."

"That's right. I've a cabin up there. Had it a few years now, but moved there permanently around six months ago." He hesitated, unsure how much more to say. It wasn't like him to reveal too much to strangers.

Ellen seemed to ignore his remarks. "I met a woman from up there this week. She's visiting from Australia."

It wasn't a question, but Mike found himself replying, "Tall and elegant, short black hair, large soulful violet eyes."

"That's her. A friend of yours?"

Mike felt embarrassed. "No, not a friend. She's staying with my neighbor."

"That one has had some challenges to face recently, and they're not over yet," Ellen stated obliquely. Jolted out of his embarrassment, Mike looked at her more closely, but Ellen was giving nothing away. "Now, the reason we're here," she began.

"Let the guy get some coffee in first." Ron held up his hand as if to forestall his sister.

"Right. I'll do that now." Mike sauntered over to the counter and put his order in. While he waited for the coffee to arrive he wondered, what was that all about? How did images of Jenny come into this? Who was Ellen, besides being Ron's sister? Well, no doubt it'd all become clear, he thought, as he carried his mug back to the table.

Mike sat down again. He took a sip of coffee then, "Okay, shoot." He looked at them both expectantly.

"You wanted to attend one of our community events," Ron began. "Well, ordinarily you'd need to be a member of the tribe to be allowed in." He looked over at his sister. "Ellen, here, she's on the tribal council so may be able to do something. If she thinks you're genuine, that is." He stopped and took a gulp of coffee, looking over at his sister again.

"We get lots of people who are just curious," Ellen explained. "I need to be sure you're not one of them, that you're really who you say you are, and that you'll provide an honest account of us."

Her words made sense to Mike, "I can provide you with my bona fides, CV, that sort of a thing. Or would you need a letter of recommendation from my university?"

"You're attached to a university, then? Ron didn't say." Ellen gave her brother a careful look.

A lot of meaningful looks going on here, Mike thought as he replied, "Not any more. I recently took early retirement from university down in San Francisco. But I taught history there for a number of years, and my research interests were widely known." And recognized, he thought, but forbore to say. "I'm working full-time on this project now. The History and Culture of the Confederated Tribes on the Oregon Coast," he added, and looked across the table to see what impact, if any, this had on his two companions. They remained impassive.

Mike drank his coffee and wondered what the other two were thinking. He was a man of few words himself, but this was unnerving. He'd come here hoping to make arrangements for the next step in his research. Now it looked as if he was going to have to jump through hoops for Ron's sister.

Finally, Ellen smiled, a wide smile that seemed to crack her face in two. She spoke again. "I think we can say you'll do. But it would be good to have the paperwork you mentioned, for the others, you understand. They'll not have met you as I have. It'll help me reassure them." She smiled again. "I have the bookshop across the way. Maybe you could drop them in there? Meantime, you can check out our newsletter on the internet. It's called *The Voice of CLUSI*." With these words she rose and held out her hand. "It's been a pleasure to meet you, Mr Halliday, Mike. And keep a lookout for that friend of yours."

As Mike watched her regal figure walk out, he turned to Ron. "Quite a woman, your sister." It was all he could think of to say. Her last words had stunned him.

"Yeah, she's one of a kind, that girl," Ron said proudly. "Well, better be going too." The men shook hands and left together, each going his separate way outside. "Be in touch," Ron said, as he walked away.

Mike jumped into his pickup and sat there for a while going over the meeting that had just taken place. On reflection, it seemed he'd been subject to some sort of a test, and he had, or he thought he had, passed it. At least as far as Ellen was concerned. But he still had to get his paperwork to her, he reminded himself. It was as bad as a job interview, something he thought he'd left behind when he retired from the university.

Driving home, Mike turned up the volume on his favorite country and western music station to drown out his thoughts, but he couldn't stop them. Images of Jenny kept popping into his head. She was an attractive woman, no doubt about that. It would be the first time he'd noticed any woman since Mary had become so ill. And he'd seen Jenny's vulnerability under the tough outer shell she liked to present.

Well, it wasn't surprising. She'd had a couple of real bad shocks recently, and there was more to come if he wasn't wrong. Who knew what she'd uncover when she started investigating her birth. Could Maddy be her birth mother? They were certainly alike, the same build, and both were strong and independent women, but where did those violet eyes come from – the ones that seemed to follow him around?

He saw the lights were on as he passed Maddy's house, but managed to control an impulse to stop and continued up the track to where Ben was waiting eagerly for his return. Mike let himself into the cold house, berating himself for allowing the stove to go out. He'd forgotten to bank it up before he left. Sighing, he went out to the woodpile and gathered an armful of logs. Looking down the way, he saw the lights twinkling again and wondered how Jenny was coping. He almost regretted his offer to help, but he told himself it was the neighborly thing to do. And she wasn't likely to take him up on it, was she? No, he was quite safe. She wasn't one of those designing women who'd been thrown at him by his former colleagues almost as soon as Mary hit the nursing home.

As he settled down for an evening of writing, Ben at his feet, Mike managed to banish all thoughts of Jenny and her challenges. He was soon lost in his favorite world; the world of the past where life seemed to have been simpler, where circles of life and rites of passage dominated, where lives were built around the migration of salmon and eels, and goods were made from local resources.

He had just poured himself a glass of red wine and was settling down for another hour or so of writing when he was startled by the ringing of the telephone.

"Hello, Mike here."

"Mike, it's Jenny." There was a pause, during which he adjusted his earlier belief that she wouldn't take him up on his offer. "I hope you don't mind but you did say..." Jenny's voice was tentative.

"Yes, yes, I did," he reassured her, mentally saying goodbye to his next chapter.

"It's just that... since I was in the hospital today..."

"Did you manage to ask Maddy?"

"No, that's it. I couldn't bring myself to mention it. And, since I've come home it's all been going round and round in my head. I'm not usually like this," she apologized. "I can cope with most things. But this has got me beat."

Mike sighed. "Would you like me to come down?" he asked deciding that, now his train of thought had been broken, he might as well go out. He fully expected her to refuse so was surprised to hear her next words.

"Would you really? I'd be very grateful." Mike could tell from Jenny's tone that it cost her a lot to say that.

"Be right down." Mike hung up the phone.

Twelve

To Jenny's surprise, she had a really good sleep and awoke refreshed next morning. Maybe the red wine had helped, she mused. Walking into the kitchen she began to clear away the remains of the previous night. She and Mike had managed to polish off a full bottle of red, and she felt sure she'd had the bulk of it. Popping her nose outside, she could feel some warmth in the air. Spring seemed to be coming at last!

Jenny was a little embarrassed she'd phoned Mike, but he'd seemed okay about it and was a good listener. She'd tried to think of all the angles of why her parents had adopted her, and why they'd felt the need to keep it secret, a secret that Maddy had been a party to. The conversation had been pretty much one-sided, Jenny remembered. She'd needed a sounding board, and had blatantly used Mike for one. The only believable solution was that Maddy had to be her birth mother. It all made sense then, and Mike had seemed to concur, even going so far as to say that she and Maddy were alike. Clearly it had been in his mind too.

What had been decided, was that she would broach the subject with Maddy today. She couldn't remain in limbo for any longer. The ignorance was killing her. She took her breakfast across to the fireside and stared up at the mantel. There was the photo of the young man in uniform who had been Maddy's fiancé before he was killed. Maybe he was... No, she did her sums. He must have died a number of years before Jenny was born. So that meant, if Maddy was her mother then she must have... Oh, this was driving her mad. She looked up at the photo again. Well, at least she was alive. She realized the poor young man in the photo had not had the luxury of living to her age. Even if she did find herself in a turmoil, it was better to be alive.

Jenny took her time dressing as she plucked up the courage to confront Maddy with her discovery. She wasn't looking forward to her visit today, but her godmother had been quite comfortable when she was there the day before, so she'd no concerns for her health.

As she poked her head around the door of Maddy's room, she was pleased to see the older woman sitting up reading a paper. "Hello there! Looks like we'll have you out of here in no time."

"Aren't you a sight for sore eyes? You haven't got all dressed up to visit me, have you? Where are you off to?" Maddy asked with a twinkle in her eye.

"Well, yes," Jenny replied awkwardly, wondering if it had been a mistake to deviate from her now usual pants and sweatshirt for this visit, but she'd felt the tailored slacks and blazer would give her the confidence she needed.

"What's the matter, honey?" Maddy pushed herself up in the bed, her look of concern seeming to bore through Jenny. Maddy wasn't easily fooled. "There's something not right, isn't there? Have you had bad news from home, or has that devil Mike been bothering you?"

"No, nothing like that." Jenny moved closer to the bed and took a seat. She looked down at her hands twisting in her lap and wondered how to begin.

"Well, out with it." Maddy looked at her expectantly.

Jenny raised her eyes to meet those looking down at her with tenderness and love. "I was sorting through your things, I found a case…"

"Yes? There's a lot of rubbish in that house. It needed going through."

"I found some letters." Jenny looked down again. "They were from Mum… and there was a photo of me, a baby photo."

Jenny saw Maddy's hands go up to her face. "Oh, my dear. You didn't…"

"I did, I read it." Jenny started to sob. "Maddy, how could you both have lied to me all these years? And how could you not have told me when I arrived here this time? Mum's gone. Surely *you* could have been honest with me at least?"

"Me, oh my God, You think that I…? Oh no, my darling girl, not me."

Jenny's eyes widened as she gazed at the older woman in surprise, the tears drying unnoticed on her cheeks. "Then who... how... why here?"

"It's a long story, and I'm not sure I can go into it all here and now." She looked up at the ceiling reflectively. "Your mother had a sister."

"A sister! I never knew."

"No, I don't expect you did. Thea was a bit of a wild child."

"Thea! That's my middle name."

"Yes. Jane gave you your mother's name, but she hoped you wouldn't turn out like her, and you haven't," she said heavily.

"But why? Why did it have to be a secret? For so long?"

"We all thought it was for the best at the time. You have to realize, Jenny Wren, times were very different in those days. And your mom had just lost her own child. It seemed to her that God had given her another chance."

"But..." Jenny was interrupted by the arrival of the nurse, who took one look at Maddy and announced, "I think that's enough visiting for today. This patient needs a rest."

Jenny felt at a loose end. All dressed up and nowhere to go. She couldn't bear the idea of returning to the house straight away, and as she started the car, she found herself driving south. Pushed to the back of her mind by all the other things which had been happening, the idea of starting a bookshop back in Oz hadn't disappeared. Maybe now was the time to have another look at the one in Florence. She didn't know what it was, but something seemed to be drawing her back there. She took the coast road down to Florence and parked in the Old Town.

Pushing open the old wooden door, Jenny paused and sniffed. There was something about the air in bookshops, she mused. Was it the smell of the books, slightly musty, or just the knowledge that there were so many words inside them? She stood for a moment, closed her eyes and breathed in deeply. She couldn't explain it, but she felt safe here.

A gentle voice in her ear took her by surprise. "So you've come back!"

Jenny's eyes flew open. "Oh, you startled me. I was just... yes, I'm back." She smiled ruefully. "There's something about this place. I'm thinking I might open one too, a bookshop that is, when I return to Australia."

It was as if she hadn't spoken. The other woman laid her hand on Jenny's arm. "I can see you're troubled, but it will all work out. There is no need to fear."

Shaken, Jenny pulled her arm away and rubbed it where the hand had touched her. "How do you know?" Her voice came out with a croak. "What do you mean?" she quickly added, unsure of what to say.

A pair of twinkling eyes met Jenny's, and the face opposite her broke into a wide grin. "I sense these things. I can feel there have been some recent challenges for you, matters you have found it difficult to cope with." Again there was a smile, but a gentler one this time. "You need to be in control, but being in control is not always possible. Nor is it always best for you."

Seeing a chair by the counter, Jenny sat down with a thump. "How... what... are you...?"

"I'm a Native American. Ellen is my name. And you are?"

She knows all this about me, but not my name, Jenny thought while her voice said, "Jenny, Jenny Sullivan."

"I met a friend of yours the other day," was Ellen's next surprising comment.

"A friend? Of mine? Here?" God, I sound like a dill, thought Jenny.

"A guy called Mike. From Seal Rock," Ellen said.

"Mike, he's not really a friend, he's a neighbor, a neighbor of my godmother."

"That's what he said, too." Ellen gave a soft laugh. "Look, I've obviously startled you. It's not something I do often. How about a cup of something? I can close this place for a bit while we go across the road."

Jenny looked out of the door, and for the first time, noticed a coffee house directly opposite. "That sounds like a good idea," she said, shaken to the core by the conversation they'd just had. A cup of tea or coffee might bring everything back to normal.

Sitting by the river with a large mug of coffee, Jenny was more at ease. She looked across at her companion. "Why did you say all that to me? I mean, where did it all come from?"

"I know it sounded odd," replied the other woman. "And I'm sorry if I spooked you. Sometimes I just get this feeling about people."

"Are you one of those psychics?"

"No, I wouldn't call myself that. It's like I see an aura around people, and I can tell when they're in trouble. Often talking about it helps," she added, taking a long drink from her mug.

Jenny didn't know why it was, but now she'd recovered from her shock, she found the company of this woman, Ellen, soothing. She was beginning to experience a calm which had been missing from her for some time – since she had read the letter, or even before that.

The two women sat in silence sipping their coffees. It was peaceful by the river. They were the only two people sitting on the deck. They watched the birds swooping down into the water, a couple of kayaks tracking their way downstream in the distance, the gentle swirl of the tide. Finally Ellen spoke, "Do you want to tell me about it?"

Jenny looked up from contemplating her coffee. "Yes," she said. She felt that here was a woman she could trust, who might even help her heal. *Now where did that word come from?* "Where do I begin?" she asked helplessly.

"At the beginning, as the white rabbit said to Alice," Ellen smiled gently and Jenny smiled too at this reference to one of her favorite tales.

"Okay." Jenny drew a deep breath. "It all began with a sand dollar."

"A sand dollar?"

"When I was little," Jenny began, "I remember visiting Maddy here in Oregon. Maddy's my godmother," she explained.

"The one you're visiting now, who's in hospital?"

"That's right. We went down to the beach, and that's where I found it."

"Maddy, look what I've found. A white penny!" The little girl swung her black pigtails back across her shoulders and held up a white disc for the adult to see.

"Let me see, Jenny Wren? Oh, that's a sand dollar, you've found. Some say that it's mermaid's money but it's really the skeleton of a tiny sea creature. It was once a live sea creature but this is all that's left of it. Would you like to look for more of them?"

"No! Mermaid's money?" The little girl completely ignored the real explanation. "This is my magic sand dollar, my very own. I'm going to keep it for ever and ever."

"And I did keep it, but it was stuffed away at the back of a drawer. Every time I moved, it came with me, even though I'd forgotten all about it."

"So what happened to remind you?"

"Everything went belly-up at work. I have… *had*," Jenny corrected herself, "a senior management position in learning and development. Things were going really well, funded projects, State awards, improved staff morale. Then they decided to restructure, and we all had to reapply for the new positions."

"And you didn't get yours?" Ellen guessed.

"Right on," Jenny said, the memory of the humiliation she had felt searing her again. She took another drink of her coffee before continuing, "Then I found my sand dollar again just as I received an email from Maddy inviting me over here. It was uncanny."

"It's amazing how things can happen like that, isn't it? Life is full of unexplainable coincidences," Ellen agreed.

"It was a good decision to come here. I was beginning to feel calmer, to heal." *That word again. Where did it come from? I've never talked that way in my life. That's hippy talk.*

"But something else has happened, hasn't it?" Ellen's eyes seemed to be probing right inside her as if she knew what she was thinking. It was a spooky feeling. The finding of the letter was a very private matter. Jenny didn't know if she could reveal that to a veritable stranger. She hesitated, then, sensing Ellen only wanted to help her, and suddenly imbued with the belief it was the right thing to do, Jenny decided to trust the other woman with her secret.

"I found a letter," she began. "I wasn't prying. Maddy and I had begun clearing out some old things from the attic when she fell." Somehow that made it better, thought Jenny. "It was a letter written when I was a baby, from my mum to Maddy. They'd been old school friends," she explained. "That's how they knew each other, and how she came to become my godmother, I guess. Well, the letter revealed Mum wasn't my mum after all. I'd been adopted as a baby."

"And you'd never known?" wondered Ellen.

"No."

"How did that make you feel?"

"Angry, upset. I don't know. I felt my whole life had been a lie, and I wanted to know the truth."

"Do you? Know the truth, now, I mean?"

"Not exactly. My first thought was that Maddy was my mother, and

I had almost come to terms with that even though I didn't understand it."

"But she's not?" Ellen prompted again.

"No. I asked her today, and she was beginning to tell me when the nurse chased me out of the room. I didn't know what to do, where to go. So I came here."

"Did she tell you anything at all?"

"Only that my real mother was Mum's sister. I didn't even know Mum had a sister."

"I believe that this was meant. That you've been sent here, at this time in your life, to find out some truths about the past," said Ellen.

"I don't believe all that stuff about predestination. I've always thought it's a load of rubbish." Although Jenny's voice was assertive, it held a dubious tone as if she didn't believe her own words.

"There's a lot we don't understand." Then Ellen added in a seeming non sequitur, "Did you know some people believe the sand dollar has religious significance, that the five-pointed star on top represents the star of Bethlehem, and the five keyholes represent the wounds Jesus received on the cross?"

"Really? I didn't know that. I just believed it was magic when I was younger." She took the sand dollar out of her pocket, and examining it closely, turned the object over in her fingers, feeling the marks with her thumb. "It brought me here." She raised her eyes to meet Ellen's. "Look, thanks for your time, for listening to me. It's helped to get it off my chest." As she said the words, she did indeed feel a lightness which she couldn't ascribe to anything other than their conversation. The two stood up.

Ellen took both of Jenny's hands in hers. "Go safely," she admonished, "and come again. You'll always find me here."

Thirteen

Mike was enjoying the slight change in the weather as he jogged along the beach with Ben. He loved it down here in the early mornings before the tourists or the scavengers started to arrive. He wondered, not for the first time, how it was that no matter how many loads of driftwood were removed from the beach, the sea always managed to provide another harvest. You only had to look at the front yards and the souvenir shops around the place to see how this harvest from the sea was being put to good use.

Stopping to allow Ben to follow after an interesting scent, he stood facing the ocean and stretched his arms above his head. He drew in an invigorating breath of air, then let it out again with a sigh. It was good to be alive on such a morning. Moving up here on a permanent basis had really been the right decision for him. He'd found peace, and his research was going well, the outline and early chapters of his book almost finished.

His mind, free from all other priorities, turned to his neighbor. He hadn't seen Jenny since the evening before last, when she'd rung him in such a state. She probably regretted it now. It hadn't been a bad night though. They'd got through a lot of wine, he remembered, and that had oiled the conversation. He wondered if she'd spoken to Maddy after all. It seemed likely she was Maddy's daughter, but you never could tell with these matters.

To Mike's surprise, his curiosity had been piqued, and he found himself wondering what Jenny had found out. As he and Ben made their way back up the track he checked his watch, deciding to take a punt on Jenny being up and about at this early hour. Knocking on the door he yelled, "Anyone home?" He didn't do it too loudly in case she was still asleep, but loud enough to be heard if she was awake.

"Mike!" Jenny's face peered around the door, which then opened wider to reveal she was not only up and about, but cooking breakfast. The apron tied around her waist bore testament to the fact that she'd been in the kitchen, even if the scent of pancakes cooking had not assailed his nostrils. "I'm making pancakes," she said. "Would you like some?"

Mike was gob smacked. His automatic reaction was to back away. Instead, he found himself accepting, and only asking, "Okay if Ben comes too?" stepped inside, Ben at his heels.

He followed Jenny into the kitchen and, leaning against one side of the bench, spoke to her back, which she'd turned to him as if regretting her invitation. "How's Maddy?" He thought that was a fairly safe opening, but Jenny's reaction shocked him.

She turned around abruptly, a dripping spatula in hand. "It's not her!"

"What's not... oh, you mean you managed to ask her?"

"Yes, and it seems my mother, the one I know that is, had a sister, a younger sister called Thea. That's where my middle name comes from. And she's my real mother."

"I don't know about real." Mike was trying to come to grips with Jenny's thought patterns. "I think they call it the birth mother, don't they?"

"Well, whatever. I didn't even know my mother had a sister. No one ever mentioned her." Jenny turned back to her pancakes. "Can you fetch some maple syrup from the pantry?" she asked, concentrating once again on the task at hand.

"Sure thing." Mike wasn't about to go where he wasn't wanted, conversation wise, but what else was there to say? Best to say nothing, he decided, so they stood in an amicable silence till Jenny turned around again.

"Breakfast's ready!"

They sat down and began to scoff the pancakes.

"Good stuff!" Mike found his voice. "Is this what you have for breakfast back in Australia?"

"No fear." Jenny seemed to want to put aside their earlier conversation, and that was fine with him. There were emotional quick sands there he didn't want to step in. "I usually have fruit and cereal. I've been having that here too, but I need to do a shop so I thought I'd go native today."

"Native, hey?"

"That reminds me. I met a woman yesterday, a Native American, who claimed she knows you. Ellen. I don't know her surname. She owns a bookshop down in Florence." Jenny hesitated as if unsure how to go on. "She seems a bit... I don't know what, but she said some strange things."

"So you met Ellen, eh? She's a weird one. I'm hoping she's going to help me with some research."

"That's right. Maddy mentioned you're doing research into the Native American Indians who lived in this region."

"They still do." Mike started to tell Jenny about his work, but could see that she wasn't paying a great deal of attention.

The conversation continued to lurch along for a short time then came to a halt. The pair seemed to have run out of things to say. There was silence while they ate their pancakes, punctuated only by the odd grunt from Ben lying under the table as he chased small creatures in his sleep.

The silence lengthened, and it seemed to Mike that Jenny had gone far away in her thoughts. This was beginning to make him feel uncomfortable. Suddenly he pushed back his chair. "Well, I'll be off," he muttered. "Thanks for the breakfast. My turn next." Now why had he added that, he wondered? Maybe knocking on this particular door this morning had not been such a good idea. Not one of his best.

*

Jenny watched Mike leave with mixed feelings. It had been a sudden impulse to invite him in for breakfast. She'd thought it would work, and it had started out all right. Then she'd begun to feel awkward. It wasn't his fault. He was a nice man. If she were honest with herself, she even found him attractive. Maybe that was the trouble. She'd managed to keep herself too busy to allow a man into her life since John had died, and if she hadn't made time for a relationship of any sort in Australia, she certainly didn't intend to do so here. It was one more complication, one she certainly didn't need.

She was conscious of taking her indignation out on the pans and dishes as she washed up. No dishwasher for her today. She needed the release the physical act of washing up gave her. As she wiped down the surfaces, she admitted to herself that Mike hadn't made any untoward advances. In fact, he'd been a gentleman. Was that the trouble, she wondered. Did she want his advances? Surely not.

She was going crazy stuck in this house on her own. How did Maddy do it? Thinking of Maddy brought Jenny full circle, back to their conversation the day before. Thea. Who was she? Then she remembered the photos, in particular the one she'd been looking at when Maddy had dashed off to answer the phone. In retrospect, it seemed as if she'd been glad of the escape the ringing phone had offered.

Drying her hands quickly, Jenny rooted out the photo albums again. It didn't take her long to find the picture she was looking for. She studied it carefully. There were the three girls she had seen before, but now she looked at them in a different light. The third girl, the leggy one, younger than the other two. Could that be Thea? Could that be her mother?

Jenny tried to see if there was any resemblance to herself, but it was an old photo and the girl's features weren't very clear. She spent the remainder of the morning searching through the other albums and found a few more which included the girl Jenny thought of as Thea, her mother's younger sister. She couldn't think of her as her mother, not yet anyway.

As she prepared to make her daily visit to the hospital, Jenny felt as if a heavy cloud was settling over her. For the first time, she was unsure about seeing her godmother. Would she or wouldn't she get more information from her, and did she want more right now?

She sighed as she drove over to the hospital. Why did everything have to be so difficult? Life certainly seemed to be throwing a few curly ones at her this year. She remembered what Ellen had said about her trip here having been meant. How could it be meant for her to go through such turmoil? What was it all in aid of? Did Ellen really have some special intuition; a sort of second sight?

At the hospital, Jenny entered Maddy's room with trepidation. She thrust a box of chocolates she'd bought in the hospital shop towards her godmother. "How are you today?" she said, determined not to be the first to bring up the 'M' word.

Maddy was beaming from ear to ear. "I'm feeling a lot better, honey. In fact, I think they're going to let me go home."

"Home? When?" Jenny couldn't believe her ears. This was the news she'd been hoping to hear for days, and the way she'd been hustled out the day before hadn't prepared her for it.

"You'll have to talk to the doctor, but it could be as soon as tomorrow or the next day. I think they need this bed," she confided, "and they're keen to get rid of me."

"As long as they think you're well enough," Jenny cautioned. "I'll check with the doctor before I leave."

"Now, what have you been up to? Tell me, have you been seeing much of Mike?" Maddy chuckled. "He's a nice lad."

"Yes he is, but don't start that." Jenny pretended to be annoyed, but was actually glad her godmother had found another topic of conversation. Though she was amused at the description of a sixty-something year old man as a lad. "We both like to live our own lives. No chance for you to match-make there."

"Pity." Maddy didn't seem too concerned. "But you *have* seen him?"

"Yes. We actually had breakfast together today," Jenny admitted.

"And how was it?" Maddy raised her eyebrows.

"Awkward." Jenny laughed. "I guess neither of us is used to dealing with members of the opposite sex, not socially anyway." As she spoke, Jenny reflected how true this was. As far as men were concerned, all her relationships had been strictly businesslike. She had eschewed a social life for work and children, and now it felt like it was too late. Not that it concerned her. She was happy on her own, or would be when she'd sorted herself out.

After a bit of inconsequential conversation, Jenny excused herself. "I'll see if I can catch the doctor now. I'll be back to let you know what she says," she assured her godmother. It was over half an hour later that Jenny came bouncing into the room, followed by a tall figure wearing a stethoscope around her neck.

"Everything's fine. I can pick you up tomorrow," she announced with a big smile, relieved Maddy was to come home at last. "I can be here at ten o'clock if that's right with you," she turned to the doctor who was clearly amused by her excitement.

"As long as this lady behaves herself between now and then," the doctor smiled at the pair.

"Listen to her. I've been treated like I'm in a first class hotel. What is there not to behave?" However Maddy looked relieved too. Jenny understood that, no matter how well the older woman was being treated here, it wasn't the same as being in her own home.

"You are in a position to take care of her?" The doctor was looking at Jenny. "Maddy's going to need a lot of help. She won't be able to move around easily or very much for a few more weeks."

"Yes, we'll be fine."

"And we have strong man living nearby," said Maddy with a grin. "Haven't we, Jenny? He can do any heavy lifting for us."

Jenny threw Maddy a weary look but, "I'm sure we can manage," were her only words as the doctor turned to leave. The two women smiled at each other. "So, tomorrow at this time you'll be tucked up in your own bed." Jenny smoothed down the top sheet and took Maddy's hand.

"Less of the tucked up bit. I'll be home, then we'll see."

Jenny was beginning to realize that once she was home, Maddy might not be the ideal patient, but she'd be glad to have her there, nevertheless.

"I'd better go now. I need to get some shopping in if you're going to be home tomorrow. Don't want to be dashing out again and leaving you to fend for yourself as soon as you get there." Patting Maddy's hand again, she moved away from the bed. "See you tomorrow," she promised.

As she walked around the supermarket filling up her basket, Jenny found she was becoming accustomed to the American brands and packaging. She made sure to include in her trolley the cinnamon rolls and macadamia nut cookies, which were her godmother's favorites. *How she doesn't get fat on all these sweet things, I don't know*, she thought as she loaded up one more package, before making her way to the checkout.

Jenny had just parked back at Seal Rock and was unloading the boot, when she heard a vehicle drive up and stop behind her.

"Need any help there?" Mike's voice rang out.

"Thanks, but I can manage," her actions seeming to give a lie to her words as she struggled with a large box of supplies.

"Fine." There was some amusement in the other's voice, but he only asked, "Did you see Maddy today? How's she getting on?"

With a sigh, Jenny moved around to balance the box on the hood of the car. "Just fine. She's coming home tomorrow. Hence the stocking up." She gestured with her head to the box sitting precariously on the car.

"Well, I guess you have things to do. Maybe I'll pop in tomorrow and say howdy to Maddy when she's back." With that parting shot, he engaged the gears and drove off leaving Jenny gazing after him in surprise.

Damn, but she could have done with some help, she considered, balancing the box on her uplifted knee while she fumbled to fit the key into the door. *Sometimes you're too independent for your own good, Jenny Sullivan, the man offered and you refused like the idiot you are.* Still carrying on the argument with herself in her head, Jenny unloaded and packed away all of the goods, before dropping panting onto the sofa. *Well, what would have happened if I had accepted his help?* she finally asked herself silently, then just as silently answered her own question: *I would have had to offer him coffee and he would probably have accepted, being the polite gentleman he is, which would have led to another awkward conversation which neither of us wanted.* Having settled all of that in her own mind she rose and went into the kitchen to brew some coffee, for herself.

Fourteen

Jenny was up at dawn. She felt exhilarated that Maddy was coming home and wanted to do a thorough clean to have the house sparkling for her godmother's return. It was lucky, she reflected, singing while mopping the floor, that the house was all on one level. It would make it easier for Maddy to move around. The hospital had said they could provide a wheelchair, though knowing her godmother, she wouldn't be willing to use it unless she really had to. Maddy would probably be content to stay in bed for a day or so, but her recovery would depend on achieving some movement, even if it was to shuffle around the house holding onto the furniture.

As Jenny put the final touches to the house and arranged a vase of rhododendrons on the dining table, she checked her watch. Time to go. She drove in to the hospital carefully, excited, but not without some misgivings. She'd managed to put her own concerns to the back of her mind while she was preparing everything for Maddy's return, and yesterday both had, as if in silent agreement, ignored their earlier conversation. Once home, however, they would be able to ignore it no longer, and while one part of Jenny was eager to hear more, there was another part of her that was dreading what she might hear.

*

In her hospital room, Maddy was sitting up eating her last breakfast there. She would be glad to be home. Despite what she'd told Jenny,

Maddy was only really happy in her own home and couldn't do with other people looking after her, even if she did need their assistance. The only fly in the ointment was that, once home, Jenny would be pestering her for more information on her parents. She hadn't expected this to crop up, and dearly wished she had been more prepared for it. *Why, in God's name, hadn't Jane told her daughter the truth about herself long ago?*

They'd all been so young then, and Thea had been even younger. It had started in school, but had all come to a head when Jane and Steve had come to visit. She hadn't had much to do with the family after Jane had emigrated to Australia, marrying the Australian guy she'd met in London when the two friends took a mad holiday there after the war. The trip had been designed to help Maddy get over her grief after Rick had been killed, but it was Jane whose life had changed.

Gosh, how her thoughts did wander as she became older. She'd been thinking about that visit, remembering it so clearly. She'd arranged to meet Jane downtown, away from the family.

"How are you? I'm so sorry. I heard about the baby." Maddy hugged her old school friend. *"It must have been tough for it to have happened on the ship."*

Jane grasped both her hands. *"Oh my dear Maddy, you don't know how glad I am to see you. It's hell at home. I wish we'd never come, but Mom wanted me to have the baby here and now…"*

"But you're all right, aren't you?"

"Yes." Jane's voice was weak giving a lie to her words. *"I'm fine."*

"How's Steve taking it… and your parents?"

"Steve's been wonderful. He says as long as I'm all right, that's all that matters. But he would have made a wonderful dad." She looked wistful.

"But surely, there'll be other babies? You're both still very young. Lots of time." Maddy tried to buck her friend up.

"No, not for us. There was damage, you see. On the ship the care was limited. It seems I was lucky to come out of it in one piece, or minus one piece." Jane tried to make a joke, but it fell flat as the two women regarded each other in dismay.

"And your parents?" Maddy repeated.

"Oh, they have other worries right now." Jane grimaced.

"What on earth do you mean?" Maddy couldn't imagine anything more earth-shattering than the fact that their eldest daughter had miscarried on

her way to visit.

"It's Thea," Jane said. "She's pregnant!"

"Oh!" Maddy was struck dumb. It was one thing for Jane to have lost her baby. That was bad enough. But for her young sister to be pregnant. That must have been more than she could take.

"She needs help, Maddy. Mom and Dad..."

"Who's the father? She's not married, is she?"

"That's the trouble. It's Jed Williams and Mom and Dad are ready to lynch him."

"It takes two," was Maddy's immediate response, then "Jed. Isn't that the guy...?"

"Yes. They've been seeing each other since school. They kept it secret as long as they could. Thea knew what Mom and Dad would be like."

"But how did she manage to keep this secret... and what did she plan to do?"

"She wore big clothes. You know what Thea's like, Maddy. She's been Dad's blue-eyed girl, the baby of the family. Could do no wrong. They want to get married, and she waited till I got here to tell them. But..." Jane shook her head. "She misjudged Dad. He went spare and even talked about locking her in her room. We've got to help them, Maddy."

"But surely your dad sees that if she's pregnant and Jed wants to marry her..."

"No!" Jane was becoming distraught. "He can't bear the thought of Thea and Jed together. They'd managed to keep their relationship secret since... since he forbade her to see him again. That was two years ago." Jane sighed. "Can't you see we must help her, help them?"

Maddy didn't quite see what she meant. "Help who do what? And who's we?"

"Help Thea and Jed get married, of course; you and I. Who else could I ask?"

"Steve?" Maddy hazarded a guess.

"Oh, Steve'll help, of course. But he's a stranger here. You and I are the ones who know the ropes."

"Well, of course I'll do what I can, but I don't know. What does Jed's family think?"

"They're just as bad as Mom and Dad. Don't want their son tied to a family like ours. Though I think they'd be more willing to come round because

of the baby. At least that's Thea's view. Her plan is that if they can run off and get married, everyone will have to accept it, and it'll all be hunky dory."

"So what's her plan for us? I presume she's got one." Thea had always been one for plans as a child, and she had often roped the older girls in. But this was more serious.

Maddy sighed, remembering. Thea did have a plan, and all looked as if it would work out. Until Jed's car turned a corner too fast. He'd been a good driver, but it was an old car, and in their rush to get away, he'd failed to check its roadworthiness. The brakes had failed at just the wrong time, and the car had flipped over.

What had happened next was almost too horrific to remember. Maddy had heard about it later when Jane had called her up in distress. Jane's voice had been catching and she was sobbing so uncontrollably that Maddy had had to listen carefully to make any sense of what she was saying.

"Oh my God, Maddy, there's been a terrible accident. Thea and Jed... the car..."

"Calm down and talk slowly." Maddy remembered saying. *"What's happened?"*

"The car, it overturned and they..." Jane broke down completely and it was several minutes before she was able to make herself understood again. "They're gone, Maddy... both gone."

"Gone...you mean...?"

"Dead, they're dead." Jane had been almost shouting by that time. "And it's our fault. We helped them."

"Don't say that." Maddy was quite firm. "They were set on this. They would have gone anyway. Jed was driving, not you." Finally Maddy managed to calm Jane, then came the shock.

"That poor baby. What's going to happen to her?"

"Baby?" Maddy took a few minutes to grasp this.

"Thea's baby. They managed to save her. She's a little girl. Dreadfully premature. She's so tiny and so beautiful." Jane began sobbing again and hung up.

Maddy met Jane for coffee several days later. She looked distraught but there was a quiet certainty underneath the despair. "We're taking her, Maddy. We're taking her back to Australia."

"Who?" Maddy asked, unable to believe her ears.

"Thea's baby. She'll be ours. The one we lost." Then she looked up at Maddy with a determined look in her eyes. "If she stays here the two families, Jed's and mine, will fight over her, as much because they don't want the other to have her as they want her themselves. No, it's better this way." She spoke as if she was trying to convince herself.

Maddy shook her head to rid herself of the memory. The anguish that had been caused to two families. Jane and Steve had whisked the baby off to Australia. She didn't even know if Jed's family had been told what had happened. Jane's father had been a force to be reckoned with. A local identity who felt he could manipulate everyone to suit his own ends. And that time, his goal had been to stop Jed's family from taking, or even having access to Thea's baby, his granddaughter. Even if it meant she was lost to him too. Maddy remembered how distressed Jane's mother had been, but to no avail. Jane had her way. And now, nearly sixty years later, Maddy, was left to try to explain everything to that baby.

"Finished, dear?" Maddy was saved from her ruminations by the arrival of the ward assistant who'd come to remove her tray. She looked distractedly at the empty dishes and handed the tray over silently.

About an hour later she was sitting in a wheelchair, washed, dressed and ready for off. She checked her watch, anxious to be gone. Ten minutes to ten. If Jenny was on time she'd be parking the car about now. Maddy couldn't wait to be shot of the place. She heard footsteps in the corridor and cautiously turned her chair to face the door. She'd never get used to this damn thing. But then she didn't want to get used to it. The sooner she was back on her own two feet the better. What did these doctors know? She'd be back to normal in no time.

The footsteps came closer. She perked up, but it was only the hospital administrator with some paperwork for her. Several cautionary words later, and just as she was beginning to feel restless, Jenny's familiar face peeped round the door.

"Hope you haven't been waiting long. They wouldn't let me in till they'd finished all their paperwork, but it seems we're good to go now." Taking hold of the handles and shrugging her handbag well up over her shoulder, Jenny carefully wheeled her godmother down the corridor and out the main door of the hospital. The fresh air hit them both, and Maddy breathed it in with relief. She'd been stuck in the ward for too long.

"They let me park right here," Jenny explained, "and there's even an orderly to help you into the car."

That done, they set off, and Maddy let out a deep breath she hadn't even realized she'd been holding. "Finally," she said. "I thought ten o'clock would never come. They had me awake and up real early, you know."

"That's hospitals for you."

"You're a good driver, dear," Maddy, who believed in giving credit where credit was due, said, as they made their way up the winding track to the house without a bump. "Good for my old bones."

"Less of the old," joshed Jenny who seemed afraid of causing Maddy any further damage. "Here we are then." They drew up in front of the house and Jenny bounced out and around to the back of the vehicle. She unloaded the wheelchair and took it around to the passenger side.

"How are you going to get me into that contraption?" Maddy asked, watching Jenny open the passenger door.

"Don't you worry. This is where all my training in patient moving comes into play. I attended enough of these sessions when I worked in Health, but I never knew how useful they'd prove to be. Here we go. Just hold on to me… here…" And, sure enough, Maddy ended up in the wheelchair before she knew what was happening.

"You chose the wrong profession. You should have been a nurse."

"Wouldn't have had the patience." Jenny maneuvered the chair into the house. "Now, how about a nice mug of coffee? And I bought some of these yummy cookies you like."

"Oh, Jenny Wren, it's so good to be home, home at last." Maddy cautiously wheeled herself around the room, checking everything was just as she'd left it. "Coffee sounds wonderful. I haven't had a proper brew since I left here. They didn't have any decent cookies in the place either. Think they were trying to put us all on a diet," she chortled.

"Oh, it's so good to have you back home." Jenny bent down to hug the older woman. "Won't be a tick." She headed to the kitchen.

"Well, I'm not going anywhere." Maddy settled back in her chair and beamed. It was a good feeling to be home again.

"Here you are." Jenny brought in a tray containing two steaming mugs of coffee and a plate of macadamia nut cookies. "Do you want to stay where you are or move to the sofa?" she asked, setting the tray down on the coffee table.

"Better stay here. I might get lost on the sofa," Maddy joked, feeling comfortable now she was in her own home. Even the wheelchair had ceased to bother her.

"You're probably right." Jenny entered into the joke and took her own place in the armchair. "You can make a quick getaway in that thing."

"Now, tell me what you've been up to while I've been incarcerated," Maddy said, giving Jenny a steely look. She had a feeling all was not well with her goddaughter, and hoped she wasn't the cause of her angst.

"We...ll," Jenny seemed to be deciding where to start. "I've been thinking about when I go back to Australia..."

"Not too soon, I hope," Maddy laughed, gesturing to her chair.

"No, I won't be leaving while you need me here. But I *will* be going back sometime and I've been thinking."

"Yes?"

"I think I might like to open a bookshop."

"A bookshop!" Maddy was surprised. "Whatever gave you that idea?"

"Well, it was when you were in hospital. One day, I went down to Florence again, to that Old Town area you took me to."

"Did you stock up on more clothes?"

"No, I wanted to check out some of the other nooks and crannies down there."

"And?"

"And I found this neat bookshop. It was strange how it drew me in. I loved the feel of it and I met the owner. She's a bit odd, though."

"Odd? In what way?"

"She seemed to sense things, things about me. It was a bit spooky to start with," Jenny admitted, "but she's really nice, and after a bit, I decided I liked her. I felt some sort of link with her, I guess." She looked wonderingly into space. "Yes, that's what it is, a sort of link," she repeated in surprise.

"Hmm." Maddy couldn't be doing with this sort of whimsy. "You'll be saying next you were meant to go there," she chortled. "Where's my pragmatic Jenny Wren gone?"

"It's funny you should say that. That's what she said."

"What?" Maddy was looking at her goddaughter as if she'd taken leave of her senses.

"That my coming here had been meant," Jenny said. "I thought it was mad too, but now I've had time to think about it, and the things that have happened since I arrived. It *is* a bit strange."

"So my falling over was meant too? Get a grip, girl."

"Well, maybe not your fall, but finding old photos, the letter, the bookshop, meeting…"

"Drink up your coffee and have another cookie," Maddy advised. "Just as well I'm back to get you on the straight and narrow. You've been here on your own too long, my dear."

"Maybe you're right. Anyway, not any more. Now we have to get you back on your feet."

"Literally, I'm afraid," Maddy laughed. "But I'm determined. Don't let this old face fool you. I'm not done yet. I'm not on the scrap-heap by a long chalk."

"That's funny!" Jenny exclaimed giving her godmother a strange look. "That's exactly the phrase I used when I heard about the redundancy."

Maddy fixed the young woman with her eyes and asked, "So, you've definitely decided to take it? The redundancy, I mean."

"Yes," Jenny sighed. "I talked with my friend Rosa while you were in hospital, and she told me everything's going from bad to worse back there. I've emailed Carmel my acceptance, and I'm waiting to see exactly what they're going to offer me."

"Well, make sure they do the right thing by you. You've been there a long time." Maddy paused. "And you think you would get enough for this bookshop idea?"

"I don't know, but I think I should have the equivalent of close to a year's salary. That would be a start. I just love the atmosphere of books, and standing there in Ellen's shop, I found myself breathing it all in." She took a deep breath as if she could sense it right there.

Maddy smiled at Jenny's enthusiasm. "Well if that's what you want, I'm sure you'll get it. You were always good at getting what you wanted out of life. Just like…" She stopped short. Time enough to talk about Thea later, but Jenny was like her in so many ways. Maddy knew it had to be done, but not today.

Fifteen

"Here you are." Jenny pushed the bedroom door open with her foot and, laying the tray down by the bed, went to open the curtains. The morning sunlight poured in. "It's a beautiful morning for your first day home," she greeted her godmother. "Now, I think you should stay there for the morning at least, after all your excitement yesterday."

"Excitement? I just came home. Don't you go treating me like one of your staff members, now. I won't have it." Pulling herself up in the bed, Maddy gave Jenny a stern look. "This is *my* house and I'm not decrepit yet. I'll get up after breakfast. Thanks for bringing it in," she added more graciously. "It looks and smells delicious." She eyed the pancakes topped with chopped fruit and drizzled with maple syrup in delight. "I certainly didn't get treated like this where I've been."

"And you may not get treated like this every morning here either," said Jenny. "Especially if you don't behave. I'll leave you to eat it in peace," she added, leaving the room.

"We'll talk when I come through," Maddy's words followed Jenny out of the room, and she stopped in her tracks outside the door. Taking a deep breath, she returned to the kitchen to eat her own breakfast and clean up, but she found her stomach was churning at the thought of what Maddy might have to tell her. In fact Jenny had found herself tossing and turning all night. She'd tried to put the thought of Thea out of her mind, but it had been niggling away at the back of it for days, ever since her name was first mentioned.

Hearing a sound behind her, Jenny turned to see Maddy shuffling slowly towards her. "Are you sure you should be doing that?" she asked anxiously, fearing her godmother might take another fall.

"Probably not," grimaced the older woman, "but how am I ever going to get moving if I don't start somewhere?" She carefully maneuvered herself into a chair. "There, that's better. Now, how about some coffee and we'll get started?"

Jenny carried over the mugs in some trepidation. This was one of the few times in her life she wished she was a smoker. She certainly needed something to calm her nerves, and coffee wasn't it. "Okay," she said, steeling herself for whatever revelations Maddy had to tell.

Maddy sat silently as if wondering exactly how to begin. "Well, it was like this," she said eventually. "Thea was Jane's younger sister. She was always trailing behind us when we were young." She shook her head, as if remembering. "We never could shake her off, not till that summer. She must have been around fifteen, and Jane and I were eighteen. We were glad to be rid of her because we were becoming interested in boys, and we didn't want her cramping our style."

Jenny sat back nursing her coffee. She could almost see the three girls, the two older ones probably giggling to themselves, while trying to evade the younger one, who wanted to be part of their secrets. She turned her attention back to Maddy, who was talking again.

"She'd always been a wild child, a bit of a tomboy, really, and she was the apple of her father's eye; his baby who could do no wrong. Well, that summer she started to grow up, and we were all too engrossed in our own affairs to notice. It was during the war, you have to remember, so the adults were fixated on the news reports, and we older girls were being fascinated by men in uniform. It was a time unlike any you've known," she explained to Jenny.

"But this was long before I was born," Jenny objected. "What does it have to do with me?"

"I'm coming to you. It all started back then. You see, what none of us had noticed was that Thea was growing up too, and she'd become interested in boys earlier than we had, or one particular boy, I should say. I didn't have much to do with Jane's family for some time. I'd met Rick." She paused and looked nostalgically at the photo of the young soldier which held pride of place on the wall.

Not for the first time, Jenny wished, if she did have to be adopted,

Maddy had been her birth mother. Maddy continued, "But I found out later Thea had met a boy, someone she knew her parents wouldn't approve of, so she kept their friendship secret."

"But this was still way before I was born," objected Jenny.

"Yes, it was. But it seems the friendship grew without their parents' knowledge. Yes," she repeated, "they managed to keep it secret until her final year at school. They wanted to attend the Homecoming Dance together, and that meant her parents found out."

"And…?"

"And her father put his foot down."

"Absolutely not!" The loud voice rings through the house, coming as it does from the man standing at the foot of the stairs. "I will not have any daughter of mine consorting with such riffraff. And you're not going out dressed like that, either!"

"But Dad, it's the Homecoming Dance and Mom said…"

"I don't care what your mom said. I'm your father and what I say goes."

The girl creeps back upstairs in tears, but she is not beaten. She'd half expected this and has a back-up plan. She'd climbed out often enough before, through her bedroom window. Luckily there's a tree just outside, and with a bit of a struggle, she can swing herself over and shin down. She's never done it dressed like this before, she reminds herself, looking down at her finery, but it'll be worth it. Jed will be waiting for her outside the gate as planned. She'll wait awhile, till she feels Dad has calmed down, then make her getaway. She knows she can get back in the same way, so he'll never know she's been gone. She smiles as she locks her bedroom door and turns on her radio as cover.

The house is quiet except for the sound of the radio coming from the lounge directly below. Her father always listens to his favorite comedy program at this time, and he likes it to be loud. Thea eases open the window and props it in place with the stick she keeps for that very purpose. It would never do to be stuck outside. That would really give the game away.

She jumps to the ground, and with a quick glance back to make sure no one is watching, runs lightly across the grass and down the driveway to where her escort is waiting. She slows down once he's in sight and skips towards him putting her hand up to touch the unaccustomed topknot of curls which she has arranged, and which she considers gives her a sophisticated look.

"Wow, girl! You've outdone yourself. Hope I can live up to you tonight."

Jed uses both hands to smooth back his black hair, glossy in the moonlight, as Thea's eager eyes take in the grey double-breasted suit with its wide lapels and shoulder pads.

"Wow yourself," is her response. "Let's boogie."

"But first," Jed reaches into the front seat of the car and brings out a corsage which takes Thea's breath away. She hasn't expected one from Jed, even though she knows all the other girls will have one. Jed has never followed the crowd. But she's secretly delighted he hasn't shunned custom on this occasion. "Stand still," he says. Thea feels a shiver run up her spine as his large hands clumsily reach down to pin the flowery tribute to her shoulder, hoping he'll hurry up and won't damage the delicate fabric of her dress. It's a dress unlike any she's worn before, made of pale blue silk with a net overskirt, its puffed sleeves echoing the ruching on the bodice. 'There!' Jed stands back in admiration. "We match!" As he speaks, Thea notices her companion wears a matching flower in his own lapel.

"I guess there was a run on carnations," she jokes as she eases herself into the station wagon, taking care not to damage the netting of her skirt. As Thea looks up into the deep brown eyes of the tall young man holding open the car door for her, she feels a thrill of excitement. This is going to be a night to remember.

"Here." As he turns the key, Jed hands her a bottle. "You may need some Dutch courage tonight. Everyone is going to see us together. We won't be a secret anymore. What did your parents say?" he adds, knowing she'd planned to tell them before she left.

"Don't ask! You know what Dad's like! Forbade me to come with you, so we can't be too open even now. Let's just enjoy the dance." Thea takes a gulp from the bottle in her hand. "I'll handle them tomorrow." She reaches over to place her hand on Jed's thigh and he immediately covers it with his.

"Your word is my command," he says, and the pair roar off into the night together.

"From what I understand, he absolutely forbade Thea to attend but…"

"She went anyway," Jenny guessed.

"Yes, she did. The relationship continued to flourish, and then a couple of years later, she fell pregnant."

"So what happened to her?"

"They decided to marry and, at first, sought permission from their parents."

"What was wrong with the boy? Why did her father disapprove of him?"

"Well, my dear, you have to try to put yourself back in that time. You have to know your grandfather was someone who had a great deal of standing in the community and was a bit of a bigot. A lot of people like him were in those days, still are," she sighed.

"Yes, I get that. But what did he have against him. Surely the fact she was pregnant...?"

"Jed was a Native American and came from a poor family, the other side of the tracks, we called it back then. He was a bright kid, a bit wild like Thea. They were well matched." Maddy stopped again and looked across at Jenny. "I need to take a break at this part, honey," she said. "How about a fresh brew?" She held her mug towards Jenny.

Jenny looked down at her own half full mug in surprise. Her coffee had gone cold while she was listening to Maddy's tale. She was loath to move, but realized the sense in giving Maddy a break, so she took both mugs and went into the kitchen without saying a word, her thoughts in turmoil.

Jenny stared out of the window as the coffee was brewing, but the scene outside meant nothing to her. Instead she was seeing a younger – much younger – version of herself. But someone who was not the controlled perfectionist Jenny was. Instead, she was a risk-taker, a rebel who had met her soul mate at the age of fifteen, and hadn't deviated in her feelings for him despite all the obstacles the two encountered.

"Okay," Jenny ferried the two coffees back and found Maddy gazing into space. She visibly jumped at the sound of Jenny's voice.

"Sorry, dear, I was miles away, years really."

"Are you sure you're ready to go on?" Jenny asked gently, setting one of the mugs down by her godmother and taking the other to the sofa where she curled up, legs tucked under her.

"Ready as I'll ever be, and I can't leave you in suspense. Now where was I?" She took a sip of her coffee and, setting the mug down again, placed both hands on the arm of her chair.

"They wanted to get married, Thea and Jed," Jenny said with wonder in her voice. These were her parents she was talking about. She could scarcely believe it. The story was more like a fairy tale.

"Right. Well, as I said, your grandfather would have none of it, so they waited till your mother, Jane," she clarified, "was due to visit. She and your father were making the trip so their child would be born here. I know, it was a long way, but Jane had made a promise to her parents when she emigrated to Australia that their first grandchild would be born in America. They chose to sail and make a real holiday out of their trip."

"A child," Jenny exclaimed, "but…"

"That was the sad part, or the start of it at least. Jane lost the baby on the trip over, and when she was examined here, was told it was unlikely she would be able to have any more children." Maddy sighed again. "Despite her own misfortune, or maybe because of it," she paused, as if trying to piece it all together. "Anyway she decided to help Thea and her fellow elope and wanted to enlist my help to do it."

Jenny stared at her godmother. This was turning from fairy tale into melodrama. "And did you?"

"I did what I could, which wasn't much. Anyway they did get off."

"So?"

"Well, this is the tragic part. They didn't get far. It was an old car, the weather was bad."

"Oh," sensing what was to come, Jenny's hands rose of their own volition to cover her mouth, a cold shiver running up her spine.

"I'm sorry Jenny Wren, but the car ran off the road and overturned."

"But they survived? They must have if I'm here now." Jenny sought reassurance as her eyes began to fill with tears.

"Thea did, but she was very badly injured. The doctors managed to save you, but she didn't survive for long after your birth."

"It's a girl, a beautiful baby girl with her mother's black hair and violet eyes." Helen looks up at the nurse, "And my daughter?" she asks, tremulously.

"We won't know for some time, but it's touch and go. I think you should prepare yourselves for the worst." We've been doing that for some time, thinks Helen, ever since we read the note saying she and Jed had run off. Why didn't Jack give his consent to their marriage, then it could all have been done properly? She looks up to see the focus of her thoughts standing in front of her, tears in his eyes.

"It's our baby, our little Thea." His voice shakes as he takes Helen into his arms. 'Where did we go wrong?'

"Maybe if you hadn't been so adamant." Helen is loath to lay blame at

such a sad time, but it has to be said. "Jed's a nice boy; was a nice boy," she corrects herself. "He didn't survive. His parents have lost their child. Ours is still alive, and we have a granddaughter. She's theirs too," she adds, as an afterthought.

"Not if I have anything to do with it." His voice has regained its former strength. "That little one is nothing to do with them. When I think…"

"There's nothing more you can do here tonight." The nurse speaks gently to the older couple. "Why don't you go home and get some rest."

"Let's, darling." Helen takes her husband's arm wearily. "Jane and Steve will be waiting for news. It's a stressful time for them too. You do have another daughter, and she's recently lost her own child…"

"You can't call a miscarriage losing a child," her husband grunts.

What would a man know, thinks Helen, but she keeps her thoughts to herself. She's been married to this man for long enough to know when to hold her tongue. He's hurting, and lashing out at her and Jane is his way of assuaging that hurt.

They arrive home to be greeted at the door by their elder daughter in tears. "How are they? They're not…?"

"Now, now don't upset yourself," Steve has his arm around Jane's shoulders and is trying ineffectually to comfort her. "Come and sit down, both of you," he motions to the older couple. "You look as if you could do with a cup of tea."

"Thanks, son." The older man sits down in the armchair with a thump. "It's been quite a day."

"Well?" Jane is still waiting for an answer.

"Thea's holding on, and the baby seems to be fine. Jed didn't make it."

"The baby!" Jane's eyes become misty. "Boy or girl?"

"A little girl." Helen's voice is low.

"Like the one we lost!" Helen's voice is anguished, and she turns away to hide her tears. "It doesn't seem fair." The cry is almost lost in her sobs.

Jenny found herself crying in earnest. Her poor mother, the mother she'd never known and never would. She felt she knew the answer to her next question, but she had to ask. "And Jed, what happened to him?"

"I'm afraid he died in the crash. Come over here, my dear. You need a hug, and I can't come to you."

Putting down her mug, which she had been nursing in both hands,

Jenny crept over to lay her head in her godmother's lap. Maddy stroked her goddaughter's soft silky hair. "There, there," she soothed. "You're so like Thea in looks," she said. "But I think you managed to get your common sense from Jane. The old nature nurture debate, I guess."

Jenny's sobs subsided with Maddy's soothing hands on her head. She felt like a child again. She remained in that spot, enjoying the feeling, then stretched up and shook her head. "Thanks, I think I'm okay now. You can go on." And she returned to her place on the sofa.

"I heard the news from Jane in a phone call. She and Steve had already made the decision to adopt you and take you back to Australia. She felt it was all for the best, and that they could easily pass you off as their own child, the one she had been pregnant with when they left."

"And they did. How well they did, for the rest of their lives," Jenny exclaimed with some bitterness. "They didn't think how I would feel, learning about it at this age."

"It was you they were thinking of all the time," Maddy reassured her. "They felt it would be better for you to be just their child, and you were. I'm sure it never occurred to them you'd find out in this way. I blame myself," she added. "I should have thrown those letters away long ago."

"No, don't do that. It's not your fault. Maybe Ellen was right," she mused. "Maybe I *was* meant to come here and find out the truth about myself. Maybe the stars were aligned or whatever, and it *was* time. Certainly everything else had gone topsy-turvy, so why not this as well? I never believed in all of that rubbish, but I'm beginning to think... My God, will you listen to me?" she laughed nervously. "I sound like one of those hippy dippy types I've always despised, people who won't take responsibility for their own actions and have to find some supernatural explanation."

Maddy stretched out her hand, and Jenny reached to take it. They grasped each other's fingers firmly. "Don't, Jenny," the older woman cautioned. "There are more things in heaven and earth…"

"I know, I know. Maybe I have to be more open to things I don't understand." *Now where did that come from?* "It's this place," she stated eventually. "Oregon, I mean, not just this house. I feel different. I don't feel I need to be in control anymore," Jenny felt stunned at this realization. "It's liberating," she exclaimed with a smile. "But it's still not very comfortable for me."

"Good. I'm glad you've got that off your chest. Now, how about we look out some more of those old photos. I know there are more of Thea, and let's see if there are any of Jed among them."

"Really?" Jenny's mood underwent a sudden change, and she felt a sense of excitement well up within her. When she'd first seen the young girl in the photo a few weeks earlier, she'd had no inkling of what it might mean for her, or of her story. Now she would be looking at it all with fresh eyes.

Sixteen

"Well, that's all there is." Closing the last album, Maddy stole a glance at Jenny's radiant face.

"Oh, thank you, thank you. So that's where my eye color came from." Jenny sighed in pleasure. "I'll put these away, then we'd better have some lunch. Look at the time! We've spent the whole morning on this."

"Time well spent. You needed to find out more about your heritage. I can't fill you in any on Jed, though. I never really knew him. He and Thea were younger than Jane and me, you see," she explained, "so we didn't move in the same crowd."

"How about some soup for lunch? I'll open a can since we've let the time get away from us. You must be hungry."

"I am feeling a bit hungry, I have to admit. But it was best to keep going with the photos once we'd started. Soup with some crusty bread would be fine if we have any."

"Coming up." Jenny had just stowed away the albums and was opening the soup when there was a loud knocking at the door. "What on earth," Jenny began to say. The door opened and a bearded face peered around.

"Mind if I come in?" Mike asked and, suiting his actions to his words, stepped over the threshold. "And how are you, you old fraud?" he asked, walking straight over to where Maddy was sitting beaming at him.

"All the better for seeing you. What took you so long?"

"Thought I'd better leave you two ladies some time to get reacquainted," he joked, taking a seat near Maddy. "Now how are you really?" He looked concerned. "Is there anything I can do to help?" he added, before she had a chance to reply.

"Oh, I'm not so bad," Maddy replied. "I made it to this chair after breakfast, and I may take a rest after lunch."

"No 'may' about it." Jenny came out of the kitchen area at these words. "You've already done more than the doctor recommended on your first day home."

"See, I'm being bossed around in my own home, now." But Maddy's voice held traces of weariness, and the other two could see it wouldn't be long before she was asleep.

"Lunch will be right up. Would you like some?" Jenny turned to Mike who gave her a look of surprise.

"Just had mine," he said, "but don't let me stop you two ladies. I only came to ask after this one, and I can see she's in fine form."

"Do stay a while, Mike." Maddy stretched out her hand as Mike walked over to take it. "At least till we've eaten. Then maybe you and Jenny can talk?" She looked from Jenny to Mike and back again.

What would *we* have to talk about Jenny wondered, busying herself back in the kitchen. "I'm sure Mike has plenty of other things to do," she threw into the room behind her. "Better than spending time with me," she added, carrying in a tray containing two bowls of soup and a basket of crusty sour dough bread.

"I'll join you two ladies at the table," Mike said easily, completely ignoring Maddy's reference to the two of them. "I'll make myself some coffee if that's alright with you?" He looked in Jenny's direction as he spoke. She nodded, not quite sure how to respond. The house had reverted to being Maddy's as soon as the latter had returned. Jenny felt she'd resumed the status of visitor and was back under Maddy's guidance, to some extent at least. Glancing into the kitchen where Mike was making himself at home, she shrugged and sat down to her lunch.

Mike carried his coffee back to join the two women who were eating in silence. "Where's that wheelchair I heard you were going to bring home with you?" He looked around as if expecting it to appear out of nowhere.

"I left it in the bedroom," Maddy said almost gleefully. "It seems quite at home there."Then on a more serious note. "It'll come in handy, particularly if I want to go out, but I decided to try my old legs today and shuffle around in here."

"Shuffle is the operative word." Jenny interrupted. "I'm trying to keep her in order, but it's a full time job." She laughed ruefully as she spooned up the last of her soup and bit into a piece of bread. "Yum, this is good." She leant back in her chair. "Now, if you've finished, Maddy, I think it's time for a rest." Jenny tried to instil some authority into her voice, but was conscious the attempt fell flat.

"You're right," the older woman sighed. "A rest is certainly called for." She pushed her chair back from the table and gingerly began to rise.

"Wait there!" Mike was over to her in a flash, and lending his support, the pair made their awkward way to the bedroom.

"Seems like I'm not needed here," Jenny was muttering under her breath in a good humored fashion, when she became conscious of a presence behind her in the kitchen.

"Let me do that." And the tea towel was whipped from her hands as Mike made good his offer. "Now, how about that talk Maddy suggested. She told me in the bedroom you might need a sounding board. What about the beach? It's looking good right now." He tilted his head to the side nodding in the direction of the outdoors.

"Oh." Jenny was about to refuse, when she realized a sounding board was exactly what she did need. How astute of Maddy. And she'd used Mike in this way before with no ill effects, she remembered. "All right. Let me get these things away first," she found herself agreeing, much to her surprise.

The pair walked down the track in a companionable silence, neither willing to break it until they reached the beach. "Wow, what a glorious day!" Jenny exclaimed at last, when her feet touched the sand. She looked up to feel the sun on her face.

"We do have them here in Oregon, you know. It doesn't rain all the time. Though you can be excused for thinking it does," he added, clearly remembering the wet days they'd experienced recently. "Let's go!" And to Jenny's surprise, Mike grabbed her hand and began to run along the beach taking her with him. She was unprepared for the rush of warmth which suffused her at his touch, figuring her sudden breathlessness was due to the unaccustomed pace.

Jenny was about to call for mercy when Mike slowed down and turned her to face him. "That should have blown the cobwebs away. Now what was Maddy talking about? Has she been filling you in on your mother?" They walked on slowly, Jenny's hand still in his while she figured out how to start.

"She told me more about Thea," Jenny began slowly. "I can't think of her as my mother just yet. She doesn't sound at all like me. Seems she was a bit of a rebel. I was always the good kid." She smiled ruefully. "Like my own mother. But Maddy says I look like her, Thea, I mean." Jenny stopped again. She kicked up the sand as she walked along, and looked down at her feet. "Okay, here goes." As they made their way along the shoreline with the sun at their backs and the roar of the surf in their ears, Jenny tried to recount what she'd heard from Maddy. "And that's all I know," she finished.

Jenny felt Mike squeeze her hand. "What a bummer. To discover all this now. As if you didn't have enough to worry about. What's happening with your job anyway?" he asked, quickly changing the subject.

A bit stunned by the sudden change of topic, and shaken by the firm hand still grasping hers, Jenny took her time replying. "I've made up my mind. I won't be going back there. From what I hear the whole Learning and Development unit is going to be disbanded and outsourced. I couldn't bear to see that happening. No, my days in Health are over. I'm thinking of opening a bookshop."

"A bookshop!"

Jenny smiled at Mike's reaction, which was much like Maddy's had been. "Why not?" She defended her decision. "I've been surrounded by books all my life. I believe I'd enjoy it."

"Far be it from me to suggest it, but don't you think maybe you're jumping in too deep?" Mike's voice held concern, but even so, Jenny felt herself immediately go on the defensive.

"Why did I know you'd say that?" She stopped and drew her hand away, conscious of, but determined to ignore, the empty feeling where his warm hand had been. "I know there'd be a lot to learn, but I'm not afraid of trying something new, and I'm not afraid of hard work."

"No, that I'm sure of." Mike screwed up his eyes as the sun seemed to be shining directly into them. "Well, a bookshop, huh."

"Is that all you have to say?"

"I guess it's your decision. So you'll be on the lookout for one when you go back?"

"That's the plan. I'll do a bit of research here first. Check out a few shops and so on to get the feel of it. Decide exactly what sort of bookshop I want to set up."

"And where do you propose to start?"

Jenny looked taken aback for a moment then countered with, "Florence. You know that little shop in the old part of the town. I'll start there. I've already been in it a few times so…"

"Oh, yes, Ellen."

"That's right, you've met her too. Well, she's a bit odd, but the shop's good and I'm sure she can give me a few tips. There's something about the place," Jenny's voice dropped off as she pictured the inside of the bookshop, its unique smell and the comforting atmosphere. "I'd like to figure out just how she does it," she muttered almost to herself.

By this time the sun was beginning to get lower in the sky, and a slight breeze was blowing up causing the sand to begin whirling around their ankles.

"Better start back," Mike grasped Jenny's hand again, and though she tried to resist, she found his hold was too firm. They trudged back to the road and up the track. When they reached the first house Jenny wrenched her hand away, folding her arms against her body as if to ward off attack.

"Maddy will be awake now. I'd better get in. She may need something. No need for you to come," she added, even though Mike was making no effort to follow her.

As if emboldened by her obvious resistance, Mike took Jenny by the shoulders and gave her a quick peck on the cheek. "Take care," he muttered, as he took off to jog up the remainder of the track to his cabin.

It took Jenny a moment to realize what had happened. She stood staring after him, her hand to her cheek where his lips had touched it. How dare he! But then, she smiled as she opened the door. It hadn't been too bad really.

Seventeen

Now why had he done that? Mike metaphorically scratched his head as he walked up the track. He wasn't in the habit of kissing women, especially ones who clearly didn't want to be kissed. But, darn it, Jenny got under his skin, and he couldn't resist taking a chance to ruffle her feathers. Her skin had felt nice, soft to the touch of his lips. She'd smelt nice too; a fresh flowery aroma. But no, there was no excuse. She was going through a difficult time, and he shouldn't have taken advantage of her like that. It was only a peck, he thought, not a full-blown kiss. He shuddered at the thought. What had got into him? What had happened to the hardened misogynist he'd forced himself to become during the years of Mary's illness?

"Hi there, Ben," he called, as he stepped into a now cooling house. "I should stick to dogs," he told the panting animal. "Less complicated all round. And you're always pleased to see me, eh?" Ben lay down at Mike's feet and rolled over on his back as if to agree, asking to have his stomach tickled. His master made haste to oblige, then gave the dog a rough pat. "Need to get the fire going, buddy. It's going to be a cold night."

Dinner over, Mike found it hard to settle down to his writing. Jenny's face and her large violet eyes kept coming between him and his computer screen. Finally, he gave up and turned it off, returning to the fireside where Ben took up his favorite spot at his master's feet. Mike leaned back in his chair and considered the tale Jenny had related to him. It was difficult to believe, but then, a lot of strange things had happened back then, and the class system would have been very strong amongst the wealthy after the war. They were intent on rebuilding their fortunes, and anything that smacked of fortune hunting, or threatened their status, was to be immediately suspect, he figured.

But, he wondered, how come nothing of this had surfaced until now? What about the boy's folks? Surely they'd kicked up a fuss, or had they been paid off? Jenny hadn't mentioned her father's name, or expressed any interest in him or his family. But he'd bet his boots she would, as soon as she took time to give it some consideration. That really would upset her. He pulled himself up short again. What was with him tonight? Why was he so bothered about Jenny's story and how she was feeling? He stepped over to the drinks cabinet to pour himself a large measure of his favorite Jack Daniels. He was getting soft in his old age. Not enough to do. He needed to follow up on the visits Ron and Ellen were arranging for him. That would give him something more tangible to focus on.

*

Jenny was having trouble falling asleep. It had been an eventful day and she had a lot to digest. None of it seemed quite real to her. Thea was more like a young girl in a story who had met her prince, only to have him snatched from her before joining him in death. She couldn't think of Thea as her mother. She couldn't believe her grandparents had cut all memory of Thea, or that her own mother had denied her existence by silence.

Then there was Mike. She'd found his presence on the beach comforting, even her hand in his had helped her come to grips with retelling Thea's story, as she now thought of it. But that kiss, well, peck, really. Jenny wasn't sure what to think.

Eventually she must have drifted off, because the next thing she knew it was morning, time to rise and check on Maddy.

"How are you this morning?" she greeted her godmother as she went in and opened the bedroom curtains. "Did you sleep well?"

"Like a log," responded Maddy, "How about you? You were very quiet last night. You didn't say much about your walk with Mike. How was it?"

Darn the woman. Not much escaped her eagle eyes, regardless of her age. "So so," she muttered, adding under her breath, "you really don't want to know." In a more audible tone she asked, "Breakfast in bed this morning?"

"I think so. I get a bit stiff lying for so long, and it takes me a time to get my joints oiled up for movement. I'm a real old crock at the moment,' she chuckled then added, 'What do you have on the agenda for today?"

"Today? Nothing really," Jenny lied. Her intention was to do some research on Thea, maybe look up some newspaper records. She attempted to look unconcerned.

"Did you go to school in Florence?" Jenny tried to make the question seem inconsequential.

"Yes, we all did. I moved up here later, when I knew I was going to spend my life alone. What…?" The older woman's limbs might have been stiff, but there was nothing wrong with her mind. "I see, you want to poke around, see what you can find out? It was all a long time ago."

"I know." Jenny left it at that and set to prepare breakfast. As she fixed up the toast topped with a perfectly poached egg, she mused that she was eating more here than she ever had back home. It was pleasant to have someone to cook for, she decided, and this kitchen had quickly become familiar to her. With the sun shining in over the stove, and the birds swooping down to the feeders outside the window, cooking became a relaxing process.

The meal over, Jenny went back in to see how Maddy was.

"I think I'll stay here a bit longer today." The words surprised Jenny who immediately expressed concern, but Maddy waved her away. "I had a big day yesterday, and you *did* say I should be resting. I have the radio and a good book here, if I want to read. If you can leave me some sandwiches and a jug of juice I'll be fine. Then you can get on with what you want to do." This last was said with a twinkle in her eye.

Jenny smiled gratefully. "Well, if you're sure. I'll be off when I've fixed you up." She swung into the kitchen feeling lighter than she had when she awoke. She began to plan her day. She'd head down to Florence where it all began, where *she* began. She brushed away the thought. It was easier if she could pretend all she was doing was investigating an anonymous young couple who lived a long time ago.

The library would be her first port of call. She needed to check out school yearbooks, then the local newspapers. She could use her own birthdate as a reference point and work back from there.

Suddenly a shiver ran down her spine. Was she going to be able to handle this? What might she discover? Maddy had told her the bare bones, as much as she knew. Now it was up to Jenny to flesh out the people who had been her parents, Thea and Jed.

A couple of hours later Jenny turned into a parking spot outside the Florence library. She sat in the car looking at the beige building with its green pillars, reluctant to enter. Taking a deep breath, she checked her bag to ensure her notebook was there, then stepped out of the car. She walked into the library and stood just inside the door. It looked exactly as a library should, in her opinion. It was quiet with staff talking to clients in whispers.

Jenny walked over to the desk to inquire about use of the newspaper archives, but having been told how to access them, she went instead to check the catalogue for Siuslaw High School yearbooks. There they were! Gathering her bag and notebook, Jenny found the shelf where they were stored. She bent down to the bottom shelf and ran her finger across the line of books. Where should she start? Think, she told herself, trying to clear her head of the tumult of images which filled it. She closed her eyes. *If the accident had happened in 1950, the year of her birth, then the pair would have left school around two years earlier. That meant she should search maybe 1946 to 1948. Yes, that made sense.* She drew out the three volumes and carried them to where the seats and low tables were located. Placing the books on the table, she dropped into one of the low comfortable chairs and gazed at the three volumes in front of her, reluctant to open them.

Another deep breath – she seemed to be taking a lot of these this morning – she picked up the first volume and opened it. An hour later she was still engrossed. After finding some amusement in the fashions of the day, she'd found Thea in all three yearbooks. The girl certainly seemed to have thrown herself into the school's social life. Her lively face smiled out at Jenny from quite a number of pages. There she was in the drama group, the softball team, the yearbook committee, and as a cheeky cheerleader. She'd been very pretty, Jenny sighed. She could see some of her own younger self in these shots. What a waste of a young life. For the first time she wondered what her own life would have been like if the accident had never happened. But it had. Now for Jed. But it appeared Jed had been a fairly common name back then, and Jenny couldn't work out which one was the Jed she was looking for. Reluctantly she closed the books. Next, the more difficult task. She intended to look back into the newspaper archives to find reports of the accident and her own birth.

Jenny replaced the yearbooks on their shelf and walked across to the bank of computers. The librarian had explained how she could check out the archives of the *Siuslaw News* on the microfiche reader. It had been called the *Siuslaw Oar* back in 1950. Settling herself in the padded chair before the unfamiliar machine, she prepared herself for the search. As she scanned through the old editions of the paper, she was tempted to stop to read about a number of events which were taking place in the area at that time, but had determined to keep focused on looking for accident reports.

Okay, Jenny thought, my birthday is August fifth, so I should probably look around that week. That's where she began. She looked and looked but there was no report. Then she went back a week, nothing, then another week, then another. Bingo. The headline jumped out at her. *Local couple in tragic accident.* This was it! She peered at the small print as she read on. Then she leant back in her chair and closed her eyes. All this trouble and there had been very little detail reported. She was really no further forward. No, that wasn't true. She now knew who Jed was, at least his name. The paper had reported the deaths of Thea Miller and Jed Williams. Now she could go back to the yearbooks and find him, but first she needed a break. A coffee, she thought, there must be somewhere nearby.

Walking out into the fresh air, Jenny was almost surprised to feel the sun on her face. It had been cool in the library, and she had been engrossed in her search. It was refreshing to be outside in the fresh air again. She looked around. There didn't seem to be anywhere for the coffee she was now hanging out for. Making a decision, Jenny went to her car. She'd pop down to the old part of town. She knew she could find some good coffee there and maybe drop into the bookshop. She wasn't sure why, but it seemed to be drawing her back. Jenny shook off such weird thoughts, managing to convince herself she only wanted to do some research for her own bookshop, the one she'd set up on her return to Australia.

As she entered the bookshop feeling more energized after a bumper-sized coffee, the jangle of the doorbell brought Ellen out from behind some shelves. "Hello again, I had a feeling you'd drop by today. How are you?" Ellen was as cheerful as before, and again as before, engendered in Jenny a feeling of quietude and safety.

"I came to pick your brains," Jenny began and, seeing Ellen's puzzled look, continued, "You see, I'm thinking of opening a bookshop when I return home, and I love what you've done with this one." She hesitated, not sure how to go on. This wasn't really what she wanted to say. Ellen's presence had made her confused again, and she was even more startled to hear her next words.

"That's not really why you're here today, though, is it?"

Jenny stared at her. It was as if the tall figure standing before her could read her mind. She shivered with a feeling that was neither fear nor excitement, but something in between. She remembered her grandmother referring to something she could "feel in her waters". She'd never known what that meant till now.

"Come through and take a seat." Ellen drew her into the back of the shop where there was a tiny office. Jenny took the proffered seat, her eyes gazing around what was little more than a cubicle, containing a desk, two brightly upholstered chairs and a small fridge. On the wall was what looked like a family photo, and a dream catcher with purple and black feathers.

"Now," Ellen said. "Why are you really here?" She waited patiently while her companion searched for the words.

Finally Jenny spoke. "I don't know," she replied as honestly as she could. "Something drew me here. Something I can't explain. I was in the library then I went for a coffee, across the road." She indicated the coffee house with a tilt of her head. "And now I'm here."

"The library. What were you doing there?"

It sounded to Jenny as if Ellen were merely making polite conversation, so she saw no need to hide her reasons. "I may have mentioned to you that I discovered I'd been adopted?" Ellen nodded. "I found out a bit more, but not enough so I went to the library to see what I could unearth."

"And what did you find?"

"I found that Thea, my mother, had been the life and soul of her year at school. I found the report of the accident that killed my parents, but the dates were wrong." Jenny now realized she hadn't fully taken that in when she was conducting her search. She repeated, "The dates were wrong." She looked up at Ellen as if for guidance.

Ellen took Jenny's hands in hers and gently squeezed them. Her eyes met Jenny's as she asked, "What do you mean the dates were wrong?"

"My birthday. Maddy told me the accident happened, then Thea was taken to hospital and I was born there, but the paper said the accident was in the middle of July, and I was born on August fifth. It can't be right." Jenny pulled her hands away. "I'd better go back and check again. Maybe I'd been shuffling through the pages so quickly I misread what I was looking at. Yes, that's what must have happened." She spoke to herself as she rose to leave. "I'm sorry to have come here in such a state. I'll come back another time when we can have a proper talk."

Jenny drove home from Florence in a state of confusion. Her second visit to the library had helped her identify Jed, who had turned out to be an ace football player. It was clear how the two had got together; both were among the most popular in their year. It was a match made in heaven, but not in the eyes of her grandfather, or Jed's parents it seemed. She'd checked back in the paper too, and the dates still puzzled her, but even more puzzling, she hadn't been able to find an announcement of her birth. Why ever not? Perhaps Maddy would be able to clear this up. She certainly hoped so.

Eighteen

"What did you get up to today, dear?" Maddy greeted Jenny who'd popped her head around the bedroom door. "Did you find what you were looking for?"

"Yes and no." Jenny pulled the door closed behind her. "Are you sure you want me to talk about this now? Wouldn't you rather have something to eat first?"

"No, I'm not hungry, and I've been lying here all day." Maddy pushed herself up into a sitting position and patted the bed beside her. "Come and sit down here. You're looking a bit stressed."

"Stressed isn't the word." Jenny took the seat and settled down for a chat. "Well, first I checked out the school yearbook, and I found Thea. Boy she sure was a social butterfly. She was into everything. Must have been very popular."

Maddy's eyes took on a distant look. "She was. And always so full of life. And did you find Jed?"

"Eventually. I had to find the accident in the paper first so I'd know his surname. He was Jed Williams."

"That's right. I remember now. They were quite a big family, all very determined to succeed, and proud of their Native American heritage. It really got up your grandfather's nose, I can tell you. I seem to recall the father worked in one of your grandfather's companies."

"Yes, well Jed turned out to be the all-round sportsman too. Quite a remarkable couple."

"Your parents, honey," Maddy reminded gently.

117

"I know, but I still can't think of them that way. To me they're just a young couple who were cut short in their prime. They had so much to live for,' she said sadly. 'But there was something really funny about the dates."

"The dates? What do you mean?"

"I started looking for the accident around my birth date, but it was earlier, and the account in the paper read as if they'd both been killed in the accident. And I couldn't find any announcement of my birth. It's weird, Maddy. It felt as if I didn't exist. Are you sure about what you told me?"

"Oh dear." The older woman folded her hands over her stomach and gazed at Jenny. "It'll have been your grandfather's doing. He was an important man in the community, quite a force to be reckoned with. He had his finger in a number of pies, one of which was the local paper."

"You mean...?" Jenny could hardly believe what she was hearing. "He could have arranged to have the story doctored to make it look as if...?"

"He sure could. I don't remember reading the paper at the time. I was too shocked. But, yes, that would have been just like him. It would take away any breath of scandal from his family."

"But what about me?" Jenny couldn't help it but this came out as a pitiful cry. "Where did I fit into his plan?"

"You weren't part of his plan. You were part of Jane's. I see it all now. I bet your birth was registered to her, and there are no legal adoption papers. That's why it was easier for her to pretend you were her real child, hers and Steve's."

"I can't take this in." Jenny stood up and began to pace up and down. "Why did there have to be all this subterfuge? All these secrets?"

"My poor Jenny Wren, come here." Maddy opened her arms and Jenny fell into them in tears. "All of this doesn't change who you are. You're still the person you were when you arrived here. But it does give another dimension to you."

"Another dimension? You mean I may have a family I know nothing about, and who know nothing about me?" Suddenly the penny dropped and Jenny sat up in amazement.

"Yes, there is Jed's family."

"My Native American heritage," said Jenny in wonderment. "But…" She stopped, unsure how to proceed.

"Maybe that's something you need to pursue." Maddy's words struck a chord in her.

"You know, I think you're right. But where do I start?"

Jenny sat still for a moment then, "I'd like to find out a bit more about the Native Americans in general. I'm pretty ignorant about the history and culture and all that sort of thing."

"That'd be a good place to start, and I know just the person to help you." Maddy couldn't keep the smile off her face. "You must remember. That's Mike's specialty. He's been studying the area for years. He's currently writing a book on the very topic." She laughed at the obviously thunderstruck look on Jenny's face. "Why don't you call him?"

"I don't think…" Jenny started to move away and was almost at the door when Maddy's voice stopped her.

"You're not going to let any silly ideas get in your way, I hope. He's the best resource you'll find around here."

"Maybe I'll do it in the morning." Jenny was in two minds about this. She wanted to do the research, but to involve Mike? It *was* very personal, after all. Then she remembered she'd involved him already, by using him as a shoulder to cry on when she'd first learned of her adoption. "Oh, okay," she said, and saw her godmother give her an encouraging smile.

Ten minutes later Jenny was able to tell Maddy she'd arranged to meet with Mike the next morning. "If you're sure you won't mind being left alone again. Mike's suggested I go up to his cabin after breakfast. He has a lot of documents and things there he'd like to show me. Then he talked about a Native American museum or some such thing."

"I'll be fine, my dear. I had a good rest today, so I think I'll be getting up again tomorrow to try these old pins. No, I won't try to do too much," she reassured her goddaughter, who was about to offer to stay home. "I'll be looking forward to hearing the results of your visit. Now, how about some dinner and an early night? You look pretty much worn out."

*

Jenny spent another night tossing and turning. She realized she hadn't given Mike Jed's surname, but she guessed it didn't matter. She had a good feeling about meeting with Mike in the morning. He'd sounded really pleased to hear from her, and most willing to help. In fact he'd waxed lyrical about the history and culture of the Native American tribes in the area. He had, he said, even been in contact with some of the local Native Americans. For some reason that made her think of Ellen, the bookshop lady. What an idiot she must think me. I must go back and apologize, was Jenny's last thought before she fell into a restless sleep.

*

Mike put down the phone with a grunt of surprise. This was a turn up for the books and no mistake. Jenny's father was of Native American blood. That explained a lot about the way her grandfather had behaved. From what he'd learned of the old man from Maddy, Jenny's grandfather had been a bit of a tyrant and a bigot to boot. Well, well! He spent the remainder of the evening sorting out documents which might help Jenny understand her background. Doing a search like this made him realize just how much he'd managed to accumulate since he'd arrived in Oregon. Now, which ones would be of most interest to Jenny?

Mike realized he was enjoying this and was looking forward to their meeting the next day. He was assuming that, given her father had been from Florence, his family would have belonged to one of the tribes around there, possibly the Umqua. But that didn't really matter too much. She'd said she was completely ignorant about the Native American, apart from what she'd seen in western movies. Hardly a true depiction, he grinned. He'd be able to fill her in on the historical way of life, and how those ways had evolved with land rights in the present day.

Satisfied with his work, he settled down to a glass of red wine and stroked the dog, who had been lying at his feet, but now put his black head on his master's lap begging for attention. Mike could see Jenny's face as if it was there in front of him. He thought of his late wife.

Mary would have approved of Jenny. She wouldn't have wanted him to live this reclusive existence he had chosen. "What do you think, Mary?" He spoke as if his dead wife were sitting with him. "Am I being an old fool to think she'd be interested in me?" He sipped his wine as he remembered the feel of Jenny's skin against his hand. She hadn't flinched, he remembered. But then, she wasn't such a young thing either. They were much of an age. He remembered his horror when Maddy had first told him of Jenny's imminent arrival, and of his decision to steer clear. Well, that hadn't lasted for long, and this wasn't the first time she'd asked for his help either. That thought gave him confidence as he headed off to bed.

Nineteen

Ellen pushed the key into the lock and, walking through the shop door, stood in silence for a moment. Even though she'd owned this shop for over ten years, she still felt a small thrill each time she opened the door. It was hers, all hers, and it was beautiful. Everything was exactly as she'd left it, though there was no reason why it shouldn't be. Standing in the far corner were the two boxes of books Ellen had retrieved from her parents' home a few weeks earlier. They'd been sitting in the family home ever since her grandmother had passed away a few years ago, and her mother had insisted she didn't want them lying around any longer.

Shrugging off her rain jacket, she looked out at the dismal Oregon day. There wouldn't be many customers today, she decided. It would be a good opportunity to go through these boxes to see what was worth keeping. She'd been putting the task off for just such a day so now she had no excuse.

Time flew as she became lost in her self-imposed assignment. Many of the books she remembered seeing on the shelves as a child, while others were tomes of which she had no recollection. As she picked up one large book, she noticed it was a family bible. Surely her mother hadn't realized that one was included? As she went to open it, two photos slid out onto the floor. Retrieving them, Ellen saw they were both of a young man, and judging by the clothes, had been taken long before she was even born. She looked at them more closely. In one of the prints was a young girl who looked vaguely familiar. Must be some other family members, she thought, putting them aside to show to her mother later.

*

It was a couple of days before Ellen had a chance to talk with her mother. They'd enjoyed the usual family Sunday lunch, and were spending the afternoon relaxing around the fireplace. Ellen's father had buttonholed her brother with a discussion on fishing. They'd gone out to the garage, so she had her mother all to herself. After the usual family talk, Ellen began.

"There's something I want to ask you." She drew the two photos out of her bag. "I found these in one of the books you gave me for the shop. They fell out. I don't seem to recognize them. Where do they fit?"

"Oh, I thought they'd been thrown out years ago." Ellen's mother seemed flustered. At that moment, her father came into the room and leant over to see what they were looking at.

"Give these here," he ordered. Ellen's mother handed the two photos over. "Hmm. Not sure what you're doing with these," he muttered. "That was your Uncle Jed. Fine-looking fellow with a great future ahead of him, and he threw it all away. Wanted to get married. She was a rich bitch from one of these big houses out by the lake. There was a child. At least, they said there was a child, but we never saw it. Had it adopted out or some such nonsense. Leastways that's what we were told when we asked about it."

"Boy or girl?" Ellen was curious.

"I believe it was a girl," Ellen's mother replied in a softer voice. "She'd be just about Ron's age, your cousin. Imagine that!"

"What happened to her?"

"We never knew," Ellen's mother's voice took on a serious note. "We wanted to see her, maybe share in her upbringing, but it never happened. It was as if she disappeared off the face of this earth. Maybe she didn't survive, or they had her adopted interstate. I can't imagine anyone doing that to their own flesh and blood." She looked grim. "But he was an odd man, and his wife would never have been able to oppose him, not on something he felt would affect his standing in the community."

"How could a baby affect his standing?"

"In those days? A baby born out of wedlock? To one of us. He would never have countenanced that."

"A baby, about Ron's age, maybe adopted. I wonder." Ellen's eyes looked into space. The girl in the photo had reminded her of someone, and she suddenly had an inkling of who that someone was. "Did the family have any connection with Australia?" she asked her mother.

"Why do you ask that? I don't know. There was an older daughter who went overseas. I don't think she visited very often, but then, we didn't have anything to do with that family."

"No reason." Ellen decided to keep her ideas to herself. At least till she'd had time to check them out, but it was beginning to make sense to her now.

"If you two women have stopped jawing maybe we can have some dinner." Ellen's brother came into the room, interrupting the conversation, much to Ellen's relief.

Now was not the time to reveal the discovery she thought she'd made. She needed to talk with Jenny again first, to be certain she was not mistaken. She picked up the photos and took another look. Yes, she was pretty sure she was right, but she didn't want to raise everyone's hopes if she was wrong. She'd stay shtum for now.

Twenty

"This is really interesting!" Jenny laid down the document she was studying. "How much of it is followed these days?" she asked, looking up at the bearded face so close to her own and feeling a spark flare up.

"None." Mike laughed. "Native Americans are fully integrated into the rest of society now. They'd be most offended to hear you ask such a question. You've met Ron and Ellen when you were with me in Florence. Did they seem any different from anyone else?"

"Well, Ellen is a bit strange," Jenny admitted, "but I guess that's not the prerogative of Native Americans, I've met a few people like that back in Australia. I've managed to avoid them there. Why don't I feel the need to avoid her?" she wondered aloud.

"What did you say Jed's surname was?" Mike asked as he packed up the folders and stowed them away.

"I didn't." Jenny looked up at her companion, "But it's Williams. What?" she asked, seeing a look of surprise cross his face.

"Those two guys you met, Ron and Ellen. Ron and Ellen Williams."

"No, they couldn't be. That's too much of a coincidence."

"It may be only a coincidence, but we should find out. I wonder..."

"Let me do it," Jenny interrupted. "I was planning to go back to Ellen's bookshop anyway. There's something about it that drags me back there. No," she saw a wily gleam in his eyes, "I don't read any psychic stuff into this. It's the atmosphere, the books. I love it. Feels as if I've come home."

"If you're sure?" Mike's voice was hesitant. "Maybe I should come with you?" He put his hand tentatively on her shoulder. She felt it, warm and comforting through her sweater and, though her immediate instinct was to shrug it off, resisted the urge, allowing it to lie there. It felt good. It was a long time since anyone had comforted her like this, man or woman. She was beginning to realize how isolated she'd kept herself.

Jenny gave Mike's offer some thought before replying. "No, I need to do this on my own. Just think, Ellen may be my cousin." She hesitated, letting the thought sink in. Somehow it was easier to conceive of Ellen as her cousin than it was to believe Thea and Jed were her parents. "But why not come down to Florence with me? You could have a coffee and be there to pick up the pieces when I finish with Ellen."

"Now that makes sense. When had you thought of going?"

"How about tomorrow? Now I may be on the track of some relatives, I don't want to waste time."

"Works for me. What are your plans for now?"

"Better get back to Maddy and see how she's coping. I need to check on my emails too. I've been expecting some info from home about this redundancy package they want to offer me."

"Right. Bright and early tomorrow, then. About nine suit?" Mike leant over and touched Jenny's cheek gently with the back of his thumb. "It'll be all right, really," he reassured her.

Jenny found herself moving her face into his hand, as he continued to rub her cheek. "Thanks. Nine will be great." As she moved away she had the strangest feeling she was leaving part of herself behind. She was beginning to feel a connection with this man, something she hadn't allowed herself to feel since her husband had died when the children were little.

Jenny walked down the track in a daze. Too much was happening to her. She was having trouble coping with it all. This trip had certainly taken a turn she hadn't anticipated, a couple of turns, actually. She wanted to savor the feelings she was beginning to experience with Mike, but the issues relating to her background were taking priority at the moment. She'd put Mike on the back burner till later. And it might be very one-sided. Jenny had no real indication he might feel the same way, although... She touched her cheek where his thumb had been and smiled, taking a skip as she went on her way.

Maddy was sitting in her wheelchair when Jenny got back. "I managed to get into this on my own," she said. "I thought we could go for a stroll, if you think you can push me."

"I think I can manage that." Jenny was pleased to see Maddy taking an interest in getting out of the house, and delighted she was willing to use the wheelchair and accept some assistance. "Just give me a minute."

Once at the beach, Jenny positioned the chair facing out to the ocean and dropped down to the ground beside it. "Hope I can manage to get up again," she joked, as she began to recount her morning's discoveries. "And I might already have met a cousin. Mike thinks the two people he's been working with in Florence could be related to Jed. You know, Ellen, the woman with the bookshop, the one I told you about."

"Don't get your hopes up, Jenny Wren. It's a big world, and Williams is a common enough name. But, yes, it would be wonderful if it was the same family. What a lot your grandfather has to answer for!" She paused. "May be time to get back now," Maddy said at last, looking up at the darkening sky. "Looks like we're in for another storm, and we can't go too fast with this thing." She gestured to her wheelchair, laughing.

"You wouldn't remember much about visiting here when you were little, would you?" Maddy gave Jenny one of her piercing looks as they began their journey back.

"I remember being on the beach with you," Jenny smiled, "and finding the sand dollar, but my memories of my grandparents are a bit hazy." She thought for a moment then added, "I think I remember a fierce old man with white whiskers and a kindly old lady with warm arms and white hair." She laughed. "I guess they weren't too much older than I am now."

"They were a bit older," Maddy said, "but your grandfather never forgave Thea and couldn't warm to you." Her eyes took on a faraway look.

"You won't believe it, Maddy," Jane wailed on the phone. "Dad says he's not going to have anything to do with that half-cast baby. And you won't believe how beautiful she is! She's so like Thea with her black hair and violet eyes. That's why we're taking her back to Australia as soon as it can be arranged."

By the time they'd reached the house, large rain drops were beginning to fall, and Jenny's arms were aching, but "This thing is heavier than I thought" was her only comment.

"Better get Mike to come with us next time," Maddy suggested, Jenny's silence seeming to signal her agreement.

*

Mike was finding it difficult to concentrate. He'd been about to take Ben for a walk on the beach when he'd seen the two women struggling down the track, and had resisted the impulse to join them. "Sorry, Ben, later." He patted the disappointed labrador absentmindedly, trying to come to grips with the way he was feeling.

His thoughts went back to Mary, to when they'd first met. They'd been students together. It had been love at first sight, one which had endured. Their lack of children had been a disappointment to Mary, but not to him. She'd been enough for him, and he supposed that was why her sickness had hit him so hard. They'd been companions as well as lovers. Best friends. It had been hard for all of that to be gradually taken away from him till the day came when she hadn't even recognized him.

Their friends had been generous, always including him in their lives, but he hadn't felt comfortable. He'd always remembered how it had been with Mary by his side. That's why he'd left. He'd found peace here in this wild spot, a peace that seemed to be shattering since the advent of this dark-haired pixie.

He was still musing on this when he heard heavy drops of rain fall on the roof. He looked out at the sky which had darkened so suddenly it seemed like night out there. Giving himself a shake, he went back to the kitchen to make a start on his meal. Things had a way of working themselves out, he told himself philosophically. It might be just as well he couldn't predict what the future would bring. He grinned at the thought that, if he had known he would meet Jenny here in Seal Rock, he might have found some good reasons to remain in California. He still couldn't figure out whether that would have been a good or bad thing.

Twenty-one

Jenny stood outside the bookshop. She looked at the colorful display of books in the window, willing herself to go in. She hadn't felt this nervous since her last job interview, and look how that had turned out. Gripping her bag tightly, she clenched her teeth and pushed open the door. The bell seemed to be louder than ever in her nervous ears.

"Hello. What brings you here today?" Ellen's bright voice greeted her as the statuesque woman emerged from the back of the shop.

"I have something I need to talk with you about." Jenny looked around, fearful there might be other customers in the shop who would eavesdrop.

As if anticipating her fear, Ellen was quick to respond. "Well, you've come at a good time. I'm usually empty around now. Things don't get busy round here until closer to lunchtime. Why don't we go through to the office? I can hear the door from there if anyone does come in."

Following Ellen into the little room, Jenny tried to rehearse what she was going to say. How did you begin to ask someone if they were your long-lost relative, one you didn't even know you had? She sat down gingerly and looked across at Ellen's expectant face, which was all smiles.

"I think…" No, that wouldn't do. "Did you…?" No, just as bad. Finally Jenny blurted out, "I found out about the man who was my father. His name was Jed Williams." She stopped, hoping against hope that the other woman's uncanny psychic ability would help her here.

Ellen didn't look surprised. "I wondered," was her response.

"What?" Jenny spoke more sharply than she intended. "Do you mean you knew this all along?"

"Only recently. Since you were last here." Ellen's gentle voice held reassurance. "I found a photo, the girl reminded me of someone. I now know it was you. When I asked my parents about it, they identified the man as my uncle Jed who'd died before I was born. Hello, Cousin." Ellen smiled and held out both her hands in a welcoming gesture.

Jenny took her hands, the tears welling up in her eyes and beginning to slide down her face. Ellen's face began to blur as Jenny saw the other woman was in tears too. They stood up and embraced. "Oh I can't believe it!" Jenny exclaimed, breaking away and using the back of her hand to wipe away the tears.

"My Australian cousin!" Ellen held Jenny at arm's length, gazing intently at her as if trying to memorize her features. The two women began to laugh, a nervous laughter, both lost for words. Finally they sat down again.

"Fancy!" was all Jenny could think of to say. There was so much bubbling around inside her head she had no idea where to begin. "Tell me about your uncle," she finally said.

"I can't. I mean, I don't know anything about him. I hadn't even heard of him till I asked about the photo."

"Don't you think that's odd?" Jenny wanted to know. "I mean I'd never heard about Thea, and now you tell me you'd never heard about Jed. It's as if their whole existence had been wiped out."

"Yes, I guess so." Ellen's response was slow. "And my mother wasn't sure you really existed. She'd heard there was a baby, a girl, then you seemed to disappear. It would never have occurred to them you'd be in Australia."

"You mean they tried to find me?" Jenny asked hopefully, though what she was hoping for she wasn't sure. But if they were right about this, then these people were her aunt and uncle, maybe even her grandparents…

"You'd have to ask Mom about that. Apparently there was a lot of bitterness at the time."

"And your grandparents, and mine too. Are they alive?" Jenny was surprised how much she wanted this to be so, forgetting it was most unlikely.

"No. Gran Williams died a few years ago. It was among her books I found the photo. But you really need to talk with Mom. I'll check with her tonight. It's going to be a big shock for her too. Jed, my Uncle Jed,' she repeated wonderingly. 'He could be your father."

"Thanks, Ellen." Jenny stood up. "I'll be going now, unless you have any other dire predictions for me," she joked.

"Actually, what I see now is resolution, some fairly soon, but some will take time. You will need to be patient." Ellen's voice was serious.

"Not my strong suit, I'm afraid, though I seem to be improving on that score. Mainly since I came to Oregon," she said. "Must be the air here." She stood awkwardly for a moment, then gave Ellen a hug before heading to the door.

"I'll call you," Ellen's voice followed her.

Jenny crossed the road, glad to see Mike sitting with a mug of coffee. It was all so normal. He stood to greet her with a hug.

"I needed that." Her words were heartfelt as she took a seat opposite him.

"It was that bad?" he asked then, "Coffee?"

"Love some."

While Mike went to place the order, Jenny took stock of her situation. She'd arrived here only a few weeks ago, the only blot on her landscape a potential redundancy. In the space of a few weeks, her entire world had changed. She'd had to review her whole life, had found new relatives, a cousin, at least, and had met Mike. She looked at his strong back as he stood at the counter. He was a rock for her in this time of tumult. But her life was in Australia, so she'd better treat this as no more than a passing friendship, regardless of the attraction she was beginning to feel.

As Mike started to turn around, Jenny looked away, pretending interest in some magazines lying on the table in front of her.

"Interested in fishing now?" Mike handed her a coffee, and Jenny realized the magazine she'd been staring at intently without really seeing, was one devoted to the hunting and fishing fraternity.

"What? No."

Mike sat down stretching his legs out comfortably in front of him. "What did you find out from Ellen?"

"She *is* my cousin." Jenny tried to suppress the bubble of excitement welling up inside her. "Can you believe it? She'd found a photo of Jed and Thea, and asked her parents about them only a few days ago. She hadn't heard him mentioned before this. It's odd, isn't it?"

"Odd? What d'you mean?"

"Well, there's the business of the dates, then the fact my mother never mentioned Thea, never even mentioned she'd had a sister. And now Ellen didn't know anything about this Uncle Jed of hers. There seems to have been a conspiracy of silence - in both families."

"So what happens now?" Mike sounded very laconic, but it wasn't *his* life that had been turned upside down; it wasn't *his* family that had ignored *his* existence.

"Ellen will talk with her mother, then we'll see. I guess I'll have to meet them." She stopped, conscious yet again, of the enormity of this news.

"You're sure you don't need something stronger than coffee?" Mike sounded concerned, but Jenny shrugged it off.

"At this time of day? I don't think so. I'll finish this, then we'd better make tracks and get back to Maddy. If that's right with you?" she added.

Jenny's thoughts were going around in circles during the drive back to Seal Rock. She'd wondered, hoped, even, but for Ellen to have come to the same conclusion quite independently was uncanny. "She'll be having me believe all this funny stuff if she goes on like this," Jenny muttered to herself, after they'd driven in silence for some time.

"There's a lot we still don't understand," was Mike's unequivocal reply.

"Not you too?" Jenny turned to look at her companion, not sure whether he was being serious or having her on.

"It's strange, I admit." Mike shot a glance at her. "But I can't say I haven't had some strange experiences myself. When Mary died, for instance, I could have sworn I sensed her presence a few times. Kept me on the straight and narrow." He concentrated on driving again, leaving Jenny to ponder this surprising admission.

They were almost back at Seal Rock when Mike took a deep breath and, without looking at Jenny, began to speak. "I've been thinking." He stopped, then seemed to take courage. "There's a museum down in Klamath Falls that would most likely interest you - lots of artifacts and stuff. I've been meaning to make a trip there myself. Maybe when

Maddy's a bit better...? It's a five hour drive so it'd be a two day trip. It's near Crater Lake, and that's worth a visit too." He stopped as Jenny turned to look at him.

What was he hinting at? Was he asking her to go away with him for a couple of days or was this just what it seemed – an invitation to visit the museum. Was she reading too much into it?

"Mmm," was all she could think of to reply. "That might be nice." What a twit I must seem, she thought, and they made the last part of the trip in silence.

As they drove up to the house, Jenny could see Maddy was eagerly awaiting their return. She was sitting in a seat by the window so as not to miss anything going up or down the track, and they heard her voice call out through the open window immediately the vehicle came to a halt.

"I'll be with you in a minute," Jenny called, clambering out of the high vehicle. "Thanks a million, Mike." She flashed him a grateful smile. "It made all the difference having you there."

"Happy to oblige. You want me to come in now?"

Jenny waved away his offer.

"Maybe later, then? I'll drop by," he promised as he drove off.

Jenny stood watching the departing vehicle, then turned back to the house where Maddy was by now becoming impatient.

"So now I have to wait for Ellen's family to agree to see me, I expect." Jenny finished her account of her trip to Florence, concluding with Ellen's surprise announcement. "They seem to have been as secretive about all this as my own family. Maybe they won't want to see me." She was conscious of a forlorn note in her voice quite unlike her usual confident self, but these were unusual times and unusual goings on.

"You need something to take your mind off it," Maddy decided. "What say you take me for a drive this afternoon, if we can get this old carcass of mine into that little car of yours?"

"It's not as little as it looks.' Jenny was quick to defend her hire car. 'But it's a good idea if you're sure you're up to it."

*

133

After driving for about half an hour, Maddy signaled for Jenny to pull into the side of the road. "There's nothing here," Jenny said, looking at the drop to the sea on one side and the high cliffs rising from the road on the other.

"If you look closely you'll see there's a path down to the beach. Jane and I spent many a summer afternoon down there. We'd cycle up from Florence with a picnic and swimsuits in the basket. Those were the days," she sighed. "Not a care in the world."

"So?" Jenny couldn't work out why Maddy had brought her to this spot.

"Life will always throw you some curly ones," Maddy said, "but how you deal with them is up to you. When things got me down, when Rick was killed, when your mother went off to Australia, when my own parents died, I'd remember the good times we had. The carefree years, and that helped me get through the hard times."

"Are you trying to tell me something?" Jenny was becoming exasperated. She'd never been good at working out where stories like this were going.

"Be patient, honey. Don't be in too much of a hurry to judge those who lived back then. Times were different from today. It seems both families may have made some sort of an agreement, I don't really know. I wasn't party to it."

"Point taken. Can we go back now?" Jenny was wishing she hadn't agreed to this trip, and was anxious to return to what she saw as the safety of the house. There she could get back to her emails and resume contact with her world in Australia, which, at the moment, was looking a lot more attractive to her than this messy situation she found herself in here.

Half an hour later she was sitting in front of Maddy's computer with a look of amazement on her face. She couldn't believe the payout she'd receive if she accepted the redundancy. She calculated it would be more than enough to buy a bookshop and survive for the time it would take to turn it into a profitable business. With scarcely another thought, she replied, accepting the offer. As she pressed *send*, she found herself breathing more easily. That was one hurdle over.

Twenty-two

"Mom, do you have a minute?" Ellen had decided to face the issue, and dropped into her mother's house on her way home from the bookshop.

"Ellen, we don't usually see you during the week. Is everything all right?"

"Yes, very all right. Though I'm not sure if you'll agree with me." She took the tea towel from her mother's hand and led her to a chair at the kitchen table.

"My dear, I'm preparing dinner. Your father will be expecting …"

"It can wait a few minutes, can't it? Then I'll stay and eat with you," she promised.

"Well, that's a treat. You're often too busy for us old folk in your working week."

Ellen bit her lip. She knew her parents would like to see more of her, but she'd determined some years ago she wouldn't live in their pockets. Although they were a close family, they all had their own lives to lead.

"What is it that can't wait till Sunday lunch?"

Ellen sat down opposite her mother and began to fiddle with the multitude of rings on her fingers. How was she going to do this? "Remember those photos I showed you last week?"

"The old ones? What about them?" Her mother's voice held a suspicious tone.

"The couple… Jed and Thea… the baby. It *was* a girl."

"How do you know that?" The white-haired woman sounded angry.

"It's all in the past. It doesn't do any good to bring these things up again. It's all gone and forgotten."

"Well, that's just it. Oh, heck, there's no other way to put this. I've met her." Ellen's mother looked at her blankly, hand held to her chest. "Oh God, don't go and have an attack on me. Her name's Jenny and she came into the bookshop." She looked at her mother. "You're all right, aren't you?" She began to be concerned this had been too much of a shock for the old woman.

"Someone's been joshing you," her mother finally said. "How could Jed's daughter be alive, and just happen to walk into your shop after all these years. No, it's not possible. What does this woman want?" she asked suspiciously.

Ellen pulled on the end of her hair, a habit she'd developed as a child and never managed to shake. "She doesn't want anything, not from us anyway. She's as surprised as I am. She grew up in Australia…"

"Australia! That's the other end of the world. And you say she's here? Now?" She looked around as if Jenny was going to suddenly materialize in the kitchen.

"Not right here. But she would like to meet you and Dad. It's been a big shock for her to learn about us. She didn't even know she'd been adopted." And Ellen began to tell Jenny's story as Jenny had told it to her, finishing with, "So you see, while she still has difficulty in coming to grips with who she is, she wants to know us as a family. What do you say?"

"Oh dear, it was all so long ago, but I don't know what your dad will have to say." She sighed. "We went through so much at the time. Jed was his young brother. He had shown such promise, and then he got involved with this girl."

"Thea," Ellen prompted.

"Yes, Thea. She was such a livewire. I could see why he was so smitten."

"And the family didn't approve?"

"How could they? He was all set to go to college, had a football scholarship. He'd have been the first one in the family to take a degree. Your grandparents were so proud of him, and then…"

"So!" Ellen sat back and folded her arms. "Both families disapproved of their relationship. But how come I'd never even heard of him."

"We were told," Ellen's mother remembered,

"Jed is dead to us. I don't want to hear his name spoken again in this house." Dick's father laid down the law during Sunday lunch with the family bible in his hand. No one had dared disobey him. Even after Jed was in fact dead, his name had never been mentioned out loud till Ellen had brought out those photographs.

"It was as if, even before he died, he'd been wiped from the face of the earth."

"But his daughter, surely the grandparents wanted to find her?"

"I don't know. They never talked about it with us. You have to understand we were all so young. I was pregnant with your brother. We were caught up in our own lives. I do remember whisperings behind closed doors. Your dad might know more, but I doubt he'll be willing to talk about it. You know how closed he can be."

"Who can be closed?" Ellen looked up to see her father walk into the room. "What are you doing here, honey?" Ellen stood up as he reached to give her a hug.

"Thought I'd just drop in to see what's on for dinner tonight." Ellen tried to speak lightly. She wasn't quite prepared to face her father just yet, after her mother's revelations. Ellen's mother began to fuss around her husband, encouraging him to take a seat.

"There's something up." He looked from one woman to the other. "It seems it's going to be something I won't like. Okay, spill the beans. Who's in trouble?" He sat down and folded his arms, waiting for a response.

The two women looked at each other guiltily. Finally Ellen broke the silence. "No one's in trouble, Dad." She attempted a laugh which came out sounding flat. "We're a bit old for that, don't you think?" She lifted her chin and made eye contact with her father. "I found some old photos among Gran's stuff and I asked about them last time I was here. Don't you remember?"

"What's that got to do with me?"

"You told me the man in the photos was your brother, Jed, remember?" Ellen stopped, unsure how to go on.

"I don't have a brother Jed." Ellen's father sat down and picked up his paper as if to bring the conversation to an end.

Ellen continued. "Not now. Mum told me he'd died. And about

the baby…"

"Baby! There's no baby. Never was one." He slammed the paper down on the table.

"Dad, I know there was. She came into my shop."

Her father looked aghast. "Never heard such rubbish. Someone's trying to trick us, that's what. You've always been too soft." With that he picked up his paper again.

Ellen lifted her arms in disgust. How was she going to get through to him? "Dad," she tried again, but there was no response from behind the open newspaper.

"It's okay, honey, I'll talk with him after you've gone. Let's have dinner without mentioning this again, and I'll be back in touch later. It'll be all right, you'll see."

Bowing to the inevitable, Ellen sighed, and once the conversation reverted to the normal everyday things, her father's paper gradually lowered, and he deigned to take part again.

Later that night as Ellen was leaving, her mother drew her aside and repeated, "It'll be all right. I'll make it right. I'll be in touch." With these words, Ellen had to be content. She trusted her mother. She couldn't work out why her father was so obdurate about this man who had been his younger brother. Jenny had been right. There was something strange going on.

Twenty-three

Jenny's mouth was dry, and her stomach heaving. She was finally going to meet Ellen's parents. It had taken a few days to set up, and Jenny sensed they were reluctant to meet her. But Ellen, bless her heart, had been persistent, and it was finally happening.

She dressed carefully for the evening, eschewing the pants and sweaters she had come to favor since arriving in this part of the world, but refusing to revert to the business clothes with which she felt most comfortable. Instead she'd chosen a style somewhat in between. The slightly warmer weather had encouraged her to look out a tailored shirt, which she wore with black pants and a peach-colored jacket. Nothing too flamboyant. She wanted to make a good impression.

Driving down the highway, Jenny turned the radio to the country music channel, to which Mike had introduced her, and tried to hide her fear by singing along loudly. It worked for the duration of the trip, but the fluttering in her stomach returned as she pulled into the driveway of the Williams' home.

These people were her aunt and uncle. Jed's brother and sister-in-law. Ellen's father had grown up with the man Jenny was trying to accept was her own father. Walking up to the door, she wondered if they'd known Thea too. So far, Maddy was the only person who'd been able to tell her anything about the woman who had given birth to her.

Jenny rang the bell with some trepidation, relieved when it was Ellen who answered the door.

"Come on in. They're waiting in the lounge room," Ellen whispered, as she closed the outside door and ushered Jenny into a large open room. "Mom, Dad, this is Jenny."

Jenny walked into a large comfortable family room. There was a stone fireplace in the center of one wall, flanked by two soft armchairs in which her hosts sat in silence. Jenny felt awkward and immediately began to fill the silence. "I'm so glad to meet you. Ellen has told me so much about you, and it's great to meet you at last. Thanks for inviting me." Jenny dried up. *I'm babbling on. This is not like me.* She took a deep breath and sat down on the sofa, which stood opposite the fireplace, placing her between the two older people.

Ellen sat down beside her, and Jenny was grateful for her friend's presence. She still had difficulty in thinking of Ellen as her cousin. She wondered where to start, but was stymied by Ellen's father.

"So you're Thea's girl?" His deep voice boomed into the silence. Jenny looked over at the old man, whose bulky figure filled the chair, his bullet head devoid of hair, and at the red mouth from which these words had come. *And Jed's too,* she thought, but didn't put it into words.

"So I'm told," was her reply. Then her natural confidence returned. "It was news to me, but you knew about me, didn't you?" she accused, deciding to go on the offensive.

"We weren't told much at all. Dick's family was kept pretty much in the dark." Jenny turned to meet the antagonistic eyes of Ellen's mother. "Jed and Thea were a law unto themselves."

"And Thea's family wanted everything hushed up after the accident. We weren't even sure there was a baby. It's all water under the bridge. Why do you have to turn up out of the blue like this, claiming to be his daughter?" Dick Williams was beginning to sound belligerent.

"Dad, Jenny's not claiming to be anything she isn't. She didn't plan this." Ellen tried to soothe her father, to no avail.

"We don't need this, not now your grandparents are gone. Have some respect." Ellen looked at her father in dismay, and Jenny leapt into the argument.

"It's not lack of respect, Mr. Williams. I realize this has been a shock to you. It's been one to me too." She drew a shaky breath. "How do you think I feel, having my life turned upside down at this stage?" She wondered whether she should stay where she was, or if it would be better to get up and leave. If it hadn't been for Ellen sitting right beside her, she would probably have done just that. Only her ingrained politeness kept her sitting there. "I'm sorry you feel like that," she said at last, looking down at her hands.

"You're like her." It was Mrs Williams' sharp voice again.

Ignoring the tone, Jenny asked eagerly, "You knew her, Thea I mean?"

"We all knew Thea." It was said with a wry humor. "We were at school together. She was always grabbing the limelight; was in the midst of every mad prank."The woman's voice held years of disapproval.

"What we didn't know, my girl," Mr Williams said, "was that she had her hooks into our Jed." He shook his head. "But for her, he could have been alive today."

"They kept it secret?" Jenny was eager to hear more.

"Right up to almost the last minute when they wanted to get married. Why, we don't even know…"

"That's enough, Dick." Ellen's mother decided to put her oar in. "There were rumors, of course, but then there were always rumors around the school about who was seeing who. We didn't give it much credence, not until the night of the homecoming dance."

"What happened?"

"They arrived together. Late. And pretty disheveled. It was clear they were an item, but then it seemed it was over, that it had been a flash in the pan." Ellen's mother looked into the fire.

"That her father had forbidden her to see him, more like. He wouldn't want his little princess to be soiled by one of our family." Ellen's father's voice was bitter.

"Dad, it was all nearly sixty years ago. Can't you forget the family feud by now?" Again Ellen tried to make her parents see sense.

Jenny decided to take another tack. "What can you tell me about Jed?" she asked in a quiet voice. "All I know is what I've read in the school yearbook. I know he was a great sportsman and popular, but that doesn't tell me what he was like as a person."

"My little brother," began Dick Williams with a faraway look in his eyes, "was born with a smile on his face. He was a happy go lucky sort of guy. Everything went his way. He was the Williams who could succeed in everything he turned his hand to, who was going to change the world. Mom and Dad spent more time on him than on any of the rest of us. And look what happened." He rose from his chair. "And now you turn up after all this time and expect to be greeted as long-lost family. Well, I'm sorry, but it's not in my nature to be welcoming to Thea's brat." And with that rejoinder he stomped off, closing the door behind him with a bang.

"I think I'd better go." Jenny looked at Ellen for support and found her friend nodding in agreement.

"I'll let you out. I'm sorry," she mouthed, as her mother continued to stare in front of her, making no attempt to farewell her guest.

Jenny felt her face stiffen up as she stepped outside. A breeze was beginning to blow up, making her wrap her arms around her body. "I'll be in touch," she told Ellen, hurrying to her car. Her trip home was a more sober affair than the one down had been. She went over the conversation in her mind, wondering if she could have said anything to make it better. No, she decided, they were a boorish couple and she didn't care if she never saw them again. They seemed to feel the same about her. Ellen was a different matter. She looked forward to continuing their friendship.

*

Two days later Jenny read the email with growing excitement. She re-read what Rosa had written just to be sure. Yes, she hadn't been mistaken. Rosa had seen a For Sale sign outside their favorite bookshop in Noosa and had sent her a link to the website.

She clicked on the link. There it was. This could be the next step for her. Jenny pictured the inside of the shop as she remembered it. It was bigger than Ellen's little place, she realized, and there had been two or three assistants last time she was there. She couldn't wait to see Ellen again to ask her advice. In fact, why didn't she call her right now?

Ellen picked up the phone on the first ring, and her first words were ones of apology. "Jenny, what must you think of us? When you left the other night, I told my parents exactly what I thought of their behavior. I'm really sorry for their rudeness, especially my dad's." Ellen blurted all of this out without drawing breath.

"Hey, no worries!" Jenny was quick to put Ellen at ease. "I realize how difficult it must be for them. I guess it takes a bit of getting used to. I've had a few weeks to absorb it. Give them time."

"You're very generous. Your appearance certainly seemed to stir up some bad stuff for them. They've been talking about it ever since, but tend to shut up when I'm around. Mom's told me, that's how I know. Dad's never had anyone to blame for Jed's death, you see. Now you're here."

"And he can blame me! Well, indirectly I guess he's right. But Jed was driving that night."

"Give them time, Jenny. I'm sure they'll come round once they come to the realization you're all they have left of Jed. It seems Dad was really fond of his little brother. He never expected Jed's daughter to come back into his life."

Jenny heard what Ellen had to say, but didn't immediately reply. When she did, her voice was firm, "I'm not sure I want them to come round. I don't need their good opinion. My God, a few weeks ago I didn't even know of their existence. I've lived almost sixty years without them. I can live the rest quite easily. But that's not why I've called," Jenny's voice rose with excitement. "I've heard from home. Ellen, there's a bookshop for sale and I need your advice. Can I drop down sometime today?"

"Surely. Afternoon would be best. Then why not stay for dinner. We could eat out by the beach."

"The beach?" Jenny was amazed the weather would permit beach dining in Florence at this time of year.

"Well, overlooking the beach. The view's good, the food's good, and we'll be our own company. Will your godmother be all right on her own for the evening?"

"I guess so. She's an independent old woman. I can always get Mike to come down to keep her company," she added, remembering his many offers to help.

"Good! I'll book a table and see you this afternoon."

Jenny spent the morning making a list of all the questions she wanted to ask Ellen. She was comfortable back in planning mode. It was what she was accustomed to, and this trip had taken her out of her comfort zone, way out, she thought, running her fingers through her hair. It was time to get back to normal, to make some plans for the future. *Her* future. Back home in Australia.

Twenty-four

"Thanks a lot." Jenny closed her notebook and leant back in the tiny chair. "All of this will be a great help when I get back. I'm just itching to get there."

Ellen gave Jenny a long considered look. "Be sure," she said. "I don't see you being fulfilled by this bookshop you're so excited about. There's more to your life than that – more waiting for you."

Jenny folded both hands over her book. "Ellen, I know what I want. I've been out of things for too long. I need to get my life back."

"Why are you so sure that's where your journey is to be? Remember you came here to find out who you are. And you're more than the efficient career woman who has taken over for most of your life."

"I am who I am. I don't mean to offend you, but my life is there, not here. I need to be organizing things. I can't just sit back and let life happen. This has been a pleasant, no, great interlude, but that's all it can be. As soon as Maddy's on her feet again, I'll be off. My bookshop won't wait, and there's only so much I can do by email."

Ellen appeared to give up. "Okay, let's go. I booked a table for six, and it's almost that now." She checked her watch. "We'll just make it, though they shouldn't be too busy on a week night. It's not as if the tourist season has started yet."

The two women made their way out of the shop, Jenny waiting patiently while Ellen turned out the lights and locked up. She closed her eyes and listened to the door close and the key turn, picturing herself doing exactly that in her own shop in the not too distant future.

As they drove to the restaurant, Jenny knew she'd done the right thing in making this trip. It was all beginning to make sense. She was ready to close this chapter and start the next one when she returned to Australia. She also knew she'd keep in touch with Ellen, and Maddy, of course, maybe even visit again, but her future was not here.

Their meal over, the two women sat in silence finishing off the bottle of wine. Jenny gazed out of the window at the almost deserted beach where, as usual, the wind was blowing the sand horizontally, making it difficult for the few brave souls out there to stay upright. Jenny found herself staring at a young couple who'd been struggling along the beach. They stopped almost directly below the window where the two women were seated, and although distance and the reinforced glass of the window prevented Jenny and her companion from hearing the conversation, it was obvious to both of them what was happening.

First the young man knelt down in front of his companion.

"Look," Jenny exclaimed. "He's not…"

"He is."

As they watched, he rose and swung the girl around in the air, then they both hugged, oblivious to the sandstorm gusting around them.

For a moment Jenny felt an emotion she couldn't identify. It couldn't be envy. She was twice their age and had children and grandchildren of her own.

"You feel it, don't you?" Ellen swirled the wine in her glass.

"What do you mean? The expression of young love out there?" She waved the hand holding her glass in the direction of the window. "They're certainly unaware of everything except each other, but I don't yearn to be that age again." She thought for a few moments. "I guess it was like that for Thea and Jed. Seeing that young couple makes me think of them."

"And what about yourself, at the age you are?' Ellen asked, then busied herself with searching in her bag.

"No time for all that." But even as she denied it, Jenny knew she'd softened since coming to Oregon. The tough exterior she'd presented to the world for the past thirty years, through motherhood and career, had begun to crumble, and she was trying madly to regain her previous poise.

"Don't be too sure," said Ellen enigmatically.

Jenny glared, but it was a friendly glare. "You're one of the best things to come out of this trip," she told her friend and cousin. "You'll have to visit me down under."

"Hmm, but you're not off yet," she reminded Jenny.

"No. Maddy still has a few weeks to go before I'll be able to leave her, according to the doctors. What I need to do is find some support service in case she gets into trouble again once I've gone home."

"How did she manage without you all these years?"

Ellen's question was rhetorical and smacked of sarcasm, but Jenny ignored the underlying sentiment to ask, "Do you know of anyone?"

"Actually I do, or at least I know of a service in Florence, and I'm sure there's something similar up your way, if the Florence one doesn't extend that far. It's a service which can provide actual help or referrals for help, covering anything from shopping to a home handyman service. I think it works through a subscription."

"Sounds just the ticket, if I can get Maddy to agree to it."

They rose to go. "Can you drop me off?" Jenny asked, realizing she'd left her car outside the bookshop.

"Sure." They drove back in a comfortable silence. "Now don't be a stranger," reminded Ellen as Jenny climbed out of the car. "I expect to see you again soon, and the parents might even agree to see you again too," she added. Jenny grimaced, and waved as she stepped across to her car.

Twenty-five

Jenny and Mike had spent another day trawling through documents, with only a short break for lunch and a few calls next door for Jenny to check in on Maddy. They were sitting on the floor in Mike's cabin surrounded by books and folders.

"I think I'm done for the day." Jenny put down the document she'd been reading intently. "It's amazing the similarities I'm finding between the land issues for the Native Americans and the Australian Aborigines. I hadn't realized."

"Yes, indigenous people the world over have had to fight to retain their birthright. That was the focus of the conference I attended when I visited your neck of the woods."

"Of course. I'd forgotten." Jenny sat back on her heels. "You know, I've read a lot about it over the years, but it never really made much impact on me. But now, hearing about the land rights here and thinking of Jed and his family, it brings it all much closer."

"It's your birthright too, remember."

"Yeah, still can't get my head round that one. Jane and Steve were my parents, the ones who brought me up. Thea and Jed are still a fairytale to me, a couple of star-crossed lovers somewhere in my past."

"Mmm." Mike gathered the papers together and stacked them neatly beside his desk. He reached out his hand to pull Jenny to her feet. "We need some fresh air. How about a walk along the beach to blow away the cobwebs?"

"Sound like a good plan." Jenny stretched as she rose and stifled a yawn. "Wow, I hadn't realized how long we were sitting there. I'm getting quite stiff. I guess Ben would like some exercise too."

"What brought you here?" It was some time later, and the pair were strolling along the beach. Pushing her windblown hair out of her eyes, Jenny looked up at Mike's rugged face.

"To the beach?" he asked, smiling. They were walking along the edge of the ocean with the roar of the waves making conversation difficult.

"No, to Oregon, to Seal Rock. It's a pretty lonely spot." She was curious why he'd left his busy city and university life to hole up here.

"That was the attraction." Mike stopped and, picking up a pebble, hurled it into the sea. "I'd had enough of the jockeying for position, the politicking. University life isn't the esoteric searching after knowledge it seems to be. It can be as cut-throat as any big business. When Mary died, even before then," he reflected, "I knew I'd been there long enough."

"I never thought of universities in that way," Jenny replied. "To me they've always seemed like glorious halls of learning."

Mike laughed. "You are a romantic, aren't you? No, they're just like any other large organization, where you have a lot of very different individuals with different ideas of what should be done and how they should do it. Maybe a bit worse than most. Academics are all very committed to their own views."

"You mean, just like the organization I've decided to leave?"

"Pretty much. You've enjoyed your time here?" he asked, in a different tone.

"It's been wonderful. Apart from Maddy's accident and all the fuss about my parents." Jenny laughed. "I think I may have become a different person, maybe even a better person through it. But it's almost time to go back." She sighed.

"You wouldn't consider staying here?" Mike had stopped and was rubbing the toe of his shoe into the sand. Ben was running off in the distance.

"Here?" Jenny widened her eyes at the thought of it. "I couldn't do that. I have children, grandchildren, a house, a potential bookshop..." her voice tailed off.

"Of course you have." Mike looked down. Jenny's eyes followed his.

He wasn't suggesting? He couldn't be thinking? No, she was imagining it. It had merely been a casual enquiry, the sort you would make to any visitor. Then why did she feel this disappointment? Was she expecting more from him? Did she want more from him? They walked on in silence, the dog bounding back and forth retrieving the sticks Mike sent whirling ahead of them.

The pair had reached the rocks at the far end of the beach before either of them spoke again, then it was Jenny who, hugging her arms to her body in the cooling air, found her tongue. "And you, you feel you made the right decision, to come up here, I mean?"

"I know I did…" Mike paused as if searching for the right words. "San Francisco had too many memories, good ones, but sad ones too. This place," he turned around, his outstretched arm encompassing the length of beach they'd recently traversed, "it saved me. Your godmother's been a delightful neighbor, always there, never intrusive. Why," he laughed, "I think she's as much of a recluse as I am."

"Then I come along and disrupt both of your lives." Jenny tried to make light of her words, but was anxious to hear his reply.

It was some time coming, and Ben retrieved a couple more sticks before Mike ventured a response. "I wouldn't say that, Jenny." His voice seemed to savor her name. "I must admit, I wasn't pleased to hear about your arrival. You may have noticed I kept my distance for a few days."

"I did." Jenny was fearful to say too much lest she stem his confidences.

"You see, over the years, in the time I've known Maddy, she talked about you a lot to me, and to Mary too. We'd heard her sing the praises of her Australian god-daughter, the super-efficient career woman who'd managed to singlehandedly bring up two children and rise to the top of her profession, who was never flustered and had a plan for everything and whose plans always worked out. She painted you as an absolute perfectionist. Not someone I was anxious to meet."

Jenny removed the strands of hair which had blown into her mouth and smiled ruefully. "Oh dear, what a prick you must have thought I'd be. I hope I didn't live up to your expectations."

"Not quite, though you did have me worried at times." He smiled back, took her hand and gave it a light squeeze.

"I guess I was a bit like that. A control freak who panicked when everything didn't go my way." Wow, she thought, I'm talking in the past tense here.

Mike had noticed that too. "You were? But not now?"

She gave his question serious consideration before replying. "No, at least I don't think so. Both Maddy and Ellen have helped me change. I don't need to be in charge of everything and everyone anymore."

"And how does that feel?"

"Liberating."

Jenny squeezed the hand holding hers. It felt good to know she was with someone stronger than herself, someone who she could trust never to hurt her. *Now where had that come from?* "But I'm still going back to set up my bookshop." She drew her hand away and laughed, the wind carrying her laugh away.

"Ah yes, the bookshop. Was Ellen helpful?"

Jenny realized the conversation had moved on, and that Mike had decided to stick to a safer subject.

"She was. She helped me put together a workable business plan. All I have to do now is hope the sale goes through."

"But won't you have to be back there for that to happen?"

"It seems not. I know the shop well. It was one of my favorite haunts. I've been in touch with an accountant who has checked out the books to ensure all is well there. My lawyer is taking care of the rest. He'll send me the necessary papers to sign and that'll be that."

"And you'll be off, when?" Without Jenny realizing it, they'd been walking back and were almost at the other end of the beach.

"In a couple of weeks or so. I want to be sure Maddy's able to be completely independent again first. Though Ellen has put us in touch with a service which can help if necessary. When you're not around to play Prince Galahad," she joked. Mike's next words were a shock.

"I'm going to be gone for a couple of weeks myself. Down to San Francisco," he said curtly. "Have to check a few matters with my publisher, take down my latest draft, meet with my realtor and so on."

"Oh." Why did Jenny feel as if she'd just been given a body blow? "Well we won't be seeing you for a time, then?" she managed to reply insouciantly.

"I trust I'll be back before you leave, but maybe not."

By this time they'd reached the turnoff to Maddy's.

"Here, Ben," he called to the dog who was heading toward Maddy's door. "I'll say goodbye now." With a quick movement Mike dropped a kiss on Jenny's cheek and headed off up the track at a jog. Jenny gazed after him in amazement.

*

"Is that you, dear? You've been gone all day. Did you and Mike have a nice time together?" Maddy made her slow way toward her god-daughter and gave her a warm hug. "You're chilled. Where have you been? Come and sit by the fire to thaw out." Jenny was glad Maddy didn't give her time to reply. She was still shaking, whether from the kiss or the shock or Mike's leaving, she wasn't clear. She accepted her godmother's advice, dropping into a seat by the fire.

"How was your day?" Jenny asked finally.

"Glad you asked." Maddy met Jenny's eyes with her own smiling ones. "I had a call from your new cousin."

"Cousin? Oh, you mean Ellen? What did she want?"

"Good news. She sounds a nice girl. We had a good chat. Her mother wants to meet you again, not her father though. He's going to be a tougher nut to crack. Ellen has suggested the three of you meet for coffee the day after next. She'd like you to call. Why, what's the matter, Jenny Wren?" She could see Jenny's eyes were beginning to fill with tears. "Her father will come round soon, I'm sure."

"It's not that. Oh, damn." She tried to wipe away the tears with the back of her hand. "Why am I so prone to weeping these days? I never was before that stupid job thing. Now I seem to be ready to cry at the drop of a hat."

Ignoring the last words, Maddy asked, "If not that, then what's upsetting you, honey? Surely it's good news from Ellen?"

"Mike. He's going away. Back to San Francisco. Oh, damn," Jenny said again. "Why does that bother me so much?"

Twenty-six

"Great you could make it," Ellen stood up and kissed Jenny on the cheek. "Mom's over there." She nodded to a corner setting by the window, where her mother was holding her hands firmly on her lap and trying not to look towards them. "She'll be okay." Ellen's voice was reassuring, but Jenny still wasn't really sure about this meeting. The last one had gone so horribly wrong. She thought of her godmother's words to her as she'd been leaving.

"Don't expect too much, Jenny Wren," she'd said. "Remember, she's of my generation, and we don't like to have things thrust upon us. Especially reminders of the past which we've tried to hide."

"Sure," said Jenny, sounding more confident than she felt, and allowing herself to be led over to where Mrs Williams was sitting. "Hello again," she greeted Ellen's mother, who muttered something unintelligible as they sat down. While Ellen was pouring them all tea from a teapot in the center of the table, Jenny decided to try again.

"Thanks for agreeing to meet with me again. I know it must be difficult for you."

Rita Williams met Jenny's eyes for the first time and Jenny was shocked to see the other woman appeared to be holding back tears. This wasn't what she'd expected, not at all. "Ellen made me see it would be silly to refuse," she replied. "But Dick won't see you."

"No." Jenny was stuck for words. "I don't want anything from you," she said at last. "This is all as strange to me as it is to you. I'd just like to find out more about Jed, since he appears to have been my father."

Jenny paused. She felt odd saying the words out loud and noticed Rita draw herself up as if to prepare for battle.

"Strange isn't the word. Dick's family acted as if Jed had never existed, as if, when he died, they'd wiped the slate clean. I was pregnant with Ellen's brother at the time, so I had enough to think about, but Dick was devastated. Jed was his beloved younger brother." She wiped a tear from her eye. "Now you appear out of the blue and Ellen says you're his daughter. It takes a bit of getting used to." She looked over at Jenny. "Dick won't come round, you know. He won't see you." Rita's voice was flat and lacked emotion.

"I know." Jenny's voice was subdued. "But can you tell me anything about Jed? Anything that would make him more real to me? I've seen the yearbooks and know about his sporting exploits, but what about the person. What was he like?"

"Well, let me see." Rita seemed to be trying to retrieve memories from somewhere far away. Her eyes closed, and she tilted her head upwards. Opening them again she picked up her cup and took a sip before speaking. "He was a wild one, and bright too." Jenny shifted in her seat impatiently. She already knew all that and wasn't quite sure what more she had expected.

Suddenly Rita smiled. "He was a lovely boy, a good son and brother. It was such a pity..." she sighed. "But he was younger than us. I didn't really see a lot of him. Family dinners and so on, but he was always keen to rush off. Lots of other things to take care of, I expect. And then Thea..."

"I thought the family didn't know about her?" Jenny interjected.

"Mom and Dad Williams didn't, but we had our suspicions. We'd seen them together a few times, and Dick knew his brother was up to something, something he didn't want his parents to know about. How they managed to keep their relationship a secret for so long was surprising. Especially in a town this size." She nodded as if to confirm her own words.

"So you *did* know Jed and Thea?" Jenny asked. She was beginning to wonder if she was going to learn anything at all.

"Jed, yes, because he was Dick's brother, but Thea..." Rita screwed up her face. "I'm sorry, dear. She was younger, you see. I do remember Jane and Maddy. They were in the year above me. It's a funny thing, but we always remember those who were older than us at school, but the younger ones didn't figure on our radar. I'd see Jed around with a group of friends, always lots of girls among them." She smiled as if remembering. "I can't honestly say I remember Thea all that well. It was only afterwards we put two and two together. By the time they were running off to get married, Dick and I were wrapped up in our own lives and looking forward to our own baby. I vaguely remember some discussion between Mom and Dad Williams, but I didn't pay too much attention, I'm afraid."

"Mom, is there anything else about Jed growing up that would help fill in the picture for Jenny?" Ellen tried to steer her mother back on track.

"Well," Rita began, "he was a real charmer. Everyone loved him, and so good-looking. He had his pick of all the girls. And he was good at organizing things," she reflected. "I remember Dick telling me how Jed organized fundraising events for the football team. I guess that brought him into contact with all the cheerleaders. Was Thea perhaps one of them?" she asked.

"She was." Jenny was beginning to relate to this and wondered if she'd inherited her own organizational skills from Jed. She leant forward eagerly and was disappointed at Rita's next words.

"We weren't sure about the baby." Rita looked intently at Jenny. "We'd heard there was one, then nothing. It was as if it had all been a lie, as if it had never happened. Then my little Ron was born. We wanted to name him Jed, after his uncle, but Dick's dad would have none of it." She sighed and stared into the distance. "Dick was devastated. He'd loved his little brother and found it hard when his parents wanted to pretend he'd never existed."

"But…"

"Then, a couple of years later, my Ellen here came along." Rita laid her hand on her daughter's and smiled. "We managed to forget about the past and lived our own lives. Until now, when you came along to stir it all up again."

"And did…?"

"That's really all I can tell you." Picking up her cup, Rita drained it quickly. "I'm ready to go now, Ellen. I'm sorry I haven't been able to be of more help," she added, meeting Jenny's eyes.

"Talk soon," Ellen whispered, giving Jenny a quick hug before she left in her mother's wake. Jenny sat looking after them, trying to work out how she felt. Let down, she decided. She didn't know exactly what she'd expected, but it had certainly been more than Rita's few comments. She sighed, picked up her bag, and made to leave herself. Maybe she'd never really get to the bottom of this. She was still worried about the disparity in the dates.

I'll ask Maddy again, she decided as she drove home, wondering if there were any other family members still alive who could fill in the blanks. The thought enlivened her. She hadn't considered that avenue before. Maybe there were some distant relatives on her mother's side. They would be Thea's relatives too. She just wanted to shed some light on what seemed to be the mystery of her birth, then she could return to Australia with a clear heart.

When she reached the turnoff to the track, Jenny noticed a figure running along the beach with a dog. On impulse she stopped the car, and trying to see if it was Mike and Ben out there, she stepped out and walked slowly down to the edge of the ocean. She stood, hand over her eyes, and peered into the distance. It certainly looked like them, and she had to admit she'd never seen anyone else down here with a dog, not a black one like Ben, anyway.

Then she remembered. He was in California, so whoever it was, it wasn't Mike. Swallowing her disappointment, Jenny made her way back to the car and slowly drove the remainder of the way. Opening the door gently, she wasn't surprised to see Maddy's erect figure sitting quietly reading by the fire. Maddy looked up at Jenny's entrance. "How did it go?" She laid down her book.

Jenny dropped down onto the sofa, her bag falling to the floor at her feet. She raked her hands through her hair, destroying her customary tidy appearance. After a moment's silence she rubbed her eyes with both hands. "I'm not much further forward," she said finally, and imparted the conversation with Rita. "So, you see," she concluded, "it seems everyone was at great pains to hide what actually happened. I don't suppose there are any other distant relatives hidden away who might have been around at the time?" She looked at her godmother hopefully.

"Not that I can recall." Maddy paused and closed her eyes, clearly thinking back over the years. "Wait on."

"Yes?" Jenny's voice lifted, and she leaned forward, hands on knees.

"You've thought of someone?"

"We…ll, maybe." Maddy's voice was hesitant. "I seem to remember Jane had some cousins. Now where did they live? It'll come to me."

Jenny moved impatiently in her seat. "How about the photo albums? Any help there?" But there was no immediate reply. Realizing she wouldn't get an answer any time soon, Jenny decided to leave her godmother to her thoughts. She'd been in such a rush to go to Florence earlier, she hadn't checked her emails. She'd do it now.

Sitting down at the large desk overlooking the bushy yard, Jenny was soon lost in another world. The report her accountant had been preparing on the bookshop was there, and as she perused the lengthy document, she became even more convinced her future lay with her own bookshop back in Australia. She could already picture herself manning the counter surrounded by books of all shapes and sizes.

Another encouraging email from Rosa helped to confirm her decision. Rosa wrote that she'd paid the shop a visit on the weekend, and it looked ripe for some new ideas. Well, I've certainly got plenty of those, Jenny thought, opening the next email from her solicitor. He'd sent her a copy of the contract of sale, but indicated the original would be in the mail. Evidently it wasn't sufficient for a legal document such as this to be downloaded and printed out. If she intended to go ahead, she'd need to sign the original and have it witnessed here in Oregon.

She sat back, her mind going in different directions all at once. Then, drawing a piece of paper towards her, she began to make a list, then form it into a time chart. She hadn't run a successful department all those years for nothing. Head supported in both hands, Jenny looked at what she had drawn up. It all depended on Maddy, she realized. Whether she could remember the cousin, and most of all, when she'd be able to cope on her own. Eager as she was to get back to open her bookshop, Jenny determined she wouldn't leave till her godmother was self-sufficient again.

She rubbed her eyes, trying to dismiss the image which rose in her mind. The image of a bearded face with a wry smile and deep blue eyes. She wouldn't even think of him. He'd gone, and with a bit of luck, she'd be gone too before he returned. Then Jenny stretched back in her chair. She'd done enough for the day, and what a day it had been. She doubted she'd get much sleep that night.

Twenty-seven

Mike was glad he'd made an early start. It was still dark, but the sun would be up soon, and he'd have the first part of the trip over before the traffic started. Might even make it past the halfway mark before nightfall. Turning up the radio, he looked down at his faithful companion. "It's the right thing to do, Ben. Was getting a bit too steamed up for my liking. She'll be back in Australia before we know it. Better to get out now."

Just who was he kidding? Mike pulled on his beard, remembering how he'd felt last night on the beach. He'd almost heard Mary egging him on, and had been close to wrapping his arms around Jenny and giving her a kiss. A proper one, not one of these pecks he'd stolen up to now. Then she'd mentioned her return to Australia, and he'd clammed right up. He'd known he was doing it, but that didn't make it any better.

He did need to make this trip, he told himself, ignoring the small voice telling him he didn't have to make it right now. Both his publisher and the realtor had been on his back for a couple of weeks, and he'd managed to stave them off. Could have done it for a bit longer too, he guessed. But better to come now, before he was any more involved. With a bit of luck she'd be gone when he got back up there, and that would be that.

As he drove down Highway 101, he could almost hear his Mary's voice in his ear. "*You big fool. You're no good on your own. Jenny's a good woman. You let her go too easily. Remember what I wrote you? She's just the sort of woman I'd have picked for you myself.*"

"But she's going back to Australia." Somehow Mike didn't see anything strange about having this conversation with his dead wife. "What am I supposed to do, then, follow her down under?" As if understanding, Ben changed his position and placed his paw on Mike's leg. "You understand, don't you, big fellow? A man can't pick up sticks and go off to the other side of the world for a woman, not at this age." The remainder of the trip passed in silence.

*

Mike had been in San Francisco for nearly two weeks, and the buzz of the city was beginning to irritate him. He longed for the peace and tranquility he'd left behind in Oregon. One positive thing had come out of the trip, however. He'd received a good offer for the house and had agreed to the sale. That meant he now had to clear out all the furniture and other belongings he'd closed the door on when he'd headed north. He didn't relish the thought. As he knocked back his nightcap Jack Daniels, he vowed to start on the work early next morning. When he'd finished up things here, he'd head back up to Seal Rock. Surely Jenny'd be gone by now.

He wakened refreshed and with a certainty that, if Jenny was still at Seal Rock, he'd seek her out and… and what, he wasn't quite sure. But it was as if Mary had visited him in the night and set him on the right path. The path to a future with Jenny. Mike rubbed his hands through his hair. This was a weird state of affairs if ever there was one. He looked at the clock. Better get a move on. He had furniture buyers coming at ten o'clock, and there was a heap to do before then.

Dragging on a pair of track pants and a worn T-shirt, he grabbed Ben's leash. "Come, boy." That was enough for the dog who leapt to his master's bidding. They went out together into the sunshine. Looking down the suburban street already busy with commuting neighbors, Mike once again felt confident in his decision to leave.

But as he jogged along the street with Ben running by his side, Mike began to doubt his earlier plan, wondering if he'd imagined Jenny's feelings. What if she felt nothing for him? What if he made a fool of himself? There's no fool like an old fool, he thought, turning the corner and heading for home, but if I don't try I'll never know. With that resolved, he breathed a sigh of relief and prepared for what promised to be an exhausting day.

The furniture people came and went, providing quotes and promising to pick up on the following day. A couple of neighbors called round wondering what was happening to the old place. Nosey-parkers, all of them, but what could he do but be polite. Mary had been closer to them than he'd ever been. He had to admit that, since the start of her illness, he'd withdrawn into a cocoon of his own making. And stayed there, too.

It had only been at Seal Rock he'd come out of his shell. It had started with Maddy, whose gentle nature had been like a balm to his troubled soul. Then Jenny, who rather than a balm, had been more like an irritant, reminiscent of the grain of sand that irritates the oyster to form a pearl. He laughed at the comparison. Was he really comparing himself to a pearl? How Mary would have teased him at the very idea of it!

"Well," Mike sighed, "looks like we won't be able to leave for a couple more days, old fellow." Ben looked up soulfully. "You want to get back there too, don't you? You miss the wild white beach, the rough seas, the piles of bleached driftwood." As he spoke, Mike closed his eyes to see the beach at Seal Rock, deserted except for a tall figure in blue, black hair flying in the wind. In his mind's eye, the figure turned towards him. Her eyes, her deep violet eyes, met his. Her arms rose to embrace him. Her lips parted. He opened his eyes with a start. Ben had fallen asleep at his feet and was snoring away happily. Maybe he was dreaming of the beach too.

As he sluiced his face preparing for bed, Mike gave himself an assessing look in the mirror. He saw a ruddy face surrounded by faded red hair and a white beard, somewhat worn and jaded by the years. Did he have anything left to offer a woman, he wondered? He turned away. What was the point of wondering? He'd always been a believer in action. He'd make it through the next couple of days somehow, then they'd be off. He wouldn't warn Maddy and Jenny of his return. He'd just turn up and see what happened.

Next morning he was in the midst of packing when he was startled by a loud knock at the door followed by, "Hey there! Anyone home?" and a grey head popped around the door.

"Bob!" Mike's response was one of surprise. He hadn't expected to see his former colleague on this trip, having deliberately omitted to let anyone from the university know of his presence in town. "What...?"

"Heard you were back." The other man looked around the denuded room. "So this is it then? Saw the SOLD sign outside." He folded his arms and lounged against the doorway. Ben trotted over to sniff his trouser leg, then padded back to the spot by the window where the sun was spilling a puddle of warmth onto the wooden floor.

Mike, realizing he wasn't going to be able to continue his task while Bob was standing there, sighed and stretched up from where he'd been bending over a packing case. "Take a pew." He gestured to one of the few chairs which had so far escaped being stacked.

"Bit of a dark horse, aren't you?" Bob settled in, as if for a long chat. "Didn't even let your old friends know you were back. How're things up in Oregon? Miss the big city life?"

Anxious to keep the conversation as brief as possible, Mike remained standing, packing tape in one hand, scissors in the other. "Was all a bit sudden," he said. "Had a few things to finalize, then this place sold and..." He gestured at the mess around him.

"So when did you get back?" Bob's eyes were roaming around the room, apparently taking it all in. "You didn't do all this in a day. Heard you were here a week or so ago. Cathy wanted me to ring you straight away, but I said we should give you some breathing space, and now look at you. Your phone's off too," he added.

"Yeah." Mike looked down. "You know how it is. I'd already left. Said all there was to say. New life and all that."

"And is it? A new life, I mean. Are you happy up there? What do you do all day?"

Happy? Mike mused. What did that mean? His voice came slowly. "I guess. It's different. A different pace of life." Then he grew more enthusiastic. "Bob, you should see the wild seas up there, the white foam of the waves breaking on the sand, throwing up masses of driftwood. And the skies..."

"Don't go waxing all lyrical on me now," Bob muttered awkwardly. "And your work, your magnum opus, how's it going? Plenty to research?"

"As a matter of fact there is." Mike finally put down his packing materials and folded his arms. "Met a couple of Native Americans who've been real helpful. It's good to be on the spot."

"And did you get to that museum you were going on about? Where was it again?"

"Klamath Falls." As he uttered the words, Mike remembered the last time he'd said them. He'd promised to take Jenny to the museum when Maddy was well enough to be left. His eyes glazed over, remembering her face turned up to his, the sound of the waves behind them and the smell of the sea in his nostrils.

As if realizing his friend had gone off to Oregon in his mind, Bob rose. "I'll be off." Then, as if suddenly recalling his reason for visiting, added, "But before I go, Cathy wanted to invite you over tonight. We're having a few people…"

Oh, God, thought Mike, another of Cathy's dos, and was about to refuse when it occurred to him this would definitely be the last one. He wouldn't be back in San Francisco, not in this house or neighborhood, anyway. He forced his face into a smile. "Sure, tell Cathy I'll be there. What time did you have in mind?"

"It'll be a barbecue. An excuse to have me do the cooking." Bob grinned, "Any time after six should be right."

"Fine. I'll probably need a break by then. But I won't stay long." Mike decided to pre-empt any attempts to set him up. "I need to be off up north again in a couple of days, so there's a lot to take care of before I go."

*

It was closer to seven before Mike felt ready to leave. "Not this time, Ben," he told his companion, as the dog beat him to the door, "but I won't be long." Driving the short distance to Bob's home, Mike reflected that, as Mary had often warned him, he was coming close to relying on Ben for conversation. Nothing too bad about that, he thought, parking by the curb. He noticed quite a few cars had already arrived. So it was going to be one those things. The sort of evening he'd hoped never to have to face again. "Here goes," he spoke the words aloud then, taking a deep breath, jumped down from the pickup and locked the door.

A couple of hours and not a few beers later, Mike had decided it wasn't too bad. At least Cathy hadn't tried to pounce, nor had she appeared at his side with a strange woman in tow. He was beginning to relax and had just taken his first bite of a tasty hamburger, when he came face to face with a tall ascetic-looking gent who greeted him with a big smile. "It's Mike, isn't it? Mike Halliday?"

Racking his brains trying to figure out who the heck this was, Mike played for time. He took another bite of his bun then a gulp of beer, wiping the back of his hand across his mouth before replying. "Sure is. I don't think…" he began, embarrassed. He felt he should know this guy. He recognized the face but couldn't put a name to him. One of Bob's old mates he'd met years ago, he guessed.

Mike's confusion must have been obvious to the other man who quickly offered, "Don Parker. Your late wife's pastor," he added, seeing Mike was still trying to recollect him.

"Don, of course." Mike put down his beer on a nearby bench and shook the other's hand. "Forgive me. For a moment…"

"I know," consoled the other, "happens to me all the time. People expect to see me in a church, not at a garden barbecue swilling beer. I haven't seen you since the funeral. How are you bearing up? I hear you've moved away." He looked enquiringly at Mike, clearly expecting a reply.

"Yes. Seal Rock," Mike coughed. "We… Mary and I… there's a cabin up there." He felt awkward talking with this man. Mary had been the churchgoer, and he'd had very little to do with all that side of things. He'd had the funeral at the church because he knew that's what Mary would have wanted, but he'd never really cared for all the mumbo jumbo as he saw it.

"I'm glad to have this opportunity to have a word with you," Don began. Mike grimaced. The last thing he needed was a pep talk from the God squad. "You know I visited Mary in the Nursing Home?"

"Yes." Mike wondered what was coming next. He knew Mary had derived comfort from those visits, in the periods when she understood where she was and who was talking with her.

"We spoke quite a bit, in her more lucid moments that is." The other man looked at his feet as if working out how to say it. "She was concerned about you, afraid you'd withdraw into your shell when she wasn't there to egg you on, as it were." He cleared his throat.

Out with it, man, enough of this shillyshallying. Get on with what you have to say and let me get out of here. But Mike's words were for himself alone and weren't spoken aloud.

Don finally seemed to work out what to say. "What I'm trying to say is this. Mary spoke highly of you. She didn't want you to live the rest of your life alone. She hoped you'd find someone... someone to care for. Someone who'd care for you. She was most definite about that. I don't know if she was able to tell you herself, so I'm glad to have had this opportunity."

"Yes," Mike's voice was low and scarcely audible. "She left a letter," he said abruptly, hoping to silence the pastor, but to no avail.

"It's important, in these cases," Don cleared his throat again, and turned his beer around and around in his hands. "You must step forward to accept a future without her, move on to fresh pastures, and look for another companion in your journey through life."

What a load of psychobabble, thought Mike, but all he managed to say was, "Hmm." He turned, seeking an avenue of escape, and when he saw Bob standing alone by the barbecue, seized on the opportunity. "Need to check with Bob," he muttered and took off across the yard.

"See you got pinioned by the Don." Bob grinned as he turned a line of sausages. "Don't have much time for him myself, but Cathy likes to invite him round. As long as he's part of a crowd, it seems to be okay. He didn't upset you, did he?" he added, clearly shocked by the haunted look on Mike's face.

"A bit," was all Mike could get out. Taking a final bite of hamburger and gulp of beer he added. "I'm off now, Bob. Great barbecue. Can you thank Cathy for me? She seems busy right now." He gestured to where Bob's wife was standing across the garden in the middle of a group of laughing women.

Bob stopped his cooking and looked up. "Sure. Sorry you're leaving so soon. Miss the dessert Cathy's been slaving over all day. When did you say you were off up north again?"

"Don't think I did, but it'll be in the next day or so. They're picking up the furniture tomorrow. There's nothing to keep me then, not in an empty house," he said ruefully. "Ben and I'll be back on the road and at Seal Rock by the end of the week." He felt bucked at the thought of the peace which awaited him, despite some apprehension in the pit of his stomach at the thought of seeing Jenny there too.

Twenty-eight

Jenny picked up the thick envelope and turned it over in her hands. She was almost afraid to open it. Closing the mailbox, she walked slowly back up the track to Maddy's house.

"It's come, then?" Jenny looked up, startled at the sound. Maddy was standing in the doorway holding firmly to her cane. "It's what you've been waiting for, isn't it?"

"Yes." Jenny sounded doubtful. She looked further up the track as if expecting to see a tall bearded figure walking down with his black dog. But the road was as empty as it had been for the past two weeks.

"Yes it is." Pulling herself together, Jenny quickened her pace and joined her godmother in the doorway. "Let's have a coffee."

Jenny was distracted. She kept looking at the package, but made no move to open it. This was it – what she'd been waiting for. But now it had come, she was consumed with doubt. Maddy must have guessed her feelings because she was uncharacteristically silent as they drank their coffee.

When they'd finished, Jenny slipped away to her room. She needed some quiet time – time to reflect. Now that her very own bookshop was within her grasp, Jenny began to wonder if it really was what she wanted. She remembered Ellen's strange words about there being more waiting for her. She walked to the window with its view up the track. She couldn't see Mike's house from here, but could imagine it, imagine the man who lived there, his… no. Jenny gave herself a shake. He was gone. She might never see him again. That thought brought a pang of anguish, and she sat down on the bed with a thump. Never to see Mike again…never to… Her eyes caught the sand dollar lying on the bedside table, the sand dollar that had started all of this. Was it really magical?

Then Jenny's old logical side came to the fore. What on earth would she do here? What about Helen, Hugh, her grandchildren? They needed her too. This wasn't real life. It had been a pleasant interlude; something to remember in her old age; a sign that there was still life in the old bird yet. Clearly Mike felt that way too. Otherwise he'd still be here, not haring off to California to get away from her. No, she'd made the right decision. She'd go out and sign the papers right now.

Half an hour later the two women were sitting at the table surrounded by sheets of paper. "Well," Jenny started putting them back together. "It all looks pretty simple. I just need to sign this one and have it witnessed. You could do that, Maddy, couldn't you?"

"I guess so." Maddy levered herself up. "How about we celebrate the signing with a small glass of something?"

"Maddy! It's ten o'clock in the morning," Jenny said.

"Who's to know but you and me? It's not every day you buy a bookshop, is it?"

"You're right." Jenny sounded more certain. "It's a big step. The first step for the new me. But I couldn't take a drink at this time of day. Why don't I treat you to lunch instead? We can celebrate then."

"Why not go down to Florence?" Maddy suggested, then to Jenny's surprise she added, "I'd like to meet this new cousin of yours, Ellen. Do you think I could make it into her shop?"

"Are you sure? I'd love that if you think you're up to it."

"I'm not going to sit here moldering away. How are you ever going to go back to Australia if I'm housebound?" Maddy looked at Jenny with a gleam in her eye.

"True." It occurred to Jenny that her godmother might be getting bored. Although Maddy lived a solitary existence up this track, she'd been accustomed to going out most days and was used to meeting other people and keeping up with what was going on around her. She hadn't seen anyone but Jenny and Mike since returning from hospital. "Let's do it."

An hour later Jenny was driving her PT Cruiser into Old Town. She found a parking spot outside The Reading Nook and helped Maddy out of the car. There was no wheelchair this morning, but Maddy had consented to use the walker provided by the hospital. Jenny was glad her godmother had realized she needed more help than a cane for this, her first major trip out of the house.

"I can manage." Maddy's voice was testy as Jenny tried to help her reach the shop door. "So this is where you've been running off to!" She stood, regaining her breath, and ran her eyes over the shop front. "It's amazing, but I don't remember noticing this place before. I must have walked past it dozens of times. Unless it just appeared out of thin air when you arrived." She chortled at Jenny's look of surprise. In fact Jenny did sometimes feel Ellen and her shop had magical qualities.

The two women entered with the usual jangle of the bell, and Jenny, feeling familiar in these surroundings, helped Maddy settle in one of the carefully placed chairs. There were a few customers either browsing or sitting in corners reading. The place has the feel of a library rather than a bookshop, Jenny thought, wondering how she could develop the same sort of ambiance in her own shop. A shiver ran up her spine at the realization that a bookshop of her own was within her grasp. As soon as she signed the contract and sent it off, she'd have committed herself. There would be no turning back. It was an exciting, though daunting prospect.

"Well, well, who have we here?" While Jenny had been lost in her thoughts, Ellen had entered carrying a takeaway coffee. "I've just been across the road picking up my caffeine fix," she said. "And this must be Maddy." Putting down her coffee, she walked over and took the older woman's hand in both of hers. "It's so good to meet you at last. I feel I already know you. Jenny's spoken a lot about you."

Maddy gave her goddaughter a glare. "Not too much, I hope. What would you want to know about a silly old woman like me?" They laughed, and Jenny could see that, despite the difference in age, the two women were set to become friends. That pleased her.

"We were hoping you could manage to come to lunch with us. We're celebrating."

"You are? Well, I'm always ready for a celebration. What's this one in aid of?"

Before Jenny could reply, Maddy did it for her. "This one has just received the contract for her bookshop .You certainly made an impression on her with this place. Though," she added looking around, "I can see why. You've put together something pretty special here."

"Why thank you." Ellen appeared unusually flustered. "I really appreciate you saying that. Now when were you thinking of having this lunch?"

"Right now." Maddy wasn't one to mince words. "You can tell us which is the best place down here. I usually go to the Mexican on Highway 101, but today calls for something more special. It's not every day Jenny here buys a bookshop and starts a new life."

"I'm here too." Jenny finally managed to get a word in. "I couldn't have come so far without your help, Ellen."

"We Williamses have to stick together."

Jenny did a double take. She was still trying to come to grips with her heritage and hadn't even thought of herself as being part of the Williams family. "I… guess so," she replied slowly. She'd been a Miller all of her life till she'd married John and become Sullivan. The name Williams didn't belong to her, never would. It was one thing to find out about her birth and research her birth parents, but it was quite another to think of herself as belonging to another family, one whose existence she hadn't even been aware of until recently.

*

"I think I'll have to adopt you too." The three women had enjoyed a seafood feast looking out over the river, and Maddy was looking at Ellen as she spoke.

"You can be her honorary goddaughter," Jenny chimed in, delighted the two women had bonded so well over lunch.

Ellen's voice was subdued as she replied, "That would please me. But, now we're over the celebratory part of the lunch, can I ask you something?"

Jenny looked over in surprise. She'd been the one asking questions up till now. It hadn't occurred to her that Ellen might have some unresolved issues too.

"Sure thing," Maddy replied, throwing a cautionary glance at Jenny.

"Fire away."

"It's like this," Ellen began hesitantly. "With Jenny's arrival and our discovery that we're related, I've found out about an uncle I didn't know existed. Jenny's told me you knew, or at least met him, and I wondered…"

"Hadn't you best ask your parents about him, dear?" Maddy spoke gently, but it was clear to Jenny her godmother didn't want to go into the past at this time.

"They don't want to tell me anything." Jenny was surprised to see Ellen's usual calm demeanor ruffled.

Maddy looked out over the river as if trying to collect her thoughts while her two companions exchanged glances.

"I don't…" Jenny began but was interrupted by Maddy's voice.

"It was all a long time ago, and I didn't really know him. We only met face to face that one time." Jenny listened with bated breath. This was news to her. She realized she hadn't actually asked Maddy directly about Jed.

"And that time was?" Ellen appeared to have none of Jenny's inhibitions.

"Just before he and Thea set out on their fateful trip. I really can't tell you any more." Maddy closed her lips tight as if to forestall any further discussion.

Jenny's eyes blurred at this unexpected insight. As she closed them to blink away the threat of tears, the scene unrolled behind her eyelids like a movie in slow motion. She opened them again quickly and blinked a couple of times to dismiss the image of the horrific crash. "I think lunch is over." She made to rise.

"Oh, Jenny. I upset you. I'm so sorry." Ellen came round to Jenny's side of the table and put her arms around her cousin. "I suddenly had this feeling…"

"You and your feelings." Jenny tried to laugh off her distress. "But that's the problem. No one seems to have known Jed. Or at least be willing to talk about him," she added in the realization that, of course, Ellen's parents had known him very well. "No, I've given up on finding out more about him, but I would like to know why I seem to have been born before my birthday." She tried to make a joke of it, but the attempt fell flat as the others stared at her.

"I hadn't forgotten." Maddy was quick to assure her. "I've been thinking about those relatives, and I do believe I've come up with an idea. With your contract arriving this morning, we became so excited I forgot all about it."

"You have?" Jenny couldn't believe her ears. She'd all but given up on the possibility of finding anyone else who could help her.

"I seem to recall that Jane had a Cousin Rhoda, on her father's side. She didn't live up here. She was closer to Medford."

"Where's that?" Jenny was unfamiliar with other parts of Oregon.

"About four hours south of here. But she'd be pretty old by now." She laughed at herself. "Around my age I mean."

"I know," Jenny found she was able to laugh at this comment. "Not everyone has your youthful outlook. But, four hours, that's not insurmountable. Do you think she's still alive?"

"One way to find out. We can check out the directory when we get home. She may have married, of course, which would complicate things."

They made their farewells, Jenny looking anxiously at Maddy, who appeared tired. "Hope this hasn't been too much for you," she said as she settled her godmother into the passenger seat for the return trip.

"I've been sitting down all the time," Maddy remonstrated, but Jenny could see the tiredness in her eyes. "However I will be glad to get home and have a bit of a lie down," she allowed, leaning her head back and closing her eyes.

*

Mike was glad he'd made an early start. It was still dark, but the sun would be up soon. Now he was on his way, he couldn't wait to get reach Seal Rock. Seeming to be in accord with his master's mood, Ben lay on the passenger seat, tail hanging down, ears twitching from time to time as if dreaming of chasing gophers. They'd both be glad when this trip was over. Mike shuffled restlessly in his seat and turned on the radio. Music would make the time go faster.

It was evening of the next day by the time the truck turned into the track leading up to his cabin. As he passed Maddy's home, Mike peered at the shape of the house looming out of the darkness. There were no lights to be seen, so all of the occupants must be in bed. He'd have to wait till morning to find out if he was in time to see Jenny again.

Twenty-nine

Jenny stood looking out at the ocean, reflecting how she seemed to be spending a lot of her time doing that these days. She turned her collar up to her chin to keep out the early morning breeze and let her head fall back, lifting her eyes skyward to greet the morning sun. It was going to be a glorious day, a perfect summer's day, in fact. She could hardly believe she'd been here in Oregon for almost three months. It would soon be time to return home.

She thought back to the evening before. While Maddy had been napping, Jenny had begun searching for Cousin Rhoda and, to her surprise, had found her. Or, at least, Jenny qualified her thoughts, had found an address. The directory had proved fruitless, but then she'd a brainwave. She'd logged on to the Ancestry.com website, searched the social security files and bingo! There she was, Rhoda Miller, listed in Medford as recently as four years ago. She wasn't sure where to go from there, but wondered if Maddy would have any ideas. She'd check with her this morning.

Turning to go back for breakfast, Jenny noticed a man jogging along towards her with a black dog running at his heels. It couldn't be... She shook her head. It was crazy the way she kept thinking she was seeing Mike and Ben. She knew he was in California. Something she'd said had scared him off. She was sure of that, though she couldn't quite put her finger on what it had been.

As she started up the track, she heard footsteps running behind her and suddenly was almost bowled over by a large black shape. Jenny stopped in her tracks. "You're here!" It came out like an accusation, and realizing how it must have sounded, she quickly added. "It's good to see you. Quite a surprise. When did you get back?"

Panting from the effort of running along the beach and up the track, Mike stood for a moment to regain his breath. He pushed back the lock of hair which had flopped down over his forehead. "Last night. Late. It's good to be back."

Jenny stood, drinking him in. She took a deep breath in an attempt to calm the fluttering in the pit of her stomach. "Would you like to drop in for a coffee or maybe some breakfast?" she managed to say at last. "I'm sure Maddy would love to see you."

Mike's eyes seemed to bore into hers as he accepted her invitation. "As long as Ben can come too," he said.

*

"So the house is sold and I won't need to go back down again. I'm here for good." Mike looked at the two women who'd become dear to him.

"What about your publisher? Didn't you go down to see him?" Jenny seemed puzzled by Mike's relaxed manner and his obvious delight at being back.

"Oh yes, that too," Mike said, remembering the reason he'd given for leaving so precipitously. "And what have you been up to?" He turned to Jenny as he spoke.

"Finding another relative." Jenny was smiling. "Maddy remembered Mum had a cousin in Medford and I've just managed to discover she's still there. I should have her contact details soon and then…"

"So you're not haring off to Australia just yet?"

"Not immediately, but it's still on the cards. I signed the contract for my bookshop and mailed it. Just as soon as Maddy can cope, I'll be off."

"Don't use me as an excuse. I'm pretty much okay now. Jenny and her new cousin have fixed me up with this service," Maddy explained. "If I can't get out, I can arrange for someone to do my shopping or come in and clean. I can become a lady of leisure," she laughed. "Imagine!"

"Well, I want to see if I can meet Cousin Rhoda first, then we'll see."

"Medford, eh?" Mike saw his opportunity. "That's on the way to Klamath Falls. I mentioned the museum there, didn't I? The Favell museum. It's known for its collection of Native American artifacts."

"I think so." Jenny sounded vague.

Mike sensed Jenny was having trouble recalling their earlier conversation. He felt awkward, but it was as if Mary was there at his shoulder egging him on, so he persisted.

"I need to make a trip down there. What say we go together, and you can stop in to see this cousin on the way?"

"I don't…" Jenny began, when Maddy interrupted.

"What a good idea. You young ones can go off together, and I can check out these Helping Hands, or whatever they're called. Be a bit of a trial for when you leave, Jenny."

Mike grinned. "There, it's settled. Nice to be considered one of the young ones," he joked. He was hoping Jenny would take her godmother's advice and agree to take the trip with him. Turning back to Jenny, he added more seriously. "Let me know when you hear about your cousin, Jenny, and we can arrange something. It would round off your Native American background for you."

*

"So, what do you think?" Jenny looked across to where Maddy was sitting by the window. "Is there any other way we can find her from the address I have?"

"If we can't find her in the telephone directory there's no sense to keep searching it,' she replied, 'but what about people search? It doesn't cost much, and you should be able to find her there. It'll even tell you if she's died."

"Really? Wow, what a great service! I'll check it out now." Rising, Jenny made her way to the office to fire up the computer. "Wish I'd known about this last night," she muttered, as she waited for it to start. "Would have saved some time."

In a few minutes she had found a Rhoda Miller of around the right age living in Medford. She leant back in her chair and breathed a sigh of relief. That was a start. Checking the site, it became clear there was a charge to retrieve further information, so Jenny quickly provided her credit card details and closed the system down again.

"Well, she's still in Medford. She must have moved in the last few years. I should have a report back later today, which will tell me how to reach her now."

*

Two days later Jenny looked up from the computer. "Yes!"

"Did you say something, dear?" Maddy's voice came from the next room.

Jenny left her seat and hurried through.

"I've found Cousin Rhoda. She's still in Medford, but it looks as if she's moved to some sort of retirement home, or nursing home." Her voice faltered. "Do you think that means…?"

"Doesn't mean anything. Some people move from their homes because they can't function alone anymore, but some do it to have the company, or because they need help with getting around. Why don't you call? You'll soon find out if she can be of any help."

"I'll do it in a little while. Might make a coffee first. Would you like one?"

"Sounds like delaying tactics to me. Pick up the phone and get it over with," Maddy advised.

Thirty

The mist was beginning to lift to reveal a wide expanse of grass on either side of the road. The Umpqua River flowed gently in the distance on the left, while the fields on the right, which Jenny would have called paddocks back home, seemed empty, as if waiting to be populated. The pickup slowed to a halt.

"Look over there!" Mike pointed. At first Jenny thought there was nothing to see then, following Mike's pointing finger, she looked through the rising mist to see what appeared to be branches rising through the long grass.

"What...?"

"Watch," Mike said, and sure enough, in a few moments one of the branches rose to reveal itself as antlers on the head of a large beast.

"It's magnificent! I've never seen a large deer like that before."

"Elk," Mike corrected. "Keep watching." As the mist cleared, other animals arose till there was a veritable herd of them ambling around looking quite at home. "It's a reserve," Mike explained. "They sometimes wander across the road. There are signs." He waved his arm in the general direction of the highway. "Worth the early start?"

"Absolutely!" Jenny gazed at the unfolding sight, then almost as soon as they had appeared, the beasts vanished into the distance. She let out a breath she hadn't been aware she was holding. Mike's hand found hers, and she gripped his fingers tightly. They sat in silence for a few moments, then Mike drew his hand away and patted the back of Jenny's.

"We'd best get a move on if you want to make Medford by

lunchtime," he reminded her. "We'll have a coffee stop in around an hour or so. Okay with you?"

"Great!" Jenny was feeling wide awake, but a coffee stop sounded good. Her stomach was beginning to turn summersaults at the prospect of the meeting ahead of her in Medford. Although Maddy had warned her not to get her hopes up, Jenny couldn't control her excitement. She felt sure Cousin Rhoda would provide all the answers she needed to put her uncertainties to rest. Then she could get on with the rest of her life. She sighed and Mike looked over.

"Not still tired are you?"

"Not a bit. Where will we stop? Shall I get out the map?"

Mike laughed. "No need. Been up this way a few times. There's a neat spot further on called Grants Pass. I think you'll be surprised." He stopped talking and turned up the radio. They travelled along comfortably, each lost in thought and occasionally singing companionably along to the music.

It was close to two hours later when Jenny spotted the sign welcoming them to Grants Pass. "What's so special about this place? Looks pretty sleepy to me."

"Just you wait." Mike couldn't hide his obvious anticipation as he found a parking spot in the main street. "Now what do you see?" he asked.

Jenny looked around at the quiet main street, the shoppers standing in groups or walking along, the obvious tourists with cameras. Wait, what were the group with cameras laughing at, and focusing their cameras on? "Is that a bear? In the main street? But it... it's blue." Jenny turned to Mike in surprise as she realized the bear couldn't possibly be real, given its brightly colored appearance.

Mike was laughing. "Told you you'd be surprised. They're made of fiberglass," he said. "Happens every year. It's called Bear Fest. Want to have a look around before coffee?"

"Yes please!" Jenny hopped down from the pickup and waited for Mike to join her. She made no demur when he took her hand and led her across the road to inspect the first of the bears. By the time they'd taken in the whole street, they were both laughing. "I can't believe it," she said at last. "It's amazing. How...Why...?"

"It's a celebration of the black bear and a bit of a fundraiser. They're on display all summer, painted by local artists."

"There seem to be around three or four base shapes."

"Right. They start off plain, then they're decorated to end up like this." Mike waved to the many wildly-colored shapes lining the street. "Ready for coffee now?"

Jenny felt Mike's hand tighten in hers. It was comforting, she realized. "Sure." She was becoming more Americanized every day she reflected, and wondered if, when she returned home, she'd revert to her usual way of speaking.

They lingered over coffee, enjoying the leafy outlook over the Rogue River, which abounded with watersports. When they'd been subjected to the roar of several jet skis, Mike looked at his watch and suggested it might be time to move on. "If you want to reach Medford before the old dears have their afternoon nap, that is."

Jenny gave him a playful push to hide her inner turmoil at the mention of Medford again. "I hope this is a good idea," she worried.

"What did she say when you rang?"

"I didn't actually speak to Cousin Rhoda. She was asleep or something, unavailable was what the Nursing Director said. She did say Rhoda had good and bad days, and if I caught her on one of her bad ones, she mightn't make much sense."

Mike squeezed her hand. "Then let's hope this is one of her good ones, shall we?" He gave her a wide smile which reassured her and helped settle the butterflies.

"Here we are." Mike stopped in the driveway, and stepping out, Jenny looked around. The large red-brick building seemed to have been built some time ago, as evidenced by the well-established grounds complete with rolling lawns. Jenny could see gardeners hard at work weeding and replanting. It looked more like a stately home than a nursing home. "Must be well heeled," Mike observed, echoing Jenny's thoughts. "Do you want me to come in with you?"

"No, better do this on my own." Jenny drew a deep breath and turned towards the doorway. She stood staring at the large black door for a few seconds then, giving herself a shake, rang the doorbell.

A few minutes later she was standing in the entrance hall talking with the Nursing Director, who was not encouraging. "Rhoda is in her own little world today," she said, taking Jenny's arm to lead her through a doorway. "She's in here with some of our other guests."

Jenny looked around a spacious room, with French windows along the right hand side overlooking the gardens. A large television screen hung on the wall at one end, and around the edges was an unmatched selection of armchairs occupied by a mixture of old people, so frail they managed to make Maddy look almost like a teenager. They were in various stages of decay, and appeared to be paying no attention to the soap opera playing out on the television screen. Jenny felt her spirits drop and began to wonder if she was indeed wasting her time here.

"That's your cousin over there," the Director pointed to the far corner, where a large green velvet recliner was occupied by an equally large woman wearing an incongruous selection of layers. "Be patient with her."

Jenny took a deep breath and slowly made her way over to the woman she'd come to meet. She crouched down beside her.

"Hello," she ventured, and was greeted by a blank stare, then, "Thea, is that you? Why haven't you visited me before, you naughty girl?"

"I'm Thea's daughter. I'm here to ask you about Thea." Jenny made an attempt to sound accepting, to behave as if Rhoda was making sense, but she was feeling very awkward. She began to sense the others around her were staring at her back and listening to every word.

"Thea's dead." Rhoda spoke bluntly and sounded so on the ball that Jenny thought she might be getting somewhere.

"Yes," she agreed, "and I'm her daughter. Jane took me to Australia. I'm back now. I wanted to hear how it all came about." She stopped as she noticed Rhoda's eyes glaze over then close.

"I'm afraid that's all you'll get from her today." Jenny felt a hand on her shoulder. One of the nursing staff helped her rise and led her out of the room. Jenny swallowed hard to prevent herself from bursting into tears. She'd had such hopes for this visit and to end like this. It was clear to her now Cousin Rhoda was going to be no help at all. She'd just have to make do with what she already knew, unsatisfactory as it was.

As she stumbled out of the building, Mike raced forward to catch her in his arms. At the feel of his strong arms around her shoulders, Jenny could contain herself no longer. The tears began to trickle down her cheeks.

"No good, then?" Mike put his hand under her chin to look into her face. Jenny had no words. She shook her head and buried her face in his shoulder, her own shoulders heaving at the release of tension. Mike said no more, but led Jenny to the vehicle, helped her into the passenger seat, and drove off. It was some time before either of them spoke.

"I'm sorry." Jenny wiped her eyes and essayed a smile, turning to meet Mike's eyes. "It just got to me. All those old people, probably with no idea where they are, and a television blaring away. It was weird." She tried to laugh but it came out more like a wail.

"And Rhoda?" Mike asked.

"She was just like the others. For a moment I thought I was getting through to her, but no, it was like a flash of something from the past, then it was gone again."

Mike reached his hand over to cover hers. "I don't think you're quite in the mood for museum visiting right now. How about a more relaxing stop? It's practically the same distance to Crater Lake. It's the deepest blue you've ever seen. I guarantee it'll make you feel better."

Jenny relaxed for the first time since entering the nursing home. It felt good to be cosseted, something she'd become used to doing without over the years. "Sounds good to me." She put her head back and closed her eyes, feeling the sun warm her eyelids as it shone through the window.

She must have dozed off, because suddenly she was conscious of a shadow on her face, and opening her eyes she could see they were driving through forest. "Where are we?" she pushed herself upright and looked from side to side.

"Just entered the National Park. We'll be at the rim soon, and you'll see the lake."

"What's so special about it?" Jenny began to ask, then exclaimed, "There's snow at the side of the road. How can that be? It's summer."

"We're pretty high here, and it doesn't melt completely. Look!" Mike pointed out the window to where the lake lay down below, and sure enough it was the deepest blue water Jenny had seen.

"What makes it so blue?" she asked in wonder, her earlier disappointment all but forgotten.

"Its depth. It's the deepest lake in the United States." Then, changing the subject Mike asked, "Feel like a late lunch? We can have it at the lodge. There's a great balcony looking right over the lake."

"You've been here before?" Jenny asked, then felt guilty, realizing that, on previous occasions, he would have been accompanied by his wife.

*

"I could stay here forever!" They'd finished a late lunch of cob salad washed down with a couple of glasses of Budweiser, and Jenny was feeling very relaxed. She stretched her arms above her head and lay back in the rustic rocker, one of a line of chairs along the edge of the veranda. "This view is stupendous," she said. "You were right." Jenny turned to meet Mike's eyes. She reached over and took his hand, aware this was the first time she had made this move. Feeling his fingers tighten in hers, she felt a sense of utter contentment. The problems and uncertainties of the past few weeks had disappeared. She was content in the here and now.

Appearing to sense her mood, Mike leant towards her. "We have accommodation booked at the Holiday Inn in Klamath Falls." He hesitated. "If we're to make it there, we need to be off soon. Or…"

Jenny sat up with a start. "Could we stay here?" Then she fell back again. "Oh, I expect a place like this is fully booked this time of year."

"Probably, but there's no harm in asking." Jenny lay back and closed her eyes, enjoying the high mountain air and the feel of the sunlight on her face. Cousin Rhoda had been a disappointment, but she already knew quite a bit about her birth parents, and she couldn't feel upset in a gorgeous spot like this. A niggling voice in her head was also telling her the company had something to do with her feelings, but she managed to suppress it.

"Look what I have!" Mike was back dangling two keys in his hand. "They had a sudden cancellation, just as I was standing there. Must have been meant," he joked. The phrase struck Jenny speechless. Ellen's words came back to her.

Finally she found voice enough to reply, "Great. Let's get our stuff out of the car, shall we?"

"Then a walk before dinner. I've booked us into the dining room for eight, by the way. Okay by you?"

"Very okay." Jenny had peeked into the dining room when they arrived, and was impressed by the stone walls and wooden rafters. It was, she thought, like something out of a fairy tale or a movie, at least; a real hunting lodge complete with large, stone fireplace. It was the perfect spot to fit in with her mood. This whole place seemed like a place out of time; a place where she could forget everything and enjoy being with Mike, who was proving to be the perfect companion. Time enough to worry about tomorrow when tomorrow actually arrived.

*

They lingered over dinner, the candlelight on the table throwing shadows over their faces as they talked. They talked and talked. It was as if a tap had been turned on for both of them. They found so much to say. Finally Jenny said. "I thought you were so taciturn, but now…"

"Never had any reason to say much till now," Mike replied. "I'm as surprised as you are. I don't usually go on like this, but you're a comfortable person to be with."

"Not the virago you expected, eh?"

"Far from it. I haven't felt this way since… since Mary." Mike stopped as if wondering whether he'd said too much, but Jenny smiled at him over the candle in the middle of the table.

"I'm glad. I'd hate to think it was all one-sided." Their hands were clasped together on the table by now, and Jenny was wondering what was going to come next, when abruptly Mike broke contact.

"Better make tracks if we're to have an early start tomorrow." He called for the waiter and signed the bill. "Breakfast here tomorrow?" he raised his eyebrows in enquiry to Jenny.

"Yes," she said, trying to work out if she'd been too forward. She'd thought she'd been following his lead, that she'd judged the moment. Evidently not.

"Eight o'clock then. Can you book us in?" This to the waiter, who was still hovering.

They made their way up the stairs to their rooms, one on either side of a narrow passageway. Taking her by the shoulders, Mike placed a brief kiss on Jenny's forehead. "Sleep well."

Jenny opened her door to find a strong wind had blown up outside, and her open window was rattling in its frame. "Can you…?" she turned to Mike, who was opening his own door.

"Sure thing." He let his door swing to, and crossing into Jenny's, went straight to the window. It was a small room, looking out onto the lake, and somehow, in Mike's attempt to close the window, Jenny found herself caught between him and the bed, which was really too large for the size of the room.

"That's it!" he said with satisfaction, turning round only to stagger against a chair, and taking Jenny with him, fall onto the bed. The kissing just happened naturally, as natural as the hands removing each other's clothing, as natural as two warm bodies blissfully locked together and hidden away in the most idyllic place; as natural as picking up a sand dollar. It was magical.

*

It was some time later, and the moon was shining through the still open window, when Jenny looked up at the face above hers. It bore the creases of age, and at this distance, she could see the white hairs of Mike's beard beginning to reach up into his sideburns, and then to the hair on his head. The intimacy of the moment surprised her. It was a long time since she'd been this close to a man. He had awakened feelings she'd thought gone forever. "Was this meant too?" she asked dreamily.

Jenny was awake, but lay for a time with her eyes closed. She felt… it was hard to describe, replete came nearest. The last hour had been as momentous as it had been unexpected. She turned, opened her eyes, and looked at the face on the pillow beside her, a shiver of delight running down her spine. It had been so long since… At that moment Mike's eyes opened too.

"Hi there." He smiled and drew Jenny into his arms. "This feels good." She relaxed against him, and he kissed her hair. Her eyes closed again as she drifted into slumber.

*

"Are you awake?" It was almost a whisper. Jenny opened her eyes and stretched languorously. She turned her head. Mike was at the foot of the bed, struggling into his pants. She stifled a chuckle at the picture he made, with the morning sunlight behind his red hair, giving it the effect of a halo. Pushing herself up into a seating position, Jenny smiled at the memory of the previous night. "Hmm," she said. "Looks like you're ready to leave?"

"I thought…" Mike came over to the side of the bed, and sitting down, took Jenny's face in his hands and kissed her on the lips. "You don't regret…?"

"Of course not." She kissed him back and ruffled his hair. "I didn't expect…"

"Nor did I." He smiled. "I think you may have said something about it being meant to happen."

"I did? Doesn't sound like me. I'm afraid I was dreadfully out of practice."

"I didn't notice." They both laughed. "I was going to fetch us some coffee."

"Wait, I'll get up." Jenny was about to rise when she realized she was naked under the covers. Last night had been one thing, but this morning in the cold light of day was another. Seeming to understand her dilemma, Mike drew back.

"Guess I'll take myself off, have a shower and change," he muttered, backing out of the room.

Left to herself, Jenny breathed a sigh. Last night had been as wonderful as it had been unexpected, but where to now? As she showered she felt her whole body glowing, though whether from the night's exertions or the mountain air, she couldn't be sure. It had been so long, her body was telling her. Then she brought herself up with a start. What was she thinking? She had a life back in Australia. This could only be a brief interlude. She should enjoy it while she could, but she was sure she wasn't the only one who was having second thoughts. Last night had happened, and it had been good, but that was all. It couldn't happen again.

*

Mike was whistling as he stood in the shower. This was a turn up for the books. Never, in his wildest dreams, had he imagined he and Jenny would find themselves in bed together on this trip. Well, to be accurate that wasn't quite true. Maybe in his wildest dreams he *had* imagined such a turn of events, but certainly not the way it had happened. His questions regarding Jenny's feelings had been answered, and without any awkward ones being asked. It had all happened so quickly. His fears she would reject him were unfounded.

With a spring in his step he beat a tattoo on Jenny's door. "Ready for breakfast?" There was no reply. Cautiously he tried the door and, finding it unlocked, pushed it gently. "Can I come in?" He entered, only to see Jenny standing at the window fully dressed. She was gazing out at the lake as if it held the answer to all her problems. "Breakfast?" he repeated, hesitating in the doorway.

Jenny turned awkwardly. "Oh." She appeared surprised to see him. This wasn't the reception he'd expected. He felt his good humor drain away, wondering what he'd done wrong. Was she regretting their night together? Women, he'd never understand them. This trip hadn't panned out the way he'd planned. Damn that window! Things had been going well till he tried to close it, and look what had happened. He'd planned to take things slowly, give himself time to work out what she felt. Less chance of being hurt then. He'd lost one woman. Didn't want to become attached to Jenny then lose her too.

He shook his head to dismiss the negative thoughts, and took a deep breath. "I wondered if you were ready for breakfast?" Remaining in the doorway unsure whether to enter, he leaned his hand on the doorpost and smiled.

As if coming back from a far place, Jenny's face brightened, and she smiled too as she walked towards him. "Sure thing."

They had finished breakfast, and as Mike looked across the table, Jenny wiped her mouth with her napkin. She laid it down carefully then looked up to meet his eyes. "I'm a bit new to all this."

He knew exactly what she meant. He felt the same way. "Yeah, last night…" Mike paused, unsure what to say next. He looked across the table at Jenny's wide violet eyes looking back at him and tried again. "I meant to take things slowly, get to know each other a bit, you know." God, this was hard. He wished she'd help him a bit. He decided to jump in feet first. He cleared his throat and laid both hands on the table. "Since Mary... there hasn't... I never expected." Shit, he sounded like a retard.

To his surprise, Jenny laid one of her hands over his. "I know. It took me by surprise too. It was too soon." She nodded as if to herself. "I'm not saying I wish it hadn't happened. Just..." she paused, as if unsure what to say next. Mike took the hand on his and began to slide his fingers up and down hers, keeping his eyes downcast, unable to meet Jenny's.

"Let's go back to where we were at during dinner and take it from there." He grasped her hand tightly and raised his eyes. "What do you say?" He heard a sigh and saw relief in Jenny's eyes.

"I'd like that," she breathed, smiling.

*

It was almost ten by the time they loaded the pickup ready to set off for the museum. As they entered the outskirts of Klamath Falls, Jenny looked around with interest. She was feeling much more relaxed now they'd dealt with the awkwardness engendered by the previous night, and was looking forward to seeing the Native American artifacts. She was still trying to come to grips with her newly discovered heritage. It felt as if it all belonged to someone else, a character in a book she was reading. She was still considering this when Mike's voice sounded in her ear.

"Almost there!"

Jenny turned and looked into his eyes. A mistake. She caught a glimpse of a yearning look before he quickly looked away.

"It's just around this corner." His eyes were now firmly glued on the road ahead. She followed his direction and saw they were turning into the car park of a large building.

"Is this it?" Jenny knew she sounded inane, but she felt desperate to say something to dispel the tension which had suddenly started to build up.

"Sure is." For a moment Jenny wished her companion wasn't a man of such few words, then she realized this was one of the things she liked about him. He didn't beat around the bush. If he had something to say, he said it, if not, he didn't. This is what set him apart from many of the men she'd worked with over the years, men who'd talked just for the sake of hearing their own voices. Mike was a relaxing companion. He soothed her, she thought, surprised at the word which came to mind. She'd been living her life at such a fast pace for so many years, it was nice to slow down. Maybe this was what this whole trip had been about, she mused.

As she stepped down to the bitumen, the heat of the sun assailed her, and Jenny grabbed her hat from behind the seat. "Wow. This is almost like home. Wasn't this hot in Seal Rock."

"We're further inland here. Makes quite a difference, doesn't it? It'll be cooler inside. Let's get out of the heat." Mike grabbed her hand and started off towards the entrance at a fast pace.

Jenny was fascinated as they wandered around the exhibits. "To think these were my ancestors," she exclaimed on more than one occasion and to Mike's obvious amusement. "Does anyone still make these things?" she finally asked, standing in front of one large glass case of cedar bowls and baskets made from bark and plant fibers.

"I'm pretty sure they do, but Ellen would be the person to ask."

"Of course." Jenny couldn't imagine her new cousin being engaged in basket making herself, but she'd surely know about any current practices.

"For the tourist trade, I expect," Mike continued, as they moved around the exhibits.

"Have we done it?" he asked as they reached the entrance again. "If we leave now we can have lunch on the way back and be home at a decent time. Maddy's expecting you for dinner, isn't she?"

"Yes." Jenny was distracted, still thinking of the women whose days had been spent cooking and weaving. Their lives had been so different from hers. They had been part of a community, dependent on each other. Her life had been more solitary, though full. She hadn't allowed herself time for any leisure pursuits other than reading and a little gardening. This needed to change, she decided. When she got back… She hesitated and stole a look at Mike. She didn't want to think of her return to Australia just yet. Anything could happen before then. For perhaps the first time in her life she was prepared to go with the flow, as her son would say.

Thirty-one

"Hello again." Ellen looked at the tall elegant woman who had answered the door. She stood erect, even though she held firmly to a walking stick which was taking most of her weight. "Is Jenny around?"

"Ellen, come away in. They've gone down to Klamath Falls, to the museum. Should be back tonight. But it's good to see you again." The two women were the same height and eyed each other with interest. Ellen followed Maddy inside, and accepted the offer of coffee.

"Wow, I love what you've done to this place," she said looking around, her eyes taking in the high beams, the walls covered in artifacts, and the brightly covered rugs and cushions. "You've been here a while, haven't you?"

There was no immediate reply. Maddy had been studying Ellen's face. "You have a look of him, you know, your uncle."

Ellen found herself fingering her face. "Uncle Jed?" she asked, the words sitting awkwardly on her tongue. Then, collecting herself she began to apologies. "I'm sorry to arrive unannounced. It's not something I usually do, but I was visiting my brother in Yachats and it seemed foolish to drive back down when I wanted to talk to Jenny. I should have called first."

"Don't be silly. I'm delighted you called in. Gives us a chance to get to know each other, though your parents might not be so pleased you're here."

"I gave up trying to please them long ago." Ellen sighed, and shrugged. "Expectations, you know what it's like." As she spoke, she realized Maddy probably did know. She was a woman who had remained single in an era where few did. As if reading her mind Maddy spoke.

"It was different in my day. The war put paid to the hopes of a lot of women. Some found other partners," she sighed, "but there was only one for me. But you didn't come to hear my sad story. You wanted to speak with Jenny?" Maddy raised her eyebrows as she put down a mug of coffee and levered herself into a chair.

"Oh, sorry. I could have helped…" Ellen made an attempt to get up, but the coffee was already in front of her so she dropped into her seat again and took a long sip.

"Not to worry. I'm adjusting to this thing." Maddy waved her stick in the air. "I'll need to become self-sufficient again when Jenny leaves. Though the way things are going…" She stopped as if wondering if she'd said too much.

Ignoring Maddy's words Ellen began. "Well, I spoke to Mom again and…" Seeing the hope arise in Maddy's face, she was quick to dispel it. "No, she won't see Jenny again. Not yet anyway. But I did manage to get her to rack her brains for someone who might have known Jenny's parents, my uncle, you know."

"And..?"

"She came up with the name of a couple who'd been close friends of Uncle Jed and Thea. It seems they've lived in Florence all this time but, of course, our family have had nothing to do with them. They were all at school together, Bill and Ann Huggins."

"And you believe they might be able to help Jenny?"

"It's worth a try, don't you think? They may be able to fill in some of the blanks. Then Jenny can go home with a clear mind." As she said it, Ellen wondered if filling in the blanks about her birth parents would indeed satisfy Jenny. When Maddy didn't answer immediately, she asked cautiously, "What about this Mike guy? Is there anything happening between him and Jenny?"

"Now there your guess is as good as mine." Ellen breathed a sigh of relief that Maddy hadn't told her it was none of her business. "He's a good man. Lost one woman and I think he's wary of showing his feelings or getting too involved. My guess is he's afraid of his feelings for Jenny. As for her, she's been on her own for so long I don't know if she'd recognize her feelings if they came out and bit her on the ass. They're circling around each other like two cats in heat." She chortled. "That's my guess. But that's just an old woman talking."

"Not so old and plenty wise." Ellen was enjoying her talk with Maddy, realizing she and the older woman had more in common than she'd expected.

"Now tell me about you, my dear. I know you have your bookshop. You've never married?"

"No." Ellen hesitated, then feeling comfortable in the company of this wise old woman who was looking at her sagely over the rim of her coffee cup, decided here was someone in whom she could confide. "There was someone." The words stuck in her throat. She hadn't spoken about this to anyone, not for a long time.

"But it didn't…?"

"He was married." Stated baldly like that it sounded hard, and didn't remotely encapsulate the turmoil of emotions she had experienced. "I couldn't be responsible for taking someone's husband, not after I'd met her. She came into the shop, you see," she explained, "with her little boy. After that I finished with him. They moved away some time later," she added.

"And there hasn't been anyone since?"

"I've dated, if that's what you mean, but no one to match up. There was someone… I thought maybe… but it didn't come to anything. I guess it's why I've been hoping this thing with Mike works out for Jenny."

"You think if she can find love a second time, there may be hope for you too?"

"Wow, you don't pull any punches, do you?" Ellen couldn't help but feel admiration for the woman sitting opposite her. "I'd never really thought of it like that. You may be right. Did you long to find someone else all of these years?"

"No. I've been happy here, and will be as long as I'm spared." A shadow passed over her face. "As long as I can manage by myself." She looked around at the familiar surroundings. "I know Jenny won't be here for much longer." There was a long pause then Maddy spoke again. "When I go it'll all be hers."

"Don't talk like that. There's a lot of life in you yet."

"Yes." Maddy seemed to draw herself up. "But this last episode put the wind up me. I found I'm not as self-sufficient as I'd thought." She seemed about to say something else, but drank her coffee instead.

Ellen hesitated before speaking and when she did it was tentatively. "I wonder…"

"Mmm?"

"Tell me if I'm speaking out of turn, but how would you feel…" She hesitated again and swallowed, hoping Maddy wouldn't throw her out for making the suggestion. "There's a young girl in our community. She's doing an internship at the Marine Research Station in Newport next semester. I know she's looking for somewhere to stay." Ellen hesitated again. "How would you feel about a boarder?" she blurted out.

"A boarder?" Maddy repeated the word as if savoring it. "I've been many things in my life, but I've never been a landlady." She was silent for a few minutes as if digesting the idea, then she spoke slowly. "Not a boarder. Sounds too formal, too mercenary for me to be a landlady. But I like the idea of having a young person around the place. It would brighten things up. I've always liked my own company, but I've enjoyed having Jenny here. I'd have to meet this girl first, of course, see if we could rub along together. It might work."

"Great," Ellen sighed with relief. "Thanks for the coffee. It's been so good to see you again. I'd better be off now. Can you ask Jenny to ring me?" She rose and gathered her belongings.

"Sure will. They should be back later today. I'll have her call you right away. She'll be keen to contact this couple. Huggins, you said? I don't recall them, but then they were a bit younger than me." She rose and made her way to the door, walking slowly and leaning heavily on her stick. As they stood in the doorway Ellen's ears were assailed by the sound of the birds which circled the many birdhouses in the yard.

"I see you have your feathered friends up here," she joked.

"They're good company. Better than some people," Maddy laughed. "They don't quarrel or talk back and they don't want to unload their problems all the time. Be sure to let me know about the young girl you mentioned," Maddy shouted as Ellen opened her car door, then she turned back into the house.

*

It was close to six o'clock when the pickup drew into Maddy's yard. She looked out expecting to see the two of them alight, and was surprised to see only Jenny step down though she did note the two heads were pretty close before that happened.

I'm just a nosey old woman, like the nosey neighbors we had when I was young, she chastised herself, remembering how the curtain of the house next door had moved whenever she and the current boyfriend arrived home from a date. Easing herself out of the chair by the window where she'd been waiting, she picked up her stick and hobbled to the door. Jenny was there before her and practically catapulted into her arms.

"I'm back!" was her breathless greeting.

"So I see." Maddy was more restrained, but had to admit she was glad to see her goddaughter return. She managed to control her impatience till they were both sitting down and had finished their meal before asking, "Well, how did it go?" and seeing Jenny blush added, "Did you meet Rhoda?"

Jenny finished her last mouthful and laid down her knife and fork. "Yee...es," she replied slowly. "But it wasn't any good. She's really beyond it, and I couldn't get any sense out of her. So I guess that's it." She sighed and putting her elbows on the table cupped her chin in her hands.

"There may be another avenue," she said. "Ellen was here today."

"Ellen? But how? Why?"

"I'm coming to that." Maddy was enjoying Jenny's bewilderment. "She'd been talking to her mother."

"Is she coming round? Has she agreed to meet me again? Does she have more information?" Jenny's eyes brightened.

"No, she's still obdurate, but she's given Ellen the name of a couple who knew Thea and Jed."

"Where do they live?" Jenny's voice held a note of excitement.

"Right there in Florence." Maddy paused to let it sink in.

"You mean they've been there all along and we never knew about them?"

"How could we?" Maddy was delighted Jenny had included her in the 'we'. "Ellen's parents were the only ones who knew of their existence and they'd decided not to talk to you. They put the past behind them and haven't seen this couple, Bill and Ann Huggins, since Jed's death. That's a long time."

"My whole life," Jenny agreed. "You realize what this means?"

"I think I do. You finally may get to meet people who were close to Thea and Jed; who knew them as a couple."

"And who might be able to tell me why my grandparents were so against the match," Jenny finished. "Oh, it would be good. They might even be able to help explain the dates thing I've been puzzling about. Did Ellen have a number for them?"

"Oh, dear, I didn't ask. But I don't think so, or she'd have left it with me. Though she did ask you to call her."

"I'll do it now." Jenny rose and went into her room.

Maddy was a tad disappointed Jenny had left the room to make her call, but realized there were some things for which her goddaughter wanted privacy. She was a pretty private person herself, and had to respect the same trait in others, frustrating though it might be at times.

Jenny was all smiles when she emerged some time later. "All set."

"You mean?"

"Yes." Jenny beamed. "Ellen did have the number. She'd checked it out for me. I called and spoke with Bill. He sounds pretty together and agreed to meet with me tomorrow afternoon. I'm to go to their place. They live up on the bluff, above the town," she explained.

"This calls for a glass, I think." Maddy looked towards the drinks tray and made to rise.

"I'll get them." Jenny laughed.

It wasn't till they were sitting cozily side by side, drinks in hand, that Maddy dared to broach the subject which had been on her mind since Jenny's return.

"And how was the museum... and Mike?" she asked at last.

Jenny blushed again, causing Maddy to wonder just what the pair had been up to.

"The museum was fabulous. Such a wonderful collection of artifacts. Made me realize you have a number of Native American pieces here." She looked around the walls and patted the woven cushion behind her. "I didn't know before. I can appreciate them more now I have an inkling of the work which went into producing them."

Maddy was conscious that despite, or maybe because of the blush, Jenny had neatly evaded the second part of her question. She decided to try again with a different tack. "Did you stay overnight at Klamath Falls? It's not the prettiest of places."

"No." Jenny was managing to avoid making eye contact with Maddy, making her wonder exactly what had happened. "We went up to Crater Lake. It was so beautiful," she raptured. "The color, the air. I've never seen such a deep blue. And it was so peaceful looking down into the crater with the wildflowers all around us. I could have stayed there forever."

"So did you stay there? I would have thought it would be booked out at this time of year."

"Yes to both. They were booked out, but had a cancellation so we were able to have two rooms." Jenny stopped there and remained tight-lipped.

Maddy decided not to pursue it any further. *I'm not going to get any more out of her tonight, but I wonder... Crater Lake can be a very romantic spot and it wouldn't surprise me... Oh, there I go again. It's really none of my business what they got up to. They're two consenting adults. It's just that I'd like to see Jenny and Mike with some happiness in their lives and I think they suit each other very well. Oh well, time will tell, or maybe Jenny will one of these days.* She sighed.

"You sound tired. How about I help you to bed?" Jenny rose.

"I can manage," Maddy began to rise herself, then fell back into the chair. "Oh, dear, some help would be good. I'm more tired than I thought. I did manage all right when you were gone."

"But I bet you went to bed earlier and didn't have a late drink."

Maddy smiled. "You're right there. Was tucked up in bed with my hot chocolate and a book by half-eight. And nothing wrong with that, either.'

"That's for sure," Jenny responded. "It's something I used to do back home as a special treat."

*

Jenny may have managed to avoid answering Maddy's questions about

Mike but, now her godmother had gone to bed, she was left alone with her thoughts and she could no longer deny Mike played a large part in them. *How did she feel? Was she willing to risk being hurt at this late stage of her life? Did Mike share her feelings?* These were all questions she needed to ask herself, but there were no clear answers. This was an unexpected turn of events, something she hadn't anticipated when she arrived in this country. Meeting Mike had taken her completely by surprise, and so had the feelings she was now experiencing. Feelings she thought she had left far behind her. She'd never expected to have them resurrected at this stage of her life. But she wasn't old, she reminded herself. In fact, she smiled, she'd felt extremely youthful there at Crater Lake. She hugged herself at the memory. Even if nothing eventuated, she had that memory.

Thirty-two

The house was in a part of Florence Jenny hadn't visited before. It was high on a bluff with views of the angry ocean, and seemed to be a relatively new development. The houses all had a similarity which made her think of the old song about little boxes. But these homes were far from being little boxes. Judging by the size of the lots, the extensive landscaping, and the types of cars sitting in the driveways, it was an exclusive neighborhood. This friend of Jed's had done well for himself.

She closed the car door and found herself clenching her hands as she began to walk up the path. Bill had sounded friendly on the phone, but you never could tell how people would react when they were asked about their youth, especially if their youth had been sixty years earlier. As Jenny made her way to the door, she noted the well-kept garden and lawn. Either Bill Huggins was a remarkably fit eighty year old, or he had an excellent gardener. She hesitated a moment, then taking her courage in both hands, rang the bell, to have her ears assaulted with the sound of Dixie.

Momentarily taken aback, Jenny was surprised when the door was opened by a short plump white haired woman whose face immediately turned ashen.

"Thea!" she uttered, then seemed to recollect herself. "Of course it can't be, but just for a moment, you reminded me of someone, someone I knew a long time ago." She gave Jenny a closer look. "Who *are* you?"

"Jenny Sullivan. I called. I spoke with Bill and he…"

Suddenly there was a booming voice from the inside of the house. "Is that the Australian girl who wants to talk about Jed? Invite her in, hon."

"Oh, of course." Seeming to remember her manners, the woman stood aside to allow Jenny to enter. "I'm Anne, Bill's wife. Sorry if I seemed unfriendly. It was such a shock to see you standing there, just as if… Come along in. We've been expecting you." She ushered Jenny into the lounge room.

Jenny looked around taking in the comfortable, well-worn and old-fashioned furniture, which seemed to fit the couple who were now standing in front of her smiling.

"Sit down, sit down. Can I fetch you some coffee?" Anne gestured to an armchair which Jenny took gratefully.

"Coffee would be good, thanks."

"Well now, what's your interest in Jed?" Taking the seat opposite her, Bill went straight to the point. Jenny, having hoped there would have been some small talk first, gulped and looked down in an attempt to gather her thoughts. This was all happening too quickly for her.

Anne, bustling back in, appeared to see her distress. "Let the girl get her breath back first, Bill," she admonished. "Coffee will be ready soon. Now, what brings you to Florence from Australia?"

More comfortable with this approach, Jenny embarked on the story of her godmother and her decision to visit.

"And she lives in Florence?"

"She grew up here and went to school with my mother. She moved up to Seal Rock quite some time ago. You may have known her at school." She looked over at Bill. "Madeline de Ruiz."

"The name rings a bell." It was Anne who spoke. "We were schoolmates too." She looked fondly at the large bearlike man. "Sixty-five years ago. We celebrated out sixtieth wedding anniversary last year. A lifetime together and no regrets."

"Yes, I've been putting up with her chatter for all that time." Bill pretended to groan but Jenny could see they rubbed together pretty well. "Now, to get back to Jed…"

"I'll just bring in the coffee." Anne rose while Jenny took a deep breath and began.

"I don't know how to put this, so here goes. I found some photos at my godmother's house. One thing led to another, and it seems… I've been told…" She stuttered. "I want to find out about Jed Williams because Maddy told me he's my father."

Jenny was amazed at her companion's reaction. He leapt up from his chair and gaped at her before calling out to his wife. "Annie, she says she's Jed's daughter. Come here!"

"What's all the fuss about?" Anne came into the room balancing a tray containing three mugs of coffee and a plate of pastries. "What did you say?" she asked, setting the tray down on the coffee table and turning to look first at her husband then at Jenny. "Jed's daughter? How? Oh my, so there was a baby, and she lived." She sat down on the sofa with a thump. "My dear, my very dear. Thea's daughter. You really exist."

"Thea, you knew her too?" Jenny couldn't believe it. Here she was in a room with two people who had known the couple who had given birth to her.

"Knew her? I should think we did. We did everything together. Thea and Jed, Bill and I. We were a foursome. I was Thea's alibi when she wanted to get away with Jed for a while. No wonder I thought I was seeing a ghost at the door. You look just like your mother, or as she would have looked if she'd lived." Her eyes misted over. "It was such a stupid accident, and we were never told what had happened to the baby. We thought it… you," she corrected herself, "had died with Thea. Oh my goodness. I think we need something stronger than coffee."

"Coffee's fine." Jenny was trying to come to grips with what she'd just heard. She accepted a cup and a pastry, setting both down on a side table and leaning forward elbows on her knees, hands clasped under her chin. "What can you tell me about them?"

"Where to start?" Anne took a sip of her own coffee and leant back, her eyes partly closed as if she was remembering when they had all been young. "Thea and I grew up together. We met at primary school and were buddies right from the start. Oh, the scrapes she led me into!" She laughed. "Then we started high school. What a time it was! You have to remember things were different then, very different to today or even to when you were that age. The term teenager didn't exist. We were still expected to behave like children, especially Thea. Her father," she sighed.

"I've heard he was very strict," Jenny said.

"That's putting it mildly. Thea was his baby, the apple of his eye. She could do no wrong. But it didn't mean she had the freedom to do as she liked – quite the opposite, in fact. But she managed to get around it." Her eyes lit up at the memory. "He approved of me, of my family. We all went to the same church," Anne said, as if that explained everything. "Her mother was a sweetie, but deferred to the old man to keep the peace. Thea used to tell them she was coming to my house to do her homework. It worked! We'd do the homework, then get up to other exploits. Of course those times made it easier when she met Jed. She knew they wouldn't approve, especially her dad. But her parents were accustomed to Thea coming over to my house on a regular basis, so it was easy for her to slip away from there to meet him."

Jenny's mouth fell open. "And they never knew?"

"She was almost caught out a couple of times, but no, they didn't find out till the week of the Homecoming Dance. It had been going on for a couple of years by then, and they were a definite item," she smiled in reminiscence. "Because we usually went around in a crowd, it wasn't always clear to outsiders who was with whom."

"Tell me about the dance." Jenny was caught up in the story by now; a tale of star-crossed lovers which sounded so romantic.

"I'll leave you two ladies to it." Bill rose.

"Oh…" Jenny started. She was torn. She wanted to hear about Thea and the prom, but she did so want more information about Jed. She didn't want Bill to disappear.

"Don't worry, dear." Anne seemed to understand Jenny's dilemma. "He'll be back. He still likes to have his smokes and knows I won't have them in the house. He'll just be going into the garden for a little time."

"Right." Jenny tried to hide her surprise the big man could be so browbeaten by Anne who was a dainty little woman.

"Now," Anne settled back into her chair. "You wanted to know about the dance."

"Yes, please."

"Well, it was all a long time ago, but it's as fresh in my mind as if it was yesterday. They do say that as we get older we find it easier to remember long past events than what happened yesterday."

"Mmm."Jenny hoped Anne wasn't going to ramble on. She wanted her to get to the point.

"We were all very excited," Anne recalled. "We'd been talking for weeks about what we were going to wear and who was going to partner whom. Thea was very cagey about her partner. Of course, Bill and I knew it was to be Jed, but we weren't sure if they were really going to attend together. Thea kept saying it was to be a surprise."

"What about Jed?"Jenny couldn't help asking.

"Oh, typical male. He just grinned and changed the subject or said maybe he wouldn't even go. Not go to the Homecoming Dance, can you imagine?"

Jenny tried without success to imagine what it must have been like back then. She couldn't remember a similar event when she was at school, though she knew that back home these days, kids, or their parents, spent a small fortune on the school formals.

Anne didn't wait for a reply, but continued, "I managed to pinhole Thea the day before, and she admitted she and Jed intended it to be the occasion where they showed everyone they were a couple. Evidently she'd spoken to her mother, who'd been reasonable about it. She wasn't sure about her dad, but thought her mother would be able to bring him round."

"But she didn't?"

"Well, we didn't know what had happened," Anne continued, as if Jenny hadn't spoken. "The four of us had planned to meet up at the door, and when they didn't arrive, we went in without them. We didn't want to miss a minute of it. It was a very special occasion," she explained. "All the girls wore long evening dresses with corsages, and the boys were dressed up in suits and ties." She sighed, clearly remembering.

Jenny found herself picturing the scene, couples of young excited people swirling around the floor, dressed up in all their finery. It must have been quite a spectacle. "Did Thea and Jed arrive?" she asked.

"Eventually. They were very late and somewhat disheveled, I recall. Had had a bit to drink too. Not that the rest of us were completely sober," she chuckled. "The boys had been slipping out the back of the hall for reinforcements. But it wasn't something girls did in those days. They were both in very high spirits, and Thea, in particular, acted as if she hadn't a care in the world. Of course I found out later."

"Yes?" Jenny was intrigued now, and completely engrossed in the story.

"Everything had been fine until her father saw her come downstairs. He forbade her to go; even locked her in her room, I believe."

"Then how…?"

"Oh, she was a wily one, was Thea. She climbed out the window. We later found out she'd been doing that regularly to see Jed on her own late at night, when it would have been too late to use me as an excuse. Bill and I had no idea. Of course after the dance they had to keep their meetings secret again, and I have to admit I helped her there, letting her pretend she was meeting me."

"And how long did it go on?" Jenny couldn't believe the couple had kept their meetings secret for long.

"Another two years," Anne replied. Jenny's jaw dropped. "Then she became pregnant. I often wondered whether they'd done it deliberately, as a way to force the old man to agree to their marriage. But it didn't work. He was as obdurate as ever."

"So they ran away," Jenny finished for her. "But why was he, my grandfather, so against Jed? That's what I haven't been able to understand."

"There was a history there. Your grandfather was an important man in the community, highly respected. He was an elder in the church and owned a large timber yard outside town. Old man Williams, Jed's father, worked for him. He was a bit of a rabble rouser, not unlike his son." She smiled in reminiscence. "When the war began in Europe, Jed's dad was very outspoken against it. Then when your grandfather began to change the focus of his business and set up a factory to help the war effort, Williams made a nuisance of himself, writing to the paper and speaking on street corners. He lost his job and, when America entered the war, became a conscientious objector. Jed supported his dad's views and used the school paper to promote them. I'm afraid your granddad viewed him as a chip off the old block and wanted his family, especially his daughter, the apple of his eye, to have nothing to do with what he saw as a renegade."

"So it wasn't because he was a Native American and didn't belong to the same clubs? It wasn't a class thing?"

"Well, Jed's heritage probably had something to do with it, too," Anne conceded. "But I think it was mainly his politics. I only know what I remember hearing my parents say," she apologized. "You know in those days, even before the McCarthy era, communist was a dirty word, and that's how old man Williams was painted. That's why your grandfather saw red when any of the Williams family was mentioned. He viewed them as evil incarnate." Anne stopped and shook her head as if she'd run out of words.

Jenny picked up her cup, but the coffee had gone cold. She looked at her feet, unsure what to say. This was more than she'd bargained for.

"How about I freshen your cup for you?" Anne pushed herself up to take Jenny's cup. Just then, Bill walked back in and, taking in Jenny's woebegone face, gave his wife a quick look.

"What have you been saying, woman. You've frightened her half to death."

"No, I'm all right," Jenny reassured him. "It's just been a bit of a shock, hearing about my grandparents."

"It's all water under the bridge now." Bill lowered his bulk into the chair again. "Well, are you going to fix up some fresh coffee or not?" he threw at his wife as she gathered up the cups. "Give me a chance to talk to Jenny here and tell her about her dad. Then we can both hear her story."

The word sounded strange to Jenny. Her dad was Steve, the dad she'd grown up with and loved. Jed was a stranger who'd lived and died before she was born. But this was the reason for her visit. She leaned forward in her seat, eager to hear what he had to say.

"Jed," the large man smiled. 'He was a character. Always up to something. Boy, we had some good times." He stopped and gazed off into the distance, then seemed to recollect himself. "He was a good-looking fellow, had no trouble in pulling the girls. Of course he was a football star. Yes," he sighed. "It seemed to all of us he'd been born under a lucky star. Everything fell into his lap. Then he met Thea, and they were the golden couple, though," he coughed, "it was all rumor. No one but Anne and I knew for sure. Everything went his way, until he started writing against the war, that is."

"What changed, then?"

"Wasn't a popular thing to do. No siree. He was outspoken about other things too. Got himself branded a communist just like his dad." Bill shook his head. "Foolish of him, but I guess he was following in his father's footsteps. They were always a close family, and he idolized his father. Your grandfather was part of the group in town which was most outspoken against the Williams family. Wanted to drive them out of town. I can well understand why Jed and Thea wanted their relationship kept secret. Jed's parents wouldn't have approved either. When she became pregnant," he shook his head again, "we didn't know what they were going to do. They wanted to get married, but Jed knew the old man would forbid it."

"Even though she was pregnant?" Jenny gasped. "I thought back then it was important for couples to do the right thing for the sake of the baby."

"Maybe your grandmother would have seen it that way, but she was completely under her husband's thumb. I think he wanted to pretend there was no baby," he reflected.

"Well, it seems there was!" Anne reappeared carrying fresh coffee. "What's he been telling you, dear?"

Jenny looked round at her voice. "Confirming all you said and more. Did Thea and Jed confide in you? Did they tell you they were going to run away to marry?"

The two looked at each other, then both spoke at once.

"We were…"

"It was…"

They laughed. "You tell her," Bill deferred to his wife.

"We weren't there," Anne explained. "We were on our honeymoon." The pair smiled at each other across the room. "Thea and Jed didn't come to our wedding. We guessed they were trying to work out what to do. It was close to her time, and Thea was very pregnant, hard to hide at that stage. Her sister was visiting from Australia too." She suddenly gave Jenny a strange look as if realizing she was from Australia. "When we got back we heard about the accident and that Thea and Jed were dead. We couldn't believe it at first. They'd both been so full of life. They were too young to die." She wiped a tear from her cheek.

"Her sister was Mum." Jenny looked down at her lap then raised her eyes to meet the two pairs of eyes regarding her curiously. "My mum was Thea's sister," she explained. "She took me back to Australia, and I grew up there. I never knew about Thea and Jed till recently. I found a letter. How did they explain me away?" she asked, "and what about the dates?"

"The dates?" Anne appeared mystified. "What do you mean the dates?"

"My birthday is August fifth, and that's way after the accident."

"Oh, my dear!" Anne rose to take Jenny's hands. "That would be your grandfather's doing."

"How…?" Jenny felt bewildered.

Bill took it upon himself to try to explain, "When we got back, it was all over, and Thea's sister was on her way back to Australia. We thought she'd left rather abruptly after the funeral. There was no talk of a baby, and those of us in the know assumed Thea and her baby had both died in the accident. As far as everyone here was concerned, there *was* no baby. Now you turn up out of the blue."

"So, did her sister take you back with her? Pretend you were hers? How did she manage it?" Bill's voice came from the other side of the room.

"It's a long story, but in essence, that's what happened, and I only learned the truth a few weeks ago. I'm still reeling from the shock, can't quite believe it."

"Have you met the Williamses? I know some of the family still lives in town." It was Anne's gentle voice.

Before Jenny could reply, Bill butted in, "I don't expect you'd be warmly received there."

"No, you're right, at least as far as the older generation is concerned. I think it's all too hurtful for them, even after all this time, but Ellen, my cousin," Jenny's face lit up, "she's a different story. We're friends," she stated simply.

Jenny finished her coffee and looked gratefully at her hosts. "Thank you so much." She walked over and shook each by the hand, only to be enveloped in warm hugs. "You've filled in some of the blanks for me. It's been good to meet people who knew Thea and Jed."

"Your parents," Anne corrected.

"My parents," Jenny stuttered on the words.

"Together forever," Bill muttered sadly.

"Pardon?" Jenny wasn't quite sure she had heard correctly.

"Their motto," he explained. "Thea and Jed. He even had it tattooed on his shoulder." Bill sighed. "Well, I guess they are, have been for the past sixty years. Have you visited their graves?" he enquired.

"Their graves?" Jenny asked in surprise. "I didn't think..." But on reflection she realized that of course they would have been buried in Florence. "Where...?"

"Well, you won't find them together." Anne's voice held years of bitterness. "Thea was buried in the family plot, by the church, but the Williamses preferred the cemetery outside town. You should visit. It might give you some comfort."

"I will." Jenny had a lot to think about.

"And I suppose you'll be off back to Australia, then?" Anne asked. "We'd love to see you again."

Jenny met her eyes. "I'll be off soon, I expect. Maddy hasn't been well, but she'll soon be able to fend for herself again, and I'll be off." All of a sudden, Australia seemed very far away.

"Well, don't be a stranger. You know where to find us," was Anne's parting remark as Jenny opened the door of her car. She drove off, her mind full of thoughts of the couple who had been her parents, the parents she'd never known. How different her life might have been. She sighed, wondering if she would have preferred to remain ignorant of the whole matter.

Thirty-three

Jenny stood in front of the gravestone. She knelt down and traced the words with her finger.

THEA MILLER

1930-1950

BELOVED DAUGHTER AND SISTER

It was so brief, so little to remember a life as vibrant as Thea's seemed to have been. This was her mother. Unbidden, a tear ran down Jenny's cheek. She wiped it away with the back of her hand and stood up. She wished there was more she could do, wished she had known Thea. Then Jenny's usual pragmatism began to reassert itself. She'd had a good life, been happy growing up with her parents in Australia. Who could say what her life might have been like if Thea and Jed had lived? In all probability they'd have lived on the edge somewhere, shunned by both sets of parents. It may be she'd drawn the long straw after all.

Jenny walked back to the car slowly. The chirping of the birds seemed incongruous in this otherwise calm and serene spot. She stopped and looked back to imprint the scene on her mind. She saw the rhododendron bushes flowering in their whites, pinks and purple, reds and yellows, and was pleased her mother was resting in this beautiful spot.

Later in the afternoon Jenny found herself outside Ellen's bookshop without being conscious of having driven there. She was sitting in the car gazing out of the window but seeing nothing, when a tap on the glass roused her.

"Anyone home?" Ellen mouthed, bending down to look through the window. "Would you like some coffee?" Ellen held up the cup which she'd clearly just bought for herself.

Jenny pulled herself back into the present. She'd been thinking of the two young people who'd planned to be together forever and who were now buried several miles apart. Now she'd visited both graves, she felt a need to do something for them, but what? She opened the window. "That'd be great. I'll get some and join you."

"What have you been up to that's left you looking so despondent?" The two women were sitting in Ellen's little office. Jenny carefully placed her coffee on the floor beside her and looked up at her friend.

"I've just been to visit their graves – Thea and Jed's. I don't know why it didn't occur to me before. It was the Huggins, Bill and Anne. They suggested it."

"Now why didn't I think of that? I don't even know where Uncle Jed is buried. I'd have come with you…"

Jenny smiled weakly. "It's okay. I needed to go on my own. It was just… They're so far apart, so unconnected, and they wanted to be together, together forever, that's what Bill said."

"Drink your coffee and you'll feel better."

"It just brought them closer somehow. I'd seen photos, heard about them, read about them. But to see their names on gravestones and to realize these were my parents. It made me feel…" Jenny looked up and met Ellen's eyes. "It made me feel humble. I want to do something, but putting flowers on old graves doesn't seem enough. I want to do something that would have meaning for them. Do I sound crazy?"

"What's with this together forever thing?" Ellen seemed to be changing the subject.

"Didn't I tell you? It was their motto, Bill said. Jed even had a tattoo. And I bet Thea would have had one too, if girls had tattoos in those days."

"Who's to say she didn't?"

Jenny gave a weak laugh. "But that doesn't help me. Even their gravestones make no mention of each other, though I suppose it's to be expected, given the parents. It's as if all they had together has been wiped out."

"There's your answer."

"What? Deface the gravestones? I don't think so." Jenny was beginning to wonder if her friend had gone mad.

"No. Add something… something, oh, I don't know. Something to signify their attachment to each other. Something like…"

"Together forever," both spoke at once.

"But will we be allowed to alter the stones?" Jenny wondered.

"Well, you seem to be the last of the Miller family around."

"Except for Cousin Rhoda, and she's in no position to object. What about your family, though. They might not be so agreeable."

"I don't really think they'd care. It's not as if they visited Jed's grave or anything. I'll run it past Mom and see what she thinks. She can probably persuade Dad to sign necessary paperwork."

Jenny was beginning to really warm to the idea. "It'll be a lasting memento of their love."

"I think you're that." Ellen's words were blunt.

"Yes, well. This is something I can do for them. The only thing I can do for them now. Not as if they'll know."

"Don't be too sure."

"Oh, I know. There are more things in heaven and earth. You and Maddy should get together."

"You're not a believer?"

"In what?" Jenny looked at the other woman blankly.

"Oh, never mind. It'll be a good thing to do." Ellen rose as the shop bell jangled. "Got to go."

"I'd better be off too. Maddy will be wondering where I've got to."

*

As Jenny had expected, Maddy was eagerly awaiting her return.

"Well?" Maddy greeted her. "Did you find them? It certainly took you long enough. Come sit by me and tell me what you found."

"Yes. They were both there. In separate cemeteries, just as Bill and Anne said. It was sad to see them separated in death when they wanted so much to be together. Together forever, Bill said." Jenny gazed into space. "I'm going to do something about it."

"What? Move their remains? Surely not!"

Jenny couldn't help but laugh at Maddy's shocked expression. "No, nothing so drastic. But I could add to the inscriptions on their stones. We came up with 'Together Forever'. It was their motto, you know."

"We?"

"Ellen and I. I didn't intend to go to see her, but I was driving around aimlessly, and I found myself ending up down there in Old Town outside her shop," Jenny explained.

"She's a good friend and has the connection with Jed too. Sounds like a good idea." Maddy added. "Will the Williamses be okay with it?"

"Ellen's going to talk to them, so I'll get on with finding out what I need to do."

"Mike might be of some help there," Maddy suggested.

"Yes, I thought so too. It's a long time since I had anything to do with gravestones and cemeteries. I just hope it doesn't bring back too many memories for him – memories of his wife."

"I think those memories will always *be* there," said Maddy sagely. "But he has them under control. She was a good woman, and wouldn't have wanted him to waste the rest of his life alone."

Jenny's eyes grew wide at this comment. "There's not…We aren't… Oh damn, what do you mean?"

"Come on, honey. This is me, remember? I've always been good at reading people, and if ever I saw two people suited to each other, it's you two. What are you going to do about it?"

Suddenly the defenses which Jenny had been putting up broke down. She looked over at Maddy. "I honestly don't know, Maddy. My life is in Australia. My home is there. My family is there. I can't stay here indefinitely. Yes, he's a great guy, and yes I admit we're well suited. He's someone I never expected to find at my time of life."

"Your time of life? Pouff! Wait till you get to my age before you say things like that. You're just a young thing."

"Well, yes. I guess it's all relative. Anyway, I can ask his help with this project. I'll call him tomorrow."

*

"So what exactly is it you want me to do?" Mike leant back in his chair and observed Jenny sitting opposite him. She had curled her feet up under her, and he thought she looked about nineteen. His eyes feasted on her slender figure, the silky black hair which had now grown to her shoulders, a few grey streaks the only testament to the passing of the years. He watched her impatiently sweep it back behind her ears and raise her eyes to meet his. A man could drown in these violet pools.

"I thought..." She paused and twisted a lock of hair between her fingers. "I thought you would know the procedure, who to contact and that sort of thing, you know," she said hesitatingly. "I don't want..." she gulped and went on, "I don't want to bring up memories for you of..."

"No, it's all right." Mike's voice was gruff. "I do know the procedure, and I'd be glad to help. What was it you wanted added again?"

"Together Forever."

"Shouldn't present any problems. We'll just need to do the relevant paperwork. Then you arrange it with the monument company."

"Thanks." Jenny's smile of gratitude was thanks enough by itself.

"Now, how about a stroll along the beach? The wind's died down, and the moon is up. Should be pleasant down there right now. And Ben would like some exercise, wouldn't you, old chap?" At the sound of his name, Ben rose from where he was lying under the window and padded across to put his paw on his master's knee. Mike realized he'd diffused any of the romantic nonsense his invitation for a moonlight stroll might have engendered by his reference to the dog. He wasn't good at this sort of thing. Out of practice.

As the pair walked down the track, Ben running ahead of them and turning every few minutes as if to check his humans were following, Mike took the opportunity to grasp Jenny's hand. He gave a quick squeeze and was pleased to feel an answering pressure. He was aware of their agreement at Crater Lake to take things slowly, and wasn't quite sure how to proceed. It was a good sign she'd asked for his help, he figured. Maybe the moonlight on the ocean would work its magic. He remembered how it had worked for Mary and him on their first trip up here. Strangely, thinking of Mary didn't get in the way of his relationship with Jenny. Again he had the feeling that she was at his shoulder egging him on. *Okay, Mary, give me time.*

"What did you say?"

Mike realized he must have spoken out loud.

"Just talking to myself." He tried to shrug it off, hoping she really hadn't heard the words.

"As my old gran used to say, there's a place for people who talk to themselves."

They laughed together as they reached the beach and stepped onto the sand. Ben immediately ran off trying to catch the waves, and Mike and Jenny stopped in their tracks, transfixed by the beauty of the sight which greeted them. The moon was halfway on its journey through the sky, its beams turning the ocean into a silver expanse. It was calm at this time of night, the gentle waves washing softly on the shore. The large chunks of driftwood stood out like ghostly figures in the distance. They had the beach to themselves, and the only sound was the lap-lap of the waves on the shore.

Gently, Mike drew Jenny to a soft stretch of sand and pulled her down beside him. Without uttering a word, he reached his arm around her shoulder, and to his surprise and pleasure, she leant against him with a sigh, her head dropping onto his shoulder.

Thirty-four

The pounding on the door broke into his concentration. "I'm coming!"
Mike pressed *save* and made his way to the door, Ben padding along
at his heels. It must be Jenny. Who else would come knocking on his
door? But they'd not arranged to meet till later, since he'd planned on
writing all morning. His mind was still with his Native Americans
as he opened the door. "What's the matter?" he began, then stopped
short, stunned to see a complete stranger standing there, arm upraised
to knock yet again. She looked vaguely familiar, but he couldn't place
her. He only had time to take in her windswept blonde hair, and the
compact body encased in blue pants and tailored white shirt before
she spoke.

"You're Professor Halliday, Mike Halliday." It sounded like an
accusation.

Mike dragged his fingers through his already awry hair and pulled
on his beard.

"Guilty as charged. But who are you?" he said, only to be pushed
aside as the stranger swept past him into the house. Bemused, Mike
followed, with Ben leaving his master to sniff at the strange woman
who was by now standing in the middle of the great room.

"Sue's sister. Sue Lyons," the stranger added, seeing his look of
bewilderment. Mike gazed at the woman thinking back. That's why
she looked familiar.

*Mike was distracted. He had just returned from visiting Mary in the
nursing home. She'd failed to recognize him, and he was distraught. So*

this was what it was going to be like from now on? He thought he'd been prepared, but nothing could have prepared him for the blank look in her eyes when she asked him who he was, and why he was there. Now here he was sitting with a graduate student trying to make sense as he reviewed her research proposal.

"I'm sorry. My mind is elsewhere. Maybe we can do this some other time?" He pulled on his beard and looked beseechingly at the young woman sitting opposite. She tossed her long blonde hair over her shoulder, gathered her pages together and raised her eyes to meet his.

"Professor Halliday... Mike," she added daringly. "Is there anything I can do? You seem like you need to talk. What about a coffee? I can provide an ear for you."

Mike knew it wasn't the right thing to do, but he was at his wits' end, not thinking clearly, and the opportunity to pour out his troubles to this young woman seemed like a good idea. They made their way to the campus coffee shop, and over a large mug of coffee, he found himself pouring out his grief and fears. As soon as they left, he regretted his confidences, but the act of speaking them out loud had lifted his him out of his despondency. He was able to carry on with his lecturing and tutoring, carry on with his visits to the nursing home, carry on facing up to the fact that his wife, his soul mate, no longer recognized him most of the time.

He referred the student to another supervisor, saved himself the embarrassment of having to face her again. He knew it was taking the coward's way out, but he was too ashamed of his moment of weakness to face her again.

Mike looked again at the woman opposite him. "Sue Lyons," he repeated puzzled. "She was a student of mine a couple of years ago. Her sister, you say?" He was buying time, trying to work out what this angry young woman could possibly want of him.

"She's dead!" The words shot out like bullets. "And it's all your fault."

"Now steady on." Mike put a hand down on Ben's head to restrain the dog, who was growling at the woman's angry tone. "I'm sorry about your loss, but what does it have to do with me?"

"Don't play the innocent. It's all there in her diaries, the secret meetings, the protestations of love. How could you take advantage of a girl so much younger than you... and your student to boot?"

Mike sat down with a thump, and Ben, as if realizing his master's distress, laid his head on Mike's lap and began to lick his hand. "I think you'd better sit down and tell me the whole story," he said at last.

The young woman grudgingly took a seat opposite him, and still clutching her bag to her chest, began to speak more calmly. "It happened two weeks ago," she said. "I was due to meet Sue for dinner, and when she didn't turn up I began to worry. When I couldn't reach her on the phone, I went round to her flat. I got no response so I used my key. And there she was…" The woman began to sob uncontrollably. Then she seemed to pull herself together. "There she was, lying on her bed. She looked so peaceful," she sniffed. "My baby sister. She was gone. We'd lost her, our beautiful Sue."

Mike rose, confused. "I'll fetch you a glass of water," he muttered, stepping into the kitchen. He was back a moment later. "Here, drink this." He put the glass into her outstretched hand.

She took a gulp, looking down into the glass, then drew her shoulders back and raised her eyes to meet Mike's. "She took her life, and it was all your fault," she accused, her anger beginning to surface again.

Mike stretched out his hands, palms downwards. "I don't understand. Yes, your sister was one of my students, but I passed her on to another faculty member. There was an incident. I embarrassed myself. It was best she work with someone else." The words came out awkwardly.

"Embarrassed, I'll bet," she exclaimed. "Acted improperly and unprofessionally, you mean? Seducing an impressionable young girl. How could you?"

Mike's jaw dropped. *Where had all this come from? Clearly the young woman believed her accusations, otherwise why had she gone to the trouble of seeking him out. And how had she found him? That was something he needed to find out too.*

Trying to maintain his cool, he asked, "What brought you to this conclusion? I assure you it was not the case." I'm sounding like a shop front dummy, he thought. He took a deep breath and waited for her response.

"But you did. She said so in her diary. I found it under her mattress. She'd written it all down." The woman opposite appeared stunned by his denial.

"Well… I'm sorry I didn't catch your name?" Mike paused, hoping the question would diffuse her anger.

"It's Tanya, Tanya Lyons. She'd written screeds about you. In graphic detail too. It's all there in black and white."

"Well, Tanya, all I can surmise is that your sister had an overactive imagination. There was never anything improper between us."

"Then there was something." She stood up, seemingly unwilling to hear his side of the story.

They were interrupted by the sound of light footsteps outside the door and a knock followed by a voice calling, "Hello, anyone home?" The door opened, and Jenny walked in saying "It's such a lovely day I thought I'd tempt you away from your magnum opus…" The voice stopped as its owner's gaze took in the two people now standing aggressively face to face. "Oh, I didn't know you had company." She looked from one to the other. "I'll come back later."

"It's okay, I'm leaving." Tanya turned and walked to the door. "But you haven't heard the last of this," she threw at Mike and slammed the door behind her.

"Wow, that's one angry woman. What did you do to her?" Jenny asked, seeing Mike gazing after the departing figure in stupefaction.

"Not her, her sister." Mike's voice came as if in a daze. "And I didn't do anything, but I can't make her believe me." He drew his fingers through his hair then tugged on his beard. "I need to sit down."

When they were both seated, Jenny took Mike's hand in hers. "Can you tell me what it's all about?"

Mike drew his hand away. "I'm not sure you want to be associated with someone like me," he tried to make a joke out of it, but it sounded flat even to his own ears. "Look, I don't want to talk about it. At least not now." They sat in silence while Mike tried to come to grips with his recent visitor and her unexpected accusations, then he spoke. "You're right, it's too good a day to stay inside. We should walk down to the beach. Blow the cobwebs away."

In no time they were walking along the beach, Mike throwing sticks for Ben. He couldn't bring himself to raise the subject of his visitor with Jenny and, to his relief, she didn't raise it either.

"I'm afraid I'm not great company today," he said at last, as they stood looking at the waves.

"I understand." Jenny made an attempt to put her hand on his shoulder, but instead of welcoming her advance, Mike found himself moving out of reach. He felt soiled by the encounter with this Tanya Lyons person. He needed to think about it more. By himself.

"Here Ben!" Mike called the dog to heel and turned to his companion. "I *will* explain, but I need to come to terms with this first. Can you bear with me till tomorrow? After breakfast?"

"Sure thing." Mike sensed, rather than saw, Jenny's troubled look as they made their way back. He found himself giving her a perfunctory kiss on the cheek and felt her eyes on his back as he made his way up the remaining section of the track.

*

Jenny looked after him walking slowly back to his cabin. Ben was frolicking around his master as usual, but Mike's gait showed her he was worried, very worried. She wondered who his visitor had been, and what she had said to make him so disconcerted. She turned to enter the house, a frown between her eyes.

"What's up?" Maddy, perceptive as usual, was quick to notice Jenny's bewilderment. "You're back early. Did something go wrong?"

"It's Mike." Jenny looked down at her feet and twisted her fingers. "He wasn't alone. He had a visitor; a woman, an angry one. I don't know what it was all about, but it's thrown him, that's for sure. We walked on the beach but…"

"He didn't tell you what she wanted?"

"Said he needed time to think. I'm seeing him tomorrow. After breakfast."

"Then he'll explain it to you tomorrow. What you need is something to occupy you today, take your mind off Mike and his problems."

"Yeah, I guess." Jenny's voice was low. Things had been going so well with her and Mike. Even though in the back of her mind she knew she'd be returning to Australia soon, she had been enjoying their times together, living in the moment.

"Why don't we go down to Florence for lunch? Visit your cousin Ellen?"

Jenny raised her head. "If we go there, we could visit their graves,

Thea's and Jed's. The new engraving should be done by now. I'd like to see how it looks. If you feel you're up to it," she added, with a glance at her godmother.

"Oh, my dear." Maddy took her stick and hobbled over to where Jenny was sitting. "I should have thought. Of course you want to see the results of your plan."

*

THEA MILLER
1930-1950
BELOVED DAUGHTER AND SISTER
TOGETHER FOREVER

"It looks good, honey." Leaning on her walking stick, Maddy put her other arm round Jenny.

"Well, at least I've got something right." Jenny felt a lump come into her throat. "I wish... I wish I could have known them," she whispered, more to herself than to her companion.

"They'll rest more easy now." Maddy's words were comforting as the pair turned away from the graveside.

"You don't really believe that, do you?" Jenny turned to look at her godmother.

"Well, you'll rest easier, won't you? And you're part of them, so *ipso facto...*"

Jenny essayed a smile. "Oh, you old devil," she managed to say.

'Now, how about Ellen?' Maddy changed the subject. 'She'd not like to think we came down here and didn't call in on her, would she?'

'You're right again.' Jenny sniffed and rubbed her knuckles over her eyes.

*

Mike couldn't settle to work. The visit from Tanya Lyons kept repeating and repeating in his mind. Her accusations had no truth in them, but she seemed convinced of his guilt. He had a feeling he'd not seen the last of her. How could he reason with her? He paced the room, alternately dragging his fingers through his hair and pulling on his beard till he resembled a scarecrow.

"This won't do, Mary," he said aloud to his dead wife. "You know I'd never... a student, my God. What can I do?" Feeling slightly foolish, he walked to the window and gazed out at the calm evening sky. There were some high clouds, but the setting sun gave an eerie glow. He began to feel calmer. It was as if his Mary was nearby telling him this would pass.

Thinking more clearly, he decided he needed to find out more information. He could do that by checking out some San Francisco papers, find out when this Sue girl had died, see if there were any details. His heart sank at the thought there might be some mention of the diary her sister had quoted, but he doubted it. If there had been and his name had been mentioned, he felt sure someone, probably Bob, would have been in touch with him. It wasn't something people would ignore.

Mike was loathe to contact any of his former colleagues, but if need be, he could make a call to Tony who had taken Sue on as a Graduate student. Yes, he decided, that's what he'd do. Meantime he had to work out a way to explain to Jenny. This had to crop up now, when things were going so well between them.

Thirty-five

"Well, are you going to tell me what this is all about?" The pair had been walking along the beach for almost an hour, and so far, Mike had dodged any explanation of the angry woman from the day before.

Mike drew circles in the sand with the toe of his shoe and studied the marks as if seeking wisdom. He stood apart from Jenny. He had avoided taking her hand as they walked along. He knew she'd be wondering what was wrong. The incident the previous day had left him feeling soiled. In this state, he knew he couldn't touch Jenny lest he pass the grubbiness on to her.

"I know you need an explanation," he hesitated, wondering how to begin.

"I certainly do."

Mike felt Jenny's eyes on him as he continued to work the sand with his toe. He knew he couldn't avoid this, but was worried Jenny might jump to the wrong conclusion, just as this Tanya had.

"Let's sit down." Mike led Jenny over to a large log. As he sat down his hand felt the surface of the log, worn smooth by the continuous buffeting of the sea. He was beginning to feel pretty buffeted himself at the moment.

"Well?" Jenny turned her face to his and raised her eyebrows.

Mike cleared his throat. This wasn't going to be easy. "It's... it seems..." He took a deep breath. "It's not what you think," he began.

"How do you know what I think?" Jenny countered.

"I don't, but I can imagine. We're just getting to know each other and maybe find that… when you discover me arguing with a strange woman. It doesn't look good, I know. It's not something I make a habit of." Mike drew his fingers through his hair in despair.

"That certainly hasn't been my impression of you." Jenny smiled gently as she spoke, as if to encourage him to continue.

To his embarrassment Mike's eyes filled with tears. He brushed them with the back of his hand. He was conscious of Jenny's concerned gaze. He'd dearly like to get up and walk away, but was afraid what she might think. God, she might even follow him. And it wouldn't be fair. He owed her some explanation. Best to get it over with.

"She – her name is Tanya – arrived out of the blue. Never met her before. Her sister, Sue, was a student of mine several years ago, a graduate student. She happened to be the first person I encountered, after the time that Mary…" Mike's voice broke. He began again.

"Sue had a meeting scheduled with me immediately after I returned from visiting Mary in the nursing home. She, Mary, didn't recognize me. It was the first time it had happened. She asked me who I was, what I was doing there. I couldn't think straight. I'd known her illness would progress, but it shook me when it actually happened. I couldn't concentrate, and I foolishly agreed to have coffee with this student." Mike paused, tugging on his beard in embarrassment. "And I spilled my guts out."

"Doesn't seem too bad. What happened then?"

"Oh, I quickly realized it would be too difficult and embarrassing to continue advising her, so I passed her on to another professor. I never saw her again."

"So what's happened now?"

"Seems she's committed suicide." The words sounded harsh, even to Mike.

Jenny looked puzzled. "But what's that got to do with you?"

"There's a diary."

"A diary?"

"Her sister says she wrote a lot about me."

"And they think…?"

"She appears to have had some sort of crush, and fantasized about me. Tanya accused me of being the cause of her suicide," he stated bluntly.

Mike finally turned to look at Jenny, expecting to see disgust but, to his surprise, her face held nothing but compassion.

"You poor man. She's lost her sister. She wants to blame someone. You just happen to fit the frame. What do you intend to do?"

Mike scratched his head. "I've been awake most of the night trying to work that out," he admitted. "I guess I can get back to my old colleagues, though I don't know." He pulled on his beard in agitation. "I'm not sure what I hope to find out. As this Tanya said, it's all there in black and white. And there's only my word for it that I didn't have anything to do with her after we had coffee. With Mary so sick, I'd retreated into myself even more than usual. I wasn't talking much to anyone at that time. No one would have known what I was doing... or not doing," he added.

Mike suddenly realized Jenny was gazing into space.

"You do understand, don't you? I can't let them go on thinking... Oh, God, you believe me, don't you? There was never anything between me and this student. I'd never sink to those depths." Mike followed Jenny's gaze.

"Of course. I can't imagine you getting involved with anyone when your wife was so ill, least of all a student. But is it really so important? Can't you just let it go?"

"She won't. Tanya, I mean. And to answer your question, no, I can't. It's my reputation at stake here, don't you see? I may need to go back down to California." Mike dreaded the thought of the trip, and what he needed to do. He hadn't any close friends down there. There was old Bob, he supposed. But he didn't want to go over the sordid details with him.

"Yes," he continued. "That's what I need to do. Though I'll have to be careful who I talk with. Don't want any more people involved than need be."

"You should..." Jenny stopped.

"Yes? I should what?"

"No, you shouldn't. I mean... Oh, damn. It's not up to me to tell you what to do. What you said about me when we first met, the person you thought I was, the perfectionist. You were right. I *was* that person. I was so organized I didn't have a spare minute – and I managed to organize everyone around me too. I couldn't seem to help myself."

"Funny. You've never struck me as that sort of person. I worked out a long time ago I'd been wrong about you. You might be a bit uptight at times, but I haven't seen you try to organize me. I can tell you, you wouldn't have seen me for dust if you had."

"It's this place." Jenny waved her arms around. "It has a calming effect. It's been good for me." She looked down at her feet, as if considering the sand on which she was standing, then raised her eyes again. "So what will you do?"

Mike scratched his head, unsure how to proceed. He'd thought there might be something developing between Jenny and him, but he had to settle all this stuff first. It was a bummer.

"I think," he began. He paused, then continued, thinking aloud, "I think I need a breathing space. It's not that..." He looked at Jenny beseechingly hoping she'd understand. "While I have this hanging over me I can't..." His face closed up as he saw her stunned reaction. She seemed about to move towards him, then stopped as he folded his arms around himself.

"So you don't want my help. Fine by me." Jenny stood up and started to leave.

"Don't go!" Mike rose from the log, stretching out his hand, but it was too late. Jenny had already begun to run back up the beach.

Mike sat down again with a thump, sorry he'd left his faithful Ben back home. *A man really needed his dog in a situation like this. A companion who knew when to keep quiet and who didn't take offense. Women, who needed them?*

Thirty-six

Jenny couldn't settle. She hadn't told Maddy about her conversation with Mike, though she sensed the older woman wondered what happened, when Jenny had burst into the house and gone straight to her room. And she had a niggling feeling Mike hadn't told her everything. By the time she felt fit for company again and ventured out into the living area, her godmother had taken herself to bed for a nap.

After making herself a coffee Jenny sat down on the sofa, her mind going back over her recent conversation with Mike and comparing it with earlier ones, where it had seemed there might be some connection between them. She was dragged out of her musings by the shrilling of the phone. She picked it up, and to her surprise, she was greeted by her son-in-law's voice.

"Oh, Mum, it's Helen." Jenny immediately thought the worst. Alan continued, "She had a fall in the park this afternoon and seems to have broken her ankle. We've just got back from hospital. She can't put any weight on it. I don't know how we're going to manage."

Jenny heard the implication. If she hadn't been so foolhardy as to have had a career, then taken this trip to the States, she would have been there to take over. She steeled herself to keep calm. "Are you able to take some time off work?" The question was followed by a long pause.

"Well, we'd hoped... maybe... you could..." Jenny let him bluster for a while, then pointed out that she had commitments now too.

"But, Helen thought…"

"I know. You both thought I could drop everything. Well, I can't. Maddy's been incapacitated too, you know, and she lives alone." Jenny paused to let her words sink in. She thought quickly, about to give an outright refusal then relented. "I may be able to get away next week, if you can hold the fort till then. But I'll need a few days to set things up here, and I can't stay for long, just long enough to get Helen sorted out. I have some plans I need to share with you."

Alan's sigh of relief was palpable.

"Good oh. I can cope with the weekend and maybe a few days at the beginning of the week. When do you think you can get away? The boys are looking forward to seeing you."

Realizing she'd fallen right into the trap, Jenny hesitated, but only for a moment. Helen was her daughter after all, and a broken ankle wasn't easy to cope with, even without with two young children around.

"I'll call you tomorrow and let you know. Tell me exactly how it happened." It was twenty minutes later when she finally put down the phone, her day completely ruined. Now she'd have to figure out how to tell Maddy, and to work out if her godmother could cope on her own. Then there was Mike. Helen's timing couldn't have been worse.

"Who was on the phone, dear?" Maddy shuffled through from her bedroom where she'd been resting. Seeing Jenny's stricken face, she moved to put her arm around her shoulder. "Bad news from home?"

"Yes. Oh, Maddy. It's Helen. She's broken her ankle and expects me to come and take care of her and the kids too."

"What about her husband?"

Maddy's enquiry went unheard as Jenny continued, "It's so unfair. I've been there for her, and Hugh too, all of their lives and now, when I'm doing something for myself and seem to have a chance at a new start, this happens. I couldn't say it to many people, Maddy, but sometimes my kids really piss me off."

"What you need is a glass of something stronger than that tea you're drinking." Jenny looked down at the half drunk mug sitting on the table. "Pour yourself a glass of something … and I'll have one too."

When Jenny sat down again, her head was spinning, thinking of all the things she'd need to do if she was to return to Australia in less than a week. She was so busy working it all out in her mind that she wasn't listening to Maddy. "What did you say?" she enquired, realizing Maddy had been speaking to her for some time. "Sorry, I was miles away."

"Back in Australia, I suspect," Maddy responded drily. "I was only asking you what you intended to do about Mike. You and he seemed to be getting quite close since he returned from California."

Jenny bit her lip. Her brow creased. "Yes. Helen's timing isn't the best. But I'm sure he'll understand. It's not as if…"

"No?" Maddy raised her eyebrows. "I thought it was very much as if."

Jenny waved her hands in front of her as if to bat away Maddy's words. "We were two lonely people, that's all. Ships passing in the night." She tried to deflect Maddy's curiosity. "There's nothing else happening," she added, hoping her voice didn't give her away. Mike was someone she'd have to deal with, but she had to agree to go back. Helen needed her, and she was about due to return anyway she told herself.

"You're more important. Are you going to be able to cope on your own if I go back right away?"

"Oh, don't worry about me. I'll manage. There's this young person Ellen mentioned. She's coming to see me the day after tomorrow. We'll see if we suit." Jenny suspected Maddy was putting on a brave face, but couldn't figure out how to reply, so remained silent, nursing her drink.

"I'll call Mike later, maybe walk up to his place. I can break it to him then."

*

The sun was beginning to fall below the horizon, and Jenny and Mike had been walking along the water's edge for a time in silence. Mike kicked a piece of driftwood out of his way, and Jenny heard his voice, as if coming from a long distance away. "So what is it you wanted to talk with me about? Sounded serious. Sorry I was so abrupt earlier," he added.

They stopped and Jenny turned to face him, but kept her eyes on the ground. She was trying to work out what to say, when she felt his large hand take hold of her chin and tip it up towards him.

"It can't be that bad, hon. You're not going to run off on me are you? I know I've got this bit of bother right now. But I can sort it out." Mike tugged on his beard and sighed. "Means another trip down south. I decided I need to meet with Tanya again. Maybe talk with Tony too. He's the one who took her sister on when I…" His face reddened, and he turned to face Jenny

Oh, shit, how was she going to do this? "I had a call from Alan today," she began.

"Alan? Your daughter's husband? Everything okay back there?"

"No, that's the problem." The words came out tumbling over each other. "Helen's broken her ankle, and they need me to go back home." There, she'd said it. She looked Mike in the eye to gauge how he was taking it.

"So your daughter calls, and you're off. What about your hard-sought freedom? Your determination to lead your own life? Your bookshop? She doesn't even live near you, does she?"

"I know, I know." Jenny dragged her fingers through her hair. "It's just…" She sat down on the sand, legs bent and hands clasped around her knees. Mike joined her, reaching his arm round her shoulder and giving her a squeeze.

"I'd have had to go soon anyway. It's not as if… Oh, God, Why does everything have to be so hard? It's just, coming here, finding out how my grandparents abandoned Thea and Jed. It's made me value family. I know all the stuff I said about them, but I'd hate my children to feel I'd abandoned them in their time of need. As long as I can be sure Maddy's okay, then I'll go and get Helen sorted out."

"It's not as if what?" Mike ignored the latter part of her speech, focusing on the part she'd glossed over. He took his arm away and, twisting his fingers together on his lap, gazed out at the ocean and the darkening sky. "I know I'm not in my prime, but I thought maybe…" He turned to meet Jenny's eyes. "I thought after our trip to Crater Lake that maybe I'm not such an old codger after all."

Jenny laid her hands on his, feeling their warmth, aware again of the strength in them. "You're far from being an old codger! Crater Lake was wonderful. It reaffirmed me as a woman, the woman I'd forgotten existed over the past thirty years or so. But it was just an interlude, wasn't it? For both of us?" Her eyes misted over, making it impossible to see Mike's eyes clearly.

"If that's how you feel, then there's no more to say." Mike stood up suddenly and, brushing the sand from the seat of his pants, reached down to help Jenny up. "We'd best get back. Sun's down."

*

"And that was that." Jenny recounted the conversation to Maddy, carefully leaving out the reference to the trip to Crater Lake.

"Men have feelings too," Maddy commented. "I may never have married myself, but just because I lost the love of my life at an early age doesn't mean I've lived the life of a nun."

Jenny felt herself turn red. This wasn't the sort of conversation she expected to have with her eighty-three year old godmother.

"I've been a watcher from the outside on quite a number of relationships too. What I've noticed is that men often don't put their feelings into words, but that doesn't mean they don't have any. And Mike is more closed than most. I think it may be to do with Mary's illness, but," Maddy reflected, "he always had a tendency to be closed. Mary was the one who made friends easily."

Jenny remembered Mike's words on the beach. They'd been tantamount to a declaration of his feelings, as close as he could get. She shrugged. "Well, it's all too hard, and I've been on my own too long anyway. And he's got stuff to sort out. It's better he's on his own to do that."

"Are you sure?" Maddy's voice was gentle.

"It's what he wants. And I want it too." But the tremble in Jenny's voice belied her words. She stood up and squared her shoulders. "I'd better get started. There's a lot to do if I'm going back to Australia next week.

Thirty-seven

Ten days later, Jenny picked up a hire car at Sydney airport and headed across the harbor bridge. She was experiencing a few regrets at her precipitous departure from Oregon, but quickly stifled them. She was needed here. This is where her future lay, and the pleasant Oregon episode had been just that – pleasant but temporary. She suppressed the memory of the comfort she'd felt in Mike's presence – in his arms. He had his own demons to fight right now, and she had her new life back here in Australia. There could be no future for them together.

She gazed out of the window. Sydney was at its best this bright and beautiful morning with the harbor glistening in the sunlight and the radio playing old favorites. It was a gorgeous city, one she'd visited several times over the years, more often since Helen's children had been born. She loved her grandchildren and enjoyed spending time with them, but did prefer to choose the time. She wasn't prepared to stay any longer than was needed to sort something out for Helen.

As she drove through the gates of her daughter's home, little Bradley came running out of the door and down the steps to greet her. She'd barely stepped out of the car when he yelled out,

"I knowed it was you, Grammy. Daddy said you was coming to stay with us. Mummy has a sore leg. She has a big stick."

"Oh, you dear," she laughed, lifting him up in a big hug, "Grammy loves you too. It's so good to see you." And it was. Regardless of the reason, it was good to see him again. It was so easy to miss their growing up. It was only a few months since her last visit, and he'd grown so much already. "Now, let's go in and see Mummy and Daddy, and Tom."

"I have a red Thomas and a blue Thomas." Totally engrossed in himself and his toys, Bradley led the way, meeting Alan at the foot of the steps with baby Tom in his arms.

"Didn't hear you arrive, Mum. I was changing this little tyke. Would you like to take him while I fetch your case from the car?" And without further ado, Alan thrust the little one into Jenny's arms.

Taking the large bundle, she climbed up the steps and poked her head into the lounge room.

"Helen?"

"Oh, there you are, Mum. Alan's no good in the kitchen. We've been hanging out for you to come."

Well, it was a welcome of sorts, Jenny thought to herself, putting little Tom down gently on the floor at his mother's feet.

"What about a cup of tea? I know where everything is – unless you've changed things around since I was here last."

"I don't know what Alan's been doing." Helen was sounding very sorry for herself. "I haven't been able to get around since I did this. The boys have really been looking forward to having you here, and I have too. It'll let Alan get back to work and…"

"One thing at a time." Jenny bustled into the kitchen, which unlike its usual pristine state, looked as if a bomb had hit it. Alan certainly wasn't good in the kitchen.

Rolling up her sleeves, Jenny decided to start with the sink. It looked as if Alan had used every pot and dish in the place, and the sink was filled to overflowing. First, fill the kettle, she thought, then tackle the washing up.

"Won't be long," she called through, only to have her legs grabbed from behind by a pair of small hands.

"I can help."

"I'm sure you can, darling, but let Grammy do this first." She switched on the kettle and set to tackle the sink – first emptying it and filling it up with hot water and detergent. Where was Alan?

Speak of the devil. His head appeared around the kitchen door, looking a bit sheepish.

"I'm afraid I let it get away from me a bit. But I knew you were coming. You don't mind if I drop around to the office for a bit?"

Without waiting for a reply, he was off.

"I'll leave these to soak and bring in the tea," Jenny said to his departing back as she found a tray behind the door and some chocolate biscuits in the pantry. She poured some juice for the littlies, and joined her daughter again.

"Well," she sighed, sitting down at last, "what are we going to do with you?"

"Oh, Mum, the doctor said I have to try to keep off my feet for three weeks. It'll be a godsend to have you here. The boys really miss having their grandma around. You'll be able to take them to..."

"Steady on. I'm here for now, but three weeks? I don't think that's going to be possible." She could see Helen's bottom lip trembling, just as it had when she was a child herself. She'd been good at getting her way then, and seemed to think it would still work.

"As I said, I'm here now, and I won't leave you in the lurch. I'm sure we can work out something, but let's leave that till tomorrow. Tell me all about what happened."

Helen's tea grew cold as she filled her mother in on her woes. While it was lovely to see her and the boys, Jenny realized she was really glad she hadn't given in to her daughter's demands for her to move closer. Helen could quickly move into the dependent daughter role, and it just wasn't for Jenny these days, if it ever had been.

*

By the time Jenny had been there three days, she was beginning to feel Oregon had been a dream. A nice dream, but a dream nevertheless. This was her real life. Helen was still not on top of things. If she'd been feeling less charitable, Jenny would have said she was malingering. But Helen was her daughter, and she couldn't let her down. Jenny caught herself up short. What was she thinking? Helen wasn't a teenager anymore. She was a grown woman with her own family, and she, Jenny, had a life of her own to lead.

"Helen," she called, walking through to the sitting room where her daughter was entrenched in her usual spot on the sofa in front of the TV, Bradley playing with his cars at her feet and the baby in her arms.

"Oh, Mum. I wondered where you were. Can you take the kids out for a walk or something. I need a bit of a nap."

"We need to talk."

"Sounds ominous. Oh, did you ask Alan when he'd be home. I need…"

Sitting down on one of the flowered armchairs which were angled at each side of the sofa, Jenny looked into her daughter's eyes and said gently.

"I do have another life, you know. I told you I've bought a bookshop."

"But I thought… I need you here." The remark came out piteously.

"I can't really afford to be away much longer." Jenny drew a deep breath. "I need to be home by next weekend. I have to take over the shop."

Seeing the tears begin to brim in Helen's eyes, and realizing the fourteen year old Helen wasn't really so far away, Jenny quickly added, "Let's work out a plan for when I go."

"A plan? When I'm stuck on the sofa or on crutches? I can't cope with two children like this, and Alan can't take any more time off."

Jenny was becoming tired of this side of her daughter, and wondered where she'd gone wrong in her upbringing. Surely she'd taught her to stand on her own two feet better than this. She chuckled inwardly at the pun.

"Of course Alan's job is important." This was a bit tongue in cheek. *Was it really more important to him than Jenny's own future was to her?* She doubted it. But she continued, "Maybe we can get someone to come in and help."

"A stranger. Oh, I wouldn't like that. Alan wouldn't like it either. And what about the boys, your grandchildren? They love having you here." Clearly thinking she'd played the winning card, Helen leant back.

"I love them too, but I'm starting a new life for myself, and I have plans. Let's think. Are there any neighbors who could pop in?"

"Neighbors? Mum, these are your grandchildren we're talking about. You wouldn't want strangers looking after them, would you?"

Jenny sighed, and wondered again where she'd gone wrong. Gently she tried to extricate herself from the situation. "When you and Hugh were little…," she began.

"You were at home with us," Helen said. "I remember all the activities you planned for us, the visits to the zoo." She stopped as if remembering the happy times.

Jenny continued, "I worked hard to bring you both up by myself. I'm glad you remember the times when I was home, but I was really only there in the holidays, and only some of them, when I was able to take time off. Do you remember Auntie Rosie?"

"Auntie Rosie," Helen wondered. "Didn't she have a big black bag with lots of knitting and," more enthusiastically, "didn't she make these delicious angel cakes with real cream?"

"See, you do remember."

"But wasn't she just your friend who came to visit sometimes?"

"Yes and no. She was my friend, but she didn't start out as a friend. She actually answered an ad for a babysitter."

"You found a babysitter for us through an ad?" Helen looked shocked. "I could never do that to my boys."

"Well, needs must. I was a single mother. I needed to work and," she added pointedly, "I didn't have a mother I expected to come at my beck and call."

"I know what you're trying to say, but I don't know how Alan is going to react if you tell him you're leaving. We just can't cope."

Where had this selfish daughter of hers come from? It would serve Helen right if she just packed up and left that very night. But Jenny knew she wouldn't, couldn't do that. But leave she must, or she could see she'd be here for months as Helen got used to her presence and help around the house.

"I'm not going today," she reassured her daughter, "but I must go soon. I know you'll need help for quite a while, so we need to work out a plan. If there are no close neighbors, then maybe we need to look at some paid help."

"We're not made of money," was the snappy reply. Well, thought Jenny, these words certainly hit the mark. They might start her daughter thinking of alternative solutions.

"I'll take the boys for a walk now. Have a think while I'm out at the park, and the three of us can talk it over tonight after dinner when the boys are in bed." Jenny busied herself getting the children ready for their outing. She enjoyed the feel of the soft bodies cuddling her and putting up their faces for kisses, as she helped them into their outdoor clothes and settled the baby into his pram.

Jenny was glad to get out of the house. She enjoyed her walk along the suburban streets to the park, with little Bradley toddling along beside her and the baby gurgling contentedly in his pram. It gave her time to think, something which had been in short supply in the few days she'd spent with Helen and Alan.

She reflected how her life had changed since she'd been a young mother herself. Jenny now knew, if she had ever had any doubts, she didn't want to take on the role of doting grandmother. Even though she loved her grandsons dearly, she was done with that part of her life. She'd developed other interests and was happy to leave the nurturing of her grandchildren to the next generation.

She'd throw down the gauntlet tonight. Tell Alan and Helen they had till the weekend. She'd stay till then, but no longer, and she was willing to help them find alternative help before then. Feeling relieved as always, now she'd made her decision, she was able to concentrate on Bradley, who'd been tugging at the bottom of her jacket for the past few minutes.

"Grammy, there's the park. Can you push me on the swing? Mummy won't push me very high, but Daddy does. Can you push me like Daddy?"

Laughingly she agreed and for the next half hour focused on the two children, talking mindlessly to the one in the pram and making astonished noises of approbation at the older boy's exploits on the play equipment.

When the three returned to the house, Jenny found her daughter was still showing her displeasure, but neither woman referred to their previous conversation. It wasn't till the children had been put to bed and the adult dinner was over that Helen brought up the subject.

"Alan," she began. Alan looked over at his wife, clearly surprised at the pathetic tone in her voice. "Mum wants to go back home and leave us. Tell her she can't. We need her here."

So much for us talking about a plan, thought Jenny as she waited to hear Alan's response. She thought her daughter might have come to terms with the idea by now. Evidently not.

"So you're planning to abandon us," Alan started to joke, but stopped at the grim look on Jenny's face. He looked from one woman to the other. "What's up? I thought you were going to help out till Helen was back on her feet again? Are there problems?"

Thankful that at least one of them realized she *did* have another life, Jenny relaxed.

"No," she smiled. "But I can't stay away forever. I told you I'd bought a bookshop on the coast, and the current owner is keen to hand it over. Now Helen is on the road to recovery, I think I should be getting back, and I've suggested you look for an alternative solution to help around the house."

"And I've told her she's being selfish. Family should come first," Helen burst out.

Pushing back her chair, Jenny rose from the table.

"Why don't I go out for a while? Let you two talk it over," she suggested. "It's a lovely evening, and I could do with some fresh air."

"You went for a walk with the boys just this afternoon," Helen started to object, before being silenced by a look from her husband. "Okay, Mum," she capitulated. "We'll have a talk and see you when you come back."

"We *are* grateful, Mum," Alan said quietly, walking with her to the door. "Helen just isn't herself right now, hasn't been since the bub was born. Think it's all been getting on top of her, and then the fall. Having you here has done wonders, and I'd hoped you'd be able to stay for a while longer. But I know you're planning this shop of yours. You're probably dying to get started."

Jenny smiled. She could see they'd a bit of sorting out to do. She knew very well that her daughter wasn't the easiest person to live with. She'd spoiled her as a child, she guessed. But now she was a woman with children of her own, and needed to learn to stand on her own two feet and be a helpmate to her husband. She only hoped they'd have come to some solution before she came back.

Jenny stood still on the top step as the door closed behind her. Where was she to go? Helen had been right. She'd gone for a walk that afternoon and really didn't feel like another one now. But she'd needed to get out of the house, leave the two of them to work things out without her input. It wouldn't be easy, she knew, but she had every confidence in them. Shrugging her bag up over her shoulder, Jenny set off determinedly down the street. She strode out as if she knew where she was going, but as she turned the corner, her feet slowed and she found herself looking about her in search of a café where she could rest to take stock.

The sky was dark with only a smattering of stars as her steps led her towards a brightly lit sign in the distance. Yes, it was a café. She had a vague recollection of having seen it during her earlier walk with the children. It had been busy with mothers and toddlers at the sidewalk tables then. Now the evening crowd was beginning to arrive, dinners were being served, and there were a few couples sharing bottles of wine.

Jenny ordered her coffee and took time to look around. People-watching had always fascinated her, and her eyes soon settled on an elderly couple seated at a corner table. As she watched, the gentleman, for indeed he could not be referred to as anything else, with his dapper beard and round spectacles, lifted his glass and obviously toasted the lady opposite. His companion reached over to take his hand, and they remained holding hands until their meal arrived when they, seemingly reluctantly, let go.

That could be Mike and me! Jenny was stunned at the thought. Wow. Where had it come from? She'd decided to put all thoughts of Mike behind her and concentrate on getting her life together here in Australia. Her bookshop was waiting, with settlement due in a few weeks. She had a lot to do before then, not least of which was to get herself home and settled again. Developing a business plan was high on her to do list, a list that was becoming longer by the day. The old Jenny was beginning to emerge again. She wanted to be completely organized and ready before she took over the running of the shop.

*

"I wonder if I could just check my emails?" Jenny had been back in the house for around two hours, but it seemed they were no further forward than when she left.

Booting up the computer, Jenny realized how much she was missing being in her own place. It was close to four months since she'd left

Noosa to travel to Oregon, and she'd come straight here to Sydney on her return. She hoped there would be some news from Rosa. Maybe her friend would even have visited the bookshop and could give her some firsthand news of how it looked these days.

As she scrolled down the page, Jenny was pleased to see one from Maddy. She smiled to herself as she opened it. It had been so good to see her godmother again, to renew her acquaintance. Even though it had unlocked the can of worms about her birth.

Jenny read Maddy's email then sat back in her chair and closed her eyes. Behind the lids she could clearly visualize her godmother, who wrote exactly as she spoke. Marylou, the young girl Ellen had recommended, had arrived a few days earlier, and Maddy seemed delighted with the arrangement. Jenny was pleased to read Maddy had come to terms with having some help around the house, and was even enjoying it. That was one thing less for Jenny to worry about. She'd been somewhat concerned she was leaving Maddy in the lurch.

Maddy had also provided some news about Mike, which Jenny read avidly. It seemed he'd gone back to San Francisco for an indefinite period. Jenny's brow furrowed, and she unconsciously rubbed her forefinger back and forth across the spot between her eyes. He'd be trying to find out about the student, just as he'd said he would. She wished she could have been there to offer support. She sighed. Mike had made it clear he wanted to do this by himself, and difficult though it was, she had to accept his decision. Reading Maddy's message brought back all the emotions she'd experienced over there.

But there was nothing she could do. She was back in Australia and about to get on with the next stage of her life. Oregon was behind her. So why was there a little voice in the back of her head telling her it wasn't finished? She deliberately closed her mind to it and went on to read the hoped for email from Rosa who was looking forward to her return to Noosa and had "lots to talk about".

*

"Mum, you're not listening. You're miles away." Helen's accusation broke through Jenny's thoughts. Pulling herself together she replied dreamily. "I was. In Oregon, actually."

"Why? Did something happen there, other than all this stuff about Thea and Jed you told us last night? Something you haven't mentioned?" Helen's voice sounded anxious.

"Did you meet someone?" It was Alan's gentle voice which broke into her thoughts. "A man?"

"Don't be silly," Helen chastised her husband. "How could she? It would be disgusting. Not at her age."

"I'm not over the hill yet," Jenny was quick to retort. "And as a matter of fact, I did meet a man. Mike is Maddy's neighbor, and we ended up seeing quite a bit of each other. In fact…"

"I don't want to hear any more. It's just as well you had to come back to help us or goodness knows what you might have got up to." Helen moved her leg with a groan.

Alan jumped to settle her cushion at a better angle. "Well, Helen, it seems your mother has been leading a secret life over there in the US of A. Are we going to hear more about him?" Alan turned towards Jenny and raised his eyebrows.

"No." Jenny's voice brooked no argument. Her feelings for Mike, whatever they might be – and she still wasn't clear of that herself – were her own business. She certainly didn't want them bandied about here and sullied. She drew herself up, back straight, and turned the conversation back to the younger couple. "What have you decided? I really am leaving next Monday." She looked from one to the other.

It was Alan who finally replied. "Well, Mum. We did a lot of talking while you were out and…"

"And we think we've found a solution," Helen said.

"Yes." Alan pushed back a lock of hair which had fallen down on his face. "We remembered that Rob and Jodie, friends of ours, have been arranging for an American girl, an au pair, to look after their kids. Helen rang them and…"

"She's working out well for them, and she has a friend who's currently looking for a job. She's even in Sydney," Helen finished.

"Well." Jenny breathed out. "She would certainly seem to be a solution. Can you arrange to meet this girl? I wouldn't mind casting an eye over her myself."

"Oh, you're going to take an interest in your grandchildren, now you see you can leave them?" Jenny ignored Helen's bitterness. Alan, however, was not so generous.

"You're being unkind, Helen. Your mum has always had the boys' interests at heart, and yours too." He gave Jenny a wry smile over his wife's head. "But she has her own life to lead, and it's not here in Sydney."

"I'm beginning to wish it was." Jenny felt torn. Family was important to her, even more so now. But she'd made her life north of here, so was quick to add, "I'll come back often. It's not like I'll have to ask for leave any more." She bit her lip. It would be a whole new ball game, and one which she was ready for. She was aching to get her teeth into a new challenge. It would help her forget…. She mentally shook herself.

"I'm glad you've come up with something. I'm sure an au pair will work out for you. It'll be good for the boys too, to have someone young around," Jenny smiled at Helen and Alan, who were regarding her somewhat warily. "So much better than an old fogey like me."

As Jenny closed her eyes that night, she tried to picture her new bookshop, but a gentle bearded face kept intruding and was the last image she saw before she fell asleep.

Thirty-eight

San Francisco had turned on one of its worst summer days, thought Mike as he checked into a downtown hotel. The horizon was barely discernable through the mist, and the dampness seemed to seep right through him. The weather matched his mood. He'd come down to sort this muddle out once and for all and was aiming to meet with Tony Parker later in the day. Classes were finished for the semester, but faculty members would still be around. He well remembered the hours spent marking papers, attending meetings and preparing conference papers which seemed to take up most of the summer. Then there'd been the summer schools. He shook his head to rid himself of the memories. He was well shot of that now.

Mike's gaze took in the campus as he headed across the quadrangle to his old office block. Nothing had changed, though why should it have? He'd only been gone a few months. The few months seemed more like a year, so different did he feel from the man who'd spent the majority of his working life in these hallowed grounds. He gave a wry smile.

Mike stood in front of Tony's office door, which was covered in timetables and notes to students. It was like going back in time. He took a deep breath and knocked.

"Enter!" Tony's voice boomed through the wood. How could Mike have forgotten the absurd pomposity of his former colleague who, although close to thirty years his junior, affected the demeanor and stature of a professor twice his age? Tony was bright, no doubt about it. He'd achieved a full professorship and tenure in half the time it took most faculty members. One had to respect him for that, but his academic brilliance was tempered by an arrogance which had rankled.

"Mike Halliday!" Tony swiveled the chair around from his desk as Mike stepped through the door. "What brings you back to this neck of the woods? Can't stay away, eh?" He took off his black-rimmed glasses – another affectation, thought Mike – and dangled them from his fingers by one leg.

"Just passing." Mike paused, unsure how to broach the subject now he was actually here. Best just to barge right into it, he decided. "I heard about the student who committed suicide. You know the girl, Sue Lyons. The graduate student I passed on to you?"

Was it Mike's imagination or did Tony blanch at his words? If so, he made a fast recovery.

"Sad waste of a brilliant brain. She'd have made faculty next year. These young women." Tony shook his head as if in despair. "No resilience."

Wondering at what seemed like a strange choice of words, Mike made what he hoped were sounds of agreement before asking. "Was there any warning? As her supervisor, did you have any inkling there was anything…?"

"How could I?" For once Tony's bonhomie appeared to have deserted him. "I was only her thesis supervisor, not her keeper." He stood up. "Sorry, pal, lot to do, and the wife's about to add to the family. Need to get away."

Mike left. As he drove off, something was niggling him. Something about Tony just hadn't felt right. He shrugged. Maybe he was imagining it, reading too much into the conversation. But Tony had seemed a little too anxious for Mike to leave. He'd been working away, seemingly engrossed at his desk when Mike had opened the door. Then he'd been in a hurry to get rid of him. Was it the mention of Sue that had disturbed him? Well, Mike reasoned, having a promising student commit suicide was disturbing in itself, but… Maybe he should talk with Bob. He'd know all the gossip. Feeling better now he'd made the decision, Mike's foot pressed down on the accelerator, and he reached over to pat Ben. But instead of the feel of a familiar soft warm body, his hand hit an empty seat. Oh, damn, how could he have forgotten?

He'd left his old friend back at Seal Rock. He missed him, but he'd known the sort of hotel he was staying in would have a no pets policy. Luckily there was Maddy, whose new housemate had a real soft spot for Ben. The dog would be in good hands.

*

"So, what brings you back down? Thought you'd left us for good." The noisy hotel bar was not the meeting place Mike would have chosen, but when Bob had suggested it, he hadn't been able to think of an alternative. The pair sat nursing their shots of Jack Daniels, the loud cacophony of chatter and music echoing around them.

Mike tried to choose his words carefully. "Something came up. Necessitated a quick trip." He sipped the strong spirit, then as if changing the subject, asked. "Anything new happening in the faculty?"

In his element, Bob laid down his glass and started to regale Mike with the latest happenings: the infighting, the politics and the impending promotions. After listening politely for a time, Mike ventured, "And what's happening with Tony Parker? Still the Golden Boy?"

"Funny you should ask." Bob tapped the side of his nose with his forefinger in a show of secrecy. "There have been rumblings all isn't well there."

"Oh?" Mike tried to conceal his interest. "In what way?" He took another sip and wiped his fingers across his lips.

"In every way. Rumor has it he's been playing away from home, with a student, no less." Bob paused for effect. "Of course it wouldn't be the first time, but the scuttlebutt this time is that it all blew up in his face. Wife gave him an ultimatum. Never a good idea." Bob lowered his voice, forcing Mike to lean forward in order to hear what he was saying. "Brilliant student, of course. Great loss to the faculty, now she's gone."

"Gone?" Mike could hardly contain himself.

"Left, disappeared. Here one day gone the next. Been hushed up."

"Who was she?" Mike hoped his interest wasn't giving anything away.

"Not one of yours. Though, come to think of it, she might have been. Now, what was the name?" Bob started to mutter. "Bryant, Bryan, Lygon, Lyons, that's what it was. Something Lyons."

"Sue Lyons." Mike's voice was quiet.

"That's it. Knew her did you?"

Mike felt himself letting out a breath he hadn't known he was holding. "She started as one of mine, graduate student. Didn't work out, so I handed her over to Tony. Must have been a couple of years ago. So where is she now?"

"Oh, didn't I say? Topped herself. What a waste." Bob shook his head. "Still, old Tony seems to have come out of it okay. Wife about to drop another one any day, so it's back to playing Happy Families for him, until next time. Such is life."

And death, thought Mike, but kept his thoughts to himself. The pair sat in silence as each contemplated the strange turns life could take. Finally Mike rose to go.

"Better be off."

"Sure you won't have another?" Bob seemed settled in for the night. "What's the rush?"

"No. I'd better get going." Now his curiosity had been satisfied, Mike was anxious to return to his hotel room to digest what he'd just heard.

*

Mike opened the Telephone Directory. He needed to find Tanya Lyons. It had come to him in the middle of the night, a restless night. He hadn't had much sleep. Now here he was at the L section looking for a T Lyons. It was a common name. He scratched his head and took a slug of his morning coffee. There were pages of Lyons. He put the directory down. She might still live with her parents, so maybe he shouldn't restrict his search to the initial T. Maybe her name wasn't even Lyons any more. She might have married. This could prove to be an impossible task.

Mike picked up the book again. He had to try. An hour and three cups of coffee later, his head was beginning to spin. He'd struck out about twenty times, and that was only those who'd answered. It was ten o'clock on a Saturday morning, and he was still in the T section. Better take a break and have some breakfast, he decided.

Fortified by a three egg omelet served with biscuits and gravy, Mike returned to his room, determined to crack this. Four calls later he hit pay dirt.

"Tanya? Yes, we do have a daughter Tanya, our oldest. She's Tanya Roberts now. Who did you say you were?"

"An old friend. I knew her sister Sue." Mike tried not to make it sound like a question, but it was the way he'd decided to check if he'd reached the right Tanya. "I was sorry to hear of her passing," he added.

"Hmm. Thanks." The man on the other end, presumably the father, was not forthcoming, but he did pass on a number where Tanya could be reached. Mike hung up the phone with relief. He'd cleared the first hurdle.

*

"Decided to come clean, have you?" Tanya's voice was still bitter. "Ready to own up?"

"Can we meet?" Mike had decided he wasn't going to go into details on the phone. He wasn't exactly sure how much to say. After all, he didn't have any real evidence against Tony Parker, even though it was clear to him what had been happening. The only thing he couldn't work out was why it had been *his* name in the girl's diary.

He was in luck. Tanya agreed to meet with him, and they arranged a time that afternoon at his hotel. Mike spent the morning working out a plan. His main aim was to clear his own name. It wasn't about landing Tony in the shit, but realized it was likely to happen sooner or later.

Mike was sitting in the hotel lobby with what seemed like his umpteenth coffee of the day, when he saw Tanya walk through the door. She paused for a moment to get her bearings, then strode over and stood in front of Mike, who rose to greet her.

"Sit down, please." He gestured to the chairs, and seemingly reluctantly, his guest gingerly sat down on the edge of one of them.

"Coffee?"

"No." The word shot out like a bullet. Mike drew in his breath. This wasn't going to be easy.

"What did you have to say to me? Prepared to admit you're the one in here?" She brandished a pale blue notebook which looked well-worn.

"Is that...?"

"This is Sue's diary. Do you want me to read it to you?" She began to open it.

"No, no, that won't be necessary." Mike put up both hands as if to ward her off. "What I mean is...What I wanted to say..." God, this was going to be more difficult than he'd thought. He tried again. "It's as I told you. Regardless of what your sister wrote using my name, I wasn't the one she was involved with."

"Well if it wasn't you, why is your name on almost every page? Let me read..." She opened the book again.

"I don't know." Mike shook his head. "It's like some cruel joke. I swear. Do I really look like someone a young woman would be interested in?" He spread his hands and pointed to his grey beard.

Tanya looked at him closely for the first time. "Well if not you, then who? It wasn't an immaculate conception. She was involved with someone, and from what she wrote..." She hesitated. "If her diary's to be believed, then it was someone at the university, someone she was working with." Tanya looked at Mike expecting an answer.

Mike decided on a modicum of discretion. There was no point in implicating Tony any more than he had to. 'Well, all I know is I passed your sister on to another supervisor. But the university is full of men – staff, students, grounds men. The list goes on."

Tanya closed the diary and bit her lip. "It was someone she respected, and she wrote your name, over and over. That's why I thought..." She looked Mike over as if appraising him. "But you're right. She wouldn't have gone for someone like you." Turning the diary over and over in her hands, Tanya's eyes began to fill with tears. "My little sister. She deserved better. She was such a bright star."

Mike moved awkwardly in his chair. He was no good with women's tears. From nowhere, came a picture, not of Mary, but of Jenny. She would have known what to do. But she was back in Australia. He cleared his throat and shuffled his feet, picked up his cup, found it to be empty and put it down again. What could he say?

Tanya's voice broke into his thoughts. "I want to meet him. Can you take me to him?"

"What? Who?" For a second Mike didn't know what she was on about.

"Her supervisor. Maybe he'll know."

"I don't think…" Mike began, only to be interrupted.

"You want to help, don't you? After all, it *is* your name in here." Tanya held up the blue diary again as if to threaten him.

'I guess.' Realizing there was going to be no way out, Mike reluctantly agreed, and thirty minutes later, they had driven out to the university in tandem, and he found himself retracing his steps of the previous day.

This time Tony's door was open. They could see him sitting with a young blonde student, poring over a sheaf of papers.

Tony's words reached them. "Look at what you've written here. It's not your own words. If you're quoting from my work, I'd really like you to cite me. Let's work together on this." He stretched his arm around the student's shoulders, and she gazed up at his face in adoration.

That was enough for Tanya.

"Not so fast there, professor. Couldn't wait to have Sue cold in her grave before you make a move on your next victim?" She strode in, shocking the young girl into scattering her papers all over the floor. As she rushed to pick them up and bundle them together, Tony looked round with a smile.

Mike was the first to catch his eye, and tempting though it was to fade into the distance, he stood his ground.

"Tony, this is Tanya, Sue's sister. Sue Lyons, the student who…" At his words, Tony's face whitened, but true to form, he brought his charm to the fore. He rose and stretched out his hand.

"Tanya. I'm so pleased to meet you. We were all so sorry to lose your sister. A brilliant student, quite exceptional. I'm sure…"

He was interrupted by a little voice. "I'll be off, Tony. See you at the tutorial." All three turned to look at the young student whom they had completely forgotten.

"Right, Linda," Tony replied, then turned back to Mike and his companion. "How can I help you?" He smiled a taut smile and, removing his glasses, rubbed his eyes. "I'm not sure…"

"It was you, wasn't it?" Tanya yelled. Tony rose as if to defend himself and, taking a step backwards, almost fell over his chair. Putting his hand down on the desk in an attempt to steady himself, he was clearly shaken.

"I… I…" he stuttered.

"How could you?" Enraged, Tanya advanced on him.

Looking at the pair, Mike decided he wasn't needed here. He left. It was over as far as he was concerned. He still wondered why Sue had used his name in her diary, but it really didn't matter to him anymore. He had Tanya off his back. She was Tony's problem now. It was as it should be. He had a passing feeling of sympathy for his erstwhile colleague, but not for long. Tony had brought it on himself.

Back in his hotel room, Mike packed up his few belongings, anxious to return home. Yes, he thought, Seal Rock had become home. He was looking forward to the peace he'd found in his cabin, to joining Ben again, to walk along the beach in the breeze with the sound and scent of the ocean all around him, to… He stopped. In his image of the beach and the ocean there had been another figure, a tall slim figure with windswept black hair, a blue jacket with the collar turned up against the wind, a pair of violet eyes so deep a man could lose himself in them. Jenny. But she wouldn't be there. She'd returned to Australia. He'd been so caught up in righting this wrong he'd let her go. Then he drew himself up. That wasn't quite right. She would have gone anyway. There was this bookshop she'd bought, and her daughter's broken ankle. But a small voice – which sounded very much like Mary – reminded him he could have been more forthcoming at their last meeting instead of closing her out. "You always did tell me I needed to communicate better, Mary," he said aloud. "Well, looks like I really stuffed up this time."

*

"You're back, then?" Maddy greeted him.

Ben bounded out and started running circles around his master when Maddy opened the door. "So that's all the thanks I get for looking after you for a week?" she joked to the dog, before turning back to Mike.

"Glad to see me, are you?" Mike fondled the dog, who was now standing still, tongue hanging out and tail wagging. "Thanks, Maddy." He looked up at her. "Hope he wasn't too much trouble."

"No trouble at all. Marylou did the looking after, and Ben kept me company during the day. He's good company. And what about you? Did you find what you were looking for? Do you want to talk about it?"

Starting to shake his head, Mike found he did want to go over things, and Maddy always provided a willing and nonjudgmental ear.

Several cups of coffee and macadamia nut cookies later, Mike had covered the events of his trip to San Francisco.

"So that's that," he said finally.

"But why put your name in her diary?" Maddy wondered.

"I wondered that too. Then I had a call from Tanya just before I left. She'd managed to get the whole story out of Tony Parker. Evidently the two of them had thought it a bit of a joke. It was their secret code, so if anyone found the diary, then Tony wouldn't be identified." Mike smiled ruefully. "Evidently they considered I was the most unlikely person to attract a young student like Sue. Don't know whether to be flattered or insulted at that one. Bet they had more than a few jokes at my expense."

"Don't know why these young ones need to write it all down anyway. Bit of an ego trip, I'd say. And what's happening between you and my goddaughter?" she asked, cunningly changing the subject.

"Well, since it seems I'm the most unlikely person to be attractive to the opposite sex..."

"Get away with you. Jenny's a mature woman. She's not going to be swayed by the superficial charm of someone like your rat colleague. You have finer qualities more befitting someone like her. I thought..."

"Thank you, ma'am. Yes, well. Things just didn't work out there. She's back in Australia. She had all these plans and will be getting on with her life, her family, her bookshop. I guess I was just an interlude for her."

"But she meant more to you than that." Maddy's old eyes held the wisdom of her years. "And are you going to let her go so easily? She's my goddaughter, and you're my friend. I'd like to think you'd put up more of a fight for what you want."

Mike rubbed the palm of his hand over his head. This was heavy. *What did he want?* He hadn't expected to be faced with this sort of conversation when he'd walked in the door. He was still tired from his long drive and wanted to go home and put his head down.

"Maybe I don't know what I want," he said finally. "Right now a bit of shut-eye would be welcome."

"Well, don't leave it too long," advised Maddy, as he rose to leave, Ben at his heels. "Opportunity doesn't knock too often at your age. I should know. You're a long time dead. And Australia's only a flight away," she added.

With these words ringing in his ears, Mike stepped out of the door and back into his pickup.

Tired as Mike was, sleep eluded him. He kept hearing Maddy's words and picturing Jenny as he had last seen her. She didn't ... she couldn't ... but what if...? He tossed and turned and Ben, sensing his master's unrest whined and pattered around the bed, finally placing both front paws on the pillow next to Mike's head.

"What should I do, old boy?" Mike asked, to be answered by a wet lick on the face. Finally he fell into a restless sleep and by morning he'd made his decision.

Thirty-nine

Jenny gratefully accepted a glass of white wine, the condensation beading on the glass, lay back in the rattan chair, feet up on the balcony railing and gazed out onto the Noosa River.

"Oh, it's good to be back," she exclaimed looking across at Rosa. "I've missed this place."

"My little bit of heaven! It's been a godsend these last few weeks, let me tell you. While you've been jaunting off enjoying yourself with Oregon Man, I've been going through hell."

Glowing a little at Rosa's mention of Mike, which was not altogether inaccurate and which brought up memories of beach strolls on long light evenings, Jenny took a sip of wine.

"Okay, I'm back now. What's been happening?"

"I won't bore you with the sordid details. Enough to say I'm leaving – taking early retirement – at least, that's what I'm calling it."

Jenny's feet dropped to the balcony floor with a thump. She put her glass down carefully beside her feet, and looked over at her friend.

"You don't mean it! Your job was safe. You've always said so, and besides…"

"There's no besides any longer." With a wave of her hand Rosa dismissed her six year affair with the Financial Controller. "And I don't want to talk about it. Sure, the job's safe but it's not for me anymore."

"What will you do?" Picking up her glass, Jenny took another sip and looked across at her friend.

Rosa was gazing into her own glass as if it held the key to her future.

"Haven't quite worked that out yet. I only handed in my resignation on Friday. I'm going to work out my notice, then they won't see me for dust. Don't suppose you want a partner in your book shop?" she threw at Jenny, taking another gulp of wine.

Jenny was startled. This was the last thing she'd expected. Unsure how to reply she took refuge in another sip of wine.

"No, of course you don't. Forget it. It was just an idea."

"And not a bad one." Jenny found her voice. "But is it really what you want?" As she spoke, her mind was working fast. Having a partner would be a big help. Apart from the money angle and the day to day assistance, it could free up her own time to visit family in Sydney, even to … She stopped herself. She wasn't going to go there. If Mike wanted to see her, he'd have to make the first move. And he had a few things to sort out before that could happen, quite a few. She put the thought aside and focused on Rosa again. Her friend was speaking.

"Yes," Rosa said decidedly. "I think it is. We'd work well together, and it would be something completely different. Something to focus on, a new place, new people. A complete change is what I need right now." She gulped down the wine remaining in her glass. "Another?" She held up the bottle to Jenny.

"Okay, but only if you tell me more about what's brought you to this decision."

Rosa poured them both a large glass. "Not driving anywhere tonight are we?" she joked in remembrance of a waitress who had once used the driving limit as a reason for pouring a measured glass of wine with dinner.

"Here goes," she began.

Two hours later and halfway through another bottle of wine, Jenny put down her empty glass. "No more for me. I can see why you want to get out. I have to say I think you're better off without him, but then…"

"You never did like him, but I thought…" Rosa twirled her glass sadly. "I thought we had a future."

"I'm stunned. But don't you intend to say anything about the other stuff? It's fraudulent at the very least."

"No, it'll all come out anyway, and I don't want to be involved. I still have some loyalties, even though he's done the dirty on me."

"The rat." Jenny stretched out her hand to Rosa to find it gripped firmly by the other. "Well, looks like we're partners. What do you say?"

"I say thanks." The two sat in silence while they contemplated their decision.

"Well, I'd better be off. I may not be driving, but I still have a fair walk home. Let's meet tomorrow to go over the details, and I guess we need to have some sort of agreement drawn up. I'll call you in the morning."

"Do that," Rosa agreed.

*

Four weeks later, it was almost closing time at the bookshop, and Rosa was checking the day's takings while Jenny tidied the shelves.

"Been a good day." Rosa looked over at her business partner. "Takings are way up."

"Don't I know it!" was Jenny's heartfelt response. "A big crowd always leaves the shelves in a mess. Takes ages to get them back into shape." She sighed with pleasure as she patted the last row of books as if they were her children. It had been a hectic few weeks, but the shop was finally beginning to take shape.

"Is that another customer?" Rosa was looking at the figure lurking in the doorway. "Doesn't he know we're closed?"

"I'll go tell him." Jenny gave the books one last pat and walked over to open the door. "I'm sorry," she began.

"Jenny!"

"Mike!"

They both spoke at once. It took Jenny a few seconds to recover from the shock of seeing him standing there, outside her store, in Noosa.

"What are you doing here? Why...?" she was lost for words again.

"I came to see you. Is there somewhere we can talk? Somewhere private?" Mike looked wildly around as if they could conjure up a private trysting place in the middle of the busy thoroughfare.

"Yes. But not right here. We're just closing up. If you can wait a bit?"

"Sure." Mike pulled on his beard in the old familiar way, and Jenny felt a quiver in the seat of her stomach.

"I'll just..." Jenny closed the door gently and turned to face her friend whose eyebrows had shot up at the exchange she'd seen outside. "Don't look at me like that."

"Is it him? The wild man from Oregon? He looks pretty normal, pretty damn dishy in fact. You're a dark horse. You didn't say anything about him coming over."

"I didn't know. I haven't heard from him since I left. Oh, God, how do I look?" Jenny's hands went to her hair. "I haven't been near a mirror all day. My face..."

"You look fine, great in fact. There's a glow that wasn't there five minutes ago."

"Hmm." Jenny felt her face go red. *Glow indeed!* There was a little voice singing in her head. *Mike is here, here in Noosa, here to see me!* "Okay if I leave you to finish up?"

"Off you go. I can manage here. Don't you keep him waiting."

"I'll just freshen up a bit." Jenny drifted off to the back room to repair what she was sure were the ravages of the day.

"I'm off." She came back and made for the door, unable to keep the smile from her face. Hand on the door, Jenny stopped, stood stock still and looked at her friend. "I'm not being silly, am I? I mean..." Her voice trembled. "It's been so long, and there really wasn't..."

"Get off with you. He's come halfway around the world to see you. There's definitely something... on his part anyway. Seems it's up to you now."

Jenny lifted her chin resolutely, and opened the door.

"Here you are then. I'd almost given you up. Then I remembered how women like to take their time."

"Here I am," Jenny repeated his words inanely.

"And we're going to...?"

"Oh." In her excitement, Jenny had given no further thought to where they could have a private conversation. She thought quickly. "Might be best to go back to my place, if that's okay with you?" She looked at Mike who nodded.

"I have a hire car." He gestured across the road where a bright red Holden ute was sitting. "I know, you can see me coming a mile off," he stated ruefully. "I'll follow you."

The pair sat in wicker chairs in Jenny's back courtyard. The sun had set, and the scent of jasmine filled the air. There was a bottle of Cabernet Merlot sitting on the table between them, alongside a dish of olives and a plate of cheese and biscuits Jenny had hurriedly put together. Neither seemed willing to start the conversation.

A flock of rosellas screeched through the treetops. Mike cleared his throat.

"A bit different from Oregon."

"It sure is." Jenny wasn't willing to give much away, but after another awkward silence, she couldn't resist the urge to speak. "How did you know where I was?" she asked at last.

"Maddy." Mike seemed to be having difficulty in finding the words.

"Of course." Jenny took a sip of her wine and looked down into the glass fearful her face would give away her thoughts. *Had he? Did he? And what had happened with that student affair?* She felt herself blush at her choice of words even though they hadn't been spoken aloud.

Mike cleared his throat again. "It's like this. Oh, dammit, I feel like a schoolboy." He reached over and took Jenny's hand, removing it from the rim of the glass where her fingers had been circling. "It's all sorted, about the girl, the student. You knew it wasn't me, didn't you?"

"Of course." Jenny clasped his hand tightly in hers, glad he was finally finding the words he'd been seeking. "But I knew you had to sort it all out. You did, didn't you? You went back to San Francisco?"

"I did. Yes." Mike raised his eyes to meet Jenny's, which were beginning to brim with tears. "Now I have something else to sort out. Us... I mean we, I mean...Oh, hell, I'm not sure *what* I mean."

With her hand still firmly held in his, Jenny asked, "Why did you come all this way, Mike? What did you want to say that you couldn't put in a letter or an email?"

"Put your glass down."

Jenny did as he asked, and he took both of her hands in his and looked her square in the face. "I needed to see your face, needed to know how you felt, needed to know for sure." He stopped again, then as if he couldn't help himself, he continued, "It's like this. Since Mary," he swallowed. "Since a time before she went, there hasn't been anyone. Never was anyone but her for all the years we were married, even before. I never thought..." He swallowed again and cleared his throat.

Jenny ached for him, wished there was some way she could help, but knew she had to allow him to get it out in his own time. She tightened her fingers in his and willed him to get to the point.

He seemed to sense her thoughts and after a long pause he began again.

"Meeting you, it was like a breath of fresh air. I felt young again. You fairly blew me away. That night at Crater Lake..." He shook his head. "I couldn't believe it!" He smiled, a rueful smile. "It had been a long time." He shook his head again. "What I'm trying to say is this. I have feelings, strong feelings. I... I don't know if you feel the same way. That's why I needed to see your face when I told you." He looked into Jenny's eyes, his crinkling at the corners. "What do you say? Could you... Do you care for me? Would you be willing to take on an old codger like me?"

Jenny gasped. "You mean...?"

"I mean would you be willing to take the chance and look at spending the rest of our days together? I know I don't have a lot to offer, but we seem to rub along fine, and even through all of this mess in San Francisco, I haven't been able to get you out of my thoughts."

He seemed about to go on, but Jenny loosened one of her hands from his grasp and put a finger on Mike's lips to stop him saying any more. It wasn't the most romantic proposal in the world, but it fitted the man sitting beside her.

"The feeling's mutual, I think I..." She was silenced with the touch of his lips meeting hers. It was some time before she was released, shaken to the core. His arms had encircled her shoulders, and hers had found their way around his neck. They drew back and looked at each other with big grins on their faces.

"Wow!"

"Wow, yourself. Look, I know I'm not much for romantic words, but I never thought to fall in love again, not at my age. This is a bit of a shock to the system."

"It's as much a shock for me." Jenny placed another kiss on his lips, a brief one this time. She interlaced her hands behind Mike's head and felt his arms wrap around her waist, his hands gripping her firmly. It felt good, warm, safe. Mike pulled her to him, his lips on her neck. She had a sense of belonging, of being able to surrender herself to another, one stronger than herself. It was an unfamiliar feeling for her, but one she could come to enjoy. It was some time before the pair drew apart again.

"Well!" Mike let out a long breath. "I think this calls for a celebration."

"I have just the thing." Jenny released herself from Mike's embrace and stepped into the house to return only a few moments later brandishing a bottle of Veuve Clicquot. "This was left over from the bookshop launch. I was keeping it for something special. It's a bit different from your usual Jack Daniels, but it's the best I can do."

"Maddy will be delighted," Mike said, as he tipped out the last drop of champagne from the bottle. "I suspect she'd have engineered it if she could. In fact I'm not altogether sure she didn't. She's a bit of a witch."

"Oh, don't you start. I had enough of that psychobabble stuff thrown at me in Oregon. And it's the last thing I expect from you."

"Just a turn of phrase. She's a wily old thing."

"You're right there." Jenny contemplated the look on her godmother's face when she heard the news. "Wish I could see her when we tell her." Then, she stopped, a touch of reality setting in. "But ... you're here now, but your life is in Seal Rock and mine is here. I've just got the shop off the ground. How can I...?"

"No need for major decisions right now. Things will work themselves out." Mike stood up and pulled Jenny to her feet, managing to take her in his arms as he did so. She found herself being carried into the bedroom.

Later as she lay entwined in Mike's arms, his body fitting snugly behind hers, she looked over to the bedside table. The last thing she saw before she closed her eyes was her sand dollar lying there in the moonlight. *Maybe it was magic after all.*

THE END

Thank you for purchasing this book.
If you enjoyed it, please leave a review at:

http://www.amazon.com/
http://www.goodreads.com/

Acknowledgements

This book could not have been written without the help and advice of a number of people.

Firstly, My husband Jim for listening to my plotlines without complaint, for his patience and insights as I discuss my characters and storyline with him, for confirming for me the male point of view, ensuring I had the correct American terminology, for a final proofing to ensure all was culturally correct, and for being there when I need him.

John Hudspith, editor extraordinaire for his ideas, suggestions, encouragement and attention to detail.

Jane Dixon-Smith for my beautiful cover and formatting.

My writing group, the Inkstained Groupies for their support and encouragement and my critique partner, Helen, for her continuing patience.

About the Author

Born and brought up in Scotland, and attracted by advertisements to 'Come and Teach in the Sun', Maggie Christensen emigrated to Australia in her twenties to teach in primary schools in Sydney. She now lives with her husband of almost thirty years near Peregian Beach on the Sunshine Coast of Queensland. She loves walking on the deserted beach in the early mornings and having coffee by the Noosa River on weekends. After spending many years in teaching, lecturing and education management, where she wrote course materials and reports, Maggie began writing the sort of books she enjoys reading, books about women in their prime, their issues and relationships. Now her days are spent surrounded by books, either reading or writing them – her idea of heaven! She continues her love of books as a volunteer with Friends of Noosaville Library where she helps organize author talks and selects and delivers books to the housebound.

Look out for the sequel to The Sand Dollar. The Dreamcatcher will be available in 2015.

You can find Maggie at:
http://maggiechristensenauthor.com/
https://www.facebook.com/maggiechristensenauthor

Band of Gold

Maggie Christensen

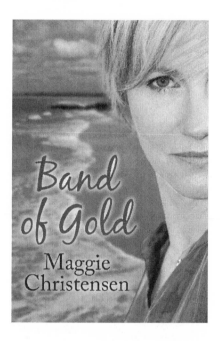

Anna Hollis believes she has a happy marriage. A schoolteacher in Sydney, Anna juggles her busy life with a daughter in the throes of first love and increasingly demanding aging parents.

When Anna's husband of twenty-five years leaves her, on Christmas morning, without warning or explanation, her safe and secure world collapses.

Marcus King returns to Australia from the USA, leaving behind a broken marriage and a young son.

When he takes up the position of Headmaster at Anna's school, they form a fragile friendship through their mutual hurt and loneliness.

Can Anna leave the past behind and make a new life for herself, and does Marcus have a part to play in her future?

The sequel to Band of Gold, The Broken Thread, will be available in 2015.